Red Handed

By Shelly Bell

BENEDICTION NOVELS

Red Handed

White Collared
Part One: Mercy
Part Two: Greed
Part Three: Revenge
Part Four: Passion

Red Handed

A BENEDICTION NOVEL

SHELLY BELL

red
AVON
IMPULSE
An Imprint of HarperCollins Publishers

Excerpt from *White Collared Part One: Mercy* copyright © 2014 by Shelly Bell.

Excerpt from *When Good Earls Go Bad* copyright © 2015 by Megan Frampton.

Excerpt from *The Wedding Band* copyright © 2015 by Lisa Connelly.

Excerpt from *Riot* copyright © 2015 by Jamie Shaw.

Excerpt from *Only In My Dreams* copyright © 2015 by Darcy Burke.

Excerpt from *Sinful Rewards 1* copyright © 2014 by Cynthia Sax.

Excerpt from *Tempt the Night* copyright © 2015 by Dixie Brown.

EPub Edition MARCH 2015 ISBN: 9780062396464

Print Edition ISBN: 9780062396471

AM 10 9 8 7 6 5 4 3 2 1

Chapter One

Tick-tock. Tick-tock.

With the loaded Glock in his hand, he leaned on the doorframe and watched her sleep.

So innocent.

So pure.

He doubted her ability to carry out this mission, but they had no choice.

In a room decorated with framed Degas prints, Danielle Walker lay on her king-sized sleigh bed, tangled in her silk sheets. Her window was open, paving the way for the moonlight to illuminate her creamy skin and the desert breeze to caress her flesh.

His fingers itched to do the same.

She wasn't his normal type. He preferred his whores thin, blonde, and tan like the California girls he'd heard sung about on the radio as a child. Although Danielle had lost weight this past year, she was still soft and curvy.

He'd studied each and every photograph his man had taken of her over the last few months, especially the ones of her sunbathing naked by the pool in her backyard. He wanted her, and damned if he would allow anyone to stop him from having her.

A sigh passed her plump lips, and she rubbed her thighs together as if inviting him to her bed.

He checked his watch and peered down the hall.

Perhaps he had time to accept her invitation.

He crossed the room and settled on the edge of her mattress, inhaling the faint scent of lilacs. His dick hardened as he traced her raven hairline with the muzzle of his gun. She stirred and licked her lips before opening her sleepy brown eyes.

It only took a moment for those eyes to widen into terror.

Before she could scream, he covered her mouth with his gloved hand and waved the gun in front of her beautifully frightened face.

Not that it mattered if she did scream. No one would help her.

"Stay quiet, Danielle, and I promise no harm will come to you." The whispered lie spilled effortlessly from his lips.

True, no harm would befall her tonight, but the countdown to the end of her life had begun years ago.

Tick-tock. Tick-tock.

She nodded as she stared at his masked face, no doubt trying to identify him. Between the mask, dark paint covering the skin underneath, and colored lenses, he could be her father come back from the dead for all she could discern. He leaned closer, trailing his gun down the length of her neck.

The echoing boom of a gunshot fired down the hall pierced the silence of Danielle's room. She startled, her body convulsing in fear and tears spilling down her face. She shouted beneath his gloved hand.

Damn it, he'd lost his chance.

Oh well. He'd take her after she finished her assignment—after she became just another whore…

Right before he killed her. His associates had ordered an efficient execution-style gunshot to the head, but after they got what they wanted, did it matter if he tortured her a bit before he ended her life? How could he resist such a sweet temptation?

"Stop yelling or next time my men will shoot your stepmother. That was merely a warning to let her know we mean business." When she quieted, he removed the hand from her mouth and patted her cheek, his gaze trained on her cleavage and the Tiffany sterling silver heart key locket that she always wore around her neck. "I'll prove to you she's alive and well. Come with me to her bedroom."

After slipping his gun into the holster at his waist, he grabbed her hand and pulled her out of bed. Thankfully, she allowed him to lead her down the hall to Tasha's room. He couldn't afford to bruise her. Yet.

The scene came into view. His three men had done their job. Bound and gagged, Tasha lay on the carpet, helpless in a shimmering silver peignoir set, a rivulet of blood trickling from the corner of her mouth.

On a sob, Danielle bolted for her stepmother. He stopped her at the entryway of the bedroom and gripped her by the shoulders, forcing her to stay in place.

"Now be a good girl and listen. There's something I want, and only you can get it for me. Until you do, I'm taking Tasha as collateral." He slid his hand into the pocket of his black leather jacket and pulled out the papers. "This is a plane ticket and your instructions. By your home's front door, you'll find a suitcase packed with everything you'll need." He checked his watch and nodded to his men. The strongest of them scooped Tasha off the floor and hoisted her over his shoulder as if she were a sack of potatoes.

Tick-tock. Tick-tock.

"I don't understand," Danielle whispered. "Why me?"

He spun her around and yanked her down the hall back to her bedroom. "The only thing you need to understand is Tasha will die if you fail. And don't even think about calling the police." He pushed her on the bed. "If you breathe a word of this to anyone, I'll not only kill her, I'll torture her first."

Taking Tasha with them, his men strode down the hall and down the staircase.

Time to go before the police arrived.

"Your plane leaves in five hours. I suggest you make the best of the situation and enjoy yourself."

Surprising him, she began laughing. "Enjoy myself? How the hell am I supposed to enjoy myself while my stepmother's life is being threatened?"

His dick swelled at the thought of how Danielle would spend her days and nights. He couldn't wait until he'd force her to bargain for her life by demonstrating her newly acquired skills on him.

He motioned to the papers in her hands. "Your application has been approved. Congratulations, you are Benediction's newest sex slave trainee."

Just as he'd expected, all humor disappeared from her face.

His watch beeped. "When the police arrive in one minute, you'll tell them you triggered the alarm accidentally. Remember, we'll be watching you. The clock is ticking, Danielle. You have a week to get me what I want."

Thirty seconds later, he disappeared into the quiet night, praying Danielle would get the job done.

For all their sakes.

Chapter Two

IN ALL THE years Danielle Walker had waited to officially meet Cole DeMarco, she'd never imagined standing in front of his home, half-naked under a mink coat in the middle of a Michigan blizzard. Fat snowflakes fell from the dark gray sky and swirled around her as though she'd shaken up one of those snow globes she'd collected as a child.

If she were smart, she'd take it as a sign to get the hell out of there and return to sunny Arizona, where she could wear full-size panties underneath her skirt. Despite the kidnapper's threats, she should've gone to the FBI.

But smart wouldn't get her the answers she needed to lay the past to rest.

Smart wouldn't save her stepmother, Tasha. Although Danielle and she hadn't always been close, she was grateful to her for the companionship she'd given her father and admired the numerous hours Tasha spent fundraising for charity. She and her son, Roman, were the only family Danielle had left, and she'd do anything to keep them safe.

Thank goodness Roman was currently in Russia on business. As her best friend, he'd know the minute he saw Danielle's face that there was something wrong. The warning that she not tell anyone about the kidnapping remained in the forefront of her mind.

As the taxi that brought her here drove away, she licked the melted snow off her lips and climbed the steps of the porch to the sprawling stone mansion known to insiders as the sex club, Benediction.

A nervous bubble tickled her belly. If anyone back home heard that she was about to become a sex slave for a billionaire recluse, they'd never believe it.

She could hardly believe it.

Yet here she was—in her Prada heels and little else— about to allow the man who'd destroyed her family to see her naked. To command her as though she were a toy existing only for his pleasure and use her body to slake his deviant lusts.

Tasha had told her all about the man who'd helped send her father to prison on charges of embezzlement and fraud. She'd warned her to stay as far away from him as she could. And despite Danielle's curiosity about the handsome man she'd spied on in her youth, she'd listened.

The wind whistled and whipped snow at her back. She had just lifted her fist to knock on the solid walnut door when it opened, and the air inside blasted her with its inviting warmth. A gorgeous blond-haired man no more than thirty years old smiled at her in greeting.

He wore black slacks, a black tie, and a silver vest over a white dress shirt, a variation on the conservative butler uniform. But oddly, his feet were bare.

She'd grown up in a mansion. All her childhood friends were raised in mansions. She'd seen her share of butlers throughout her lifetime. Not a single one looked like him.

Her gaze traveled up his body and stopped on the impressive bulge.

His laughter broke her out of her trance. She snapped up her head, embarrassment heating her cheeks.

Smoothing her hands over the soft fur of her coat, she stepped inside the entrance and glanced around the room, noting the hanging crystal chandelier and built-in desk with a coatroom behind it. If she hadn't known this was a house, she'd think she'd walked into a five-star restaurant.

"Welcome to Benediction, Danielle. I'm Adrian." He swiped his hand over his erection. "And yes, I'm proud to say it's all mine. Master Cole has decided to torture me today with a cock ring…" His gaze flicked up to a discreet video camera in the corner of the entryway. "Which I accept with most humble gratitude." He mumbled a litany of profanity under his breath. "He's waiting for you in his office. May I take your coat?"

She opened her mouth, and all that came out was a squeak.

He waited for her to respond, and when she stood there frozen, unable to move or talk, he arched a brow. "You are Danielle Walker, right?"

She swallowed the lump in her throat and nodded, her long dark hair falling in front of her eyes.

He shook his head, his lips curved in what she guessed was amusement. "Guess you can keep your coat and come with me." He pivoted and sauntered across the foyer.

A small gasp flew from her lungs. Adrian's slacks were cut in the back, exposing his perfectly toned bare ass with what looked like a humongous fake diamond wedged between the cheeks.

He stopped at another door and glanced at her over his shoulder. She jerked her head toward the camera in the corner, hoping Adrian wouldn't notice her embarrassment. From the corner of her eye, she caught the shake of his shoulders and realized he was laughing at her again.

She pressed her lips together and straightened her spine. If the sight of a man's naked behind shocked her, how would she ever get through the next week?

Since the day of her father's suicide in prison, she'd thought about what she'd do to Cole DeMarco when she finally got her chance. But now that she was here, instead of slapping him hard across his face and calling him out as the murderer he was, she would beg him to train her as a sex slave.

Adrian led her through a doorway into an ordinary Grecian-style mansion, complete with pillars and vaulted ceilings.

As she followed the blond Adonis past a sunken living room similar to the one in her home back in Arizona, she was surprised by the mixture of relief and disappointment racing through her. For some reason, she'd expected to see sex at a sex club. But the place was quiet and empty.

The butler continued down to the end of the hallway, where he stopped in front of a closed door and knocked.

Her heart pounded so loudly, she was sure Adrian could hear. She felt as though she was a gladiator facing her first battle with a lion in the Colosseum arena.

"Come in, Danielle," said a voice as smooth as Glenlivet and just as heady. A shiver raced from her head to her feet, hardening her nipples and waking the nerve endings between her thighs. It had been years since she'd heard that voice, and despite it belonging to her dangerous adversary, her body reacted exactly the same. As if he'd placed his hands on her skin and caressed her naked flesh, not sparing an inch.

Adrian motioned with a wave of his arm for her to enter first. Somehow, she managed to put one foot in front of the other until she stood inside Cole DeMarco's lair. Its chocolate walls, the walnut furniture, and the flickering flames coming from the fireplace gave the first impression of a homey, comfortable room similar to her father's before the FBI had raided it and cleaned it bare.

Her gaze fell on the man who'd haunted her in dreams and tormented her in nightmares. He didn't get up to greet her. Didn't welcome her with a smile.

From behind his desk, he sat tall in his chair, his muscular, tattooed arms folded in front of him. His brown eyes narrowed, and he scowled at her.

Her swallow caught in her throat. What could she possibly have done to anger him? She'd only just arrived.

Besides, she never elicited a strong reaction out of anyone. She usually faded into the shadows.

He glared at her, a muscle twitching in his left cheek. Then his gaze jumped to the man standing behind her, leaving her feeling as if he'd found her wanting. "Adrian, wait outside my office." He spoke softly, his voice holding none of the anger he'd directed toward her. "Sedona and Lily, I believe you're wanted in the kitchen. Thank you both for your services."

From behind the desk, two naked women suddenly popped up onto their feet, thin, red streaks marking their perky breasts and firm abdomens. Something sour burned in Danielle's belly. Something bitter and twisted.

These were the type of women Cole preferred.

The women bowed their blonde heads. In unison, they turned from Cole and strolled toward the exit. As they moved past her, they each gave a quizzical raise of their brow, as if questioning her presence.

The door shut with a gentle click, leaving her alone with a monster. Although the room was warm, she shivered.

He leveled his stare on her. "Are you cold?"

His simple black T-shirt stretched tight over a broad chest, each inhalation giving her a glimpse of the muscles underneath. He'd shaved his head clean and grown a short goatee, hiding the dimple in his chin she'd adored from afar as a teenager. He looked even better than she'd remembered and every bit as dangerous.

He gave no indication of remembering her. True, she'd lost more than fifty pounds since she was seventeen, but how could he not recognize her?

She realized she was biting her fingernail and took it out of her mouth. "No. Why?"

Glowering, he pushed his chair back and stood, drawing her attention to the fly of his army green cargo pants. She blew out a breath, relieved that not only was he wearing pants, but also that they were zipped. After discovering women on their knees with him, she hadn't known what to expect.

All six feet plus of him stomped around to the front of his desk, motioning at her with a wave of his large hand. "You're still wearing your coat. I promise no one will steal your mink. I have video cameras set up all around the house. Nothing goes on without my knowledge."

"You must not trust easily if you require so many cameras."

He moved close, towering over her, his spicy scent doing something to her body she'd rather it not. Time had been kind to this man, who despite being close to forty, appeared ageless, his skin a smooth and creamy caramel. "The slave trainees live by my rules if they choose to stay in my home, but I'm not a fool. It's always good to have backup. There are cameras everywhere except for the bathrooms and the slaves' residence." He held out his hand. "Now, since you're not cold, allow me to take your coat. I promise it will stay safe."

Her reluctance to remove her coat had nothing to do with her fear of theft. She simply wasn't prepared to reveal her body to him yet. Cole continued to offer his hand, and she had a feeling she didn't have an option of refusing if she wanted to stay.

Screw want. She *needed* to stay.

For Tasha.

And for her father.

Steeling herself for his rejection, she slowly unbuttoned her coat, starting at the top and working her way down, one by one until she ran out of buttons…and time. Pulling the flaps of her coat open, she exposed her sparsely clad body.

The kidnappers had instructed her to wear the clothes they'd provided. In the airport bathroom, she'd changed out of her conservative slacks and blouse into a black leather corset and a tiny scrap of lacy fabric that was supposed to pass for panties. Prior to an hour ago, she'd never worn either type of underclothes, having always bought comfortable full-size cotton underwear and sensible underwire bras.

The corset sucked in her stomach and cinched tight at her waist, making it more difficult to breathe. Not to mention her D-cup breasts practically spilled over the top.

As he took in the sight of her in the unflattering attire, Cole clenched his jaw, and his outstretched hand curled into a fist.

This is why she'd never given into the desire to truly expose herself to others. Why she'd limited herself to sunbathing naked by the pool and driving alone in her SUV with her skirt hiked up to her waist where she could feel exposed, even though no one could see her. Why she'd remained in the shadows at parties, bringing herself to climax by discreetly rubbing her forearms across her distended nipples and pressing her clitoris into a chair or the edge of a wall column. In addition to the fact that acting on several of her urges would be illegal, no one wanted to see her naked body.

Tears threatened, burning her eyes, but she blinked them back, refusing to admit defeat and wither away like a vine in winter. Instead she turned around and slipped the mink off her shoulders.

A warm breath caressed the shell of her ear. Antsy excitement swirled through her belly upon the realization that Cole had positioned himself right behind her, so close she felt the heat radiating from him. She swore she felt his nose in her hair, almost as though he was inhaling her scent. Her eyelids fluttered shut, and she stifled a moan when Cole's fingertips lightly brushed the tops of her arms.

"Sit, Danielle," he said, the harsh tone of the command knocking her back to reality.

He'd taken her coat while she'd continued to stand with her back to him like an idiot, lost in a fantasy where he wasn't her enemy, and she wasn't here under duress.

He set the mink on the back of a chair and perched himself on the edge of his desk. At least he no longer looked as though he wanted her out of his home. In fact, she couldn't read his emotionless face at all.

The sudden change in his demeanor threw off her equilibrium, and she didn't like it, preferring his blatant antagonism over the composed businessman in front of her. Throughout her life, she'd watched how women could manipulate men simply with a smile or a brush of a hand down a tuxedoed chest.

Unlike them, this man would prove difficult to manipulate. He'd burn as hot as lava then freeze as cold as an iceberg, burying any and all his secrets far beneath the surface. How far would she have to dig in order to expose them?

Realizing he was waiting for her to follow his order, she stifled the embarrassment of being in lingerie and toed across the carpet. She lowered herself into the padded chair and, as she'd been taught in training school, crossed her legs at the ankles like a lady.

She shifted in her seat, making her aware of the dull throbbing and the sticky mix of nervous perspiration and proof of her sexual desire between her legs. If only he'd permitted her to wear real panties, she wouldn't be so cognizant of the man's effect on her. Every moment in his presence reminded her of the power he held over her.

And he'd never had a clue. Had no idea the teenager of his business partner slid her hands under the band of her underwear every night and fantasized about what it would mean to belong to a man like Cole DeMarco.

Even then, naïve and sheltered, she'd sensed something different about him. Something that set him apart from the boys who groped with sweaty hands and her father's married friends who stared at her with lust. It hadn't been until later, when Tasha told her about Benediction, that she understood what had attracted her to Cole. Like Danielle, he was a sexual deviant.

He still hadn't mentioned their shared past. Did he know the child of the man he'd condemned to death sat before him?

His eyebrows rose, and he cocked his head as he assessed her. "Were you aroused by the sight of my slaves' submission?"

"What?" She squirmed, her heart pounding so hard she swore she could hear it. "No."

"I think you're lying." He leaned forward, pinning her to her chair with the intensity in his eyes. She felt a compulsion to avert her gaze, one stronger than the usual kind brought on by her shyness. But rather than give in, she held her ground. He smiled predatorily, his teeth white against his mocha skin and a sparkle of gold in his dark brown eyes. "Perhaps I should check."

Chapter Three

SCREW BEING LADYLIKE. She uncrossed her legs and squeezed her thighs together. "Check?"

"Yes," he said, the damn arrogant smile that made her insides quiver still on his face. "As your Master, it's my right. Of course, I always abide by my slaves' hard limits, but since your application we received last month indicated you have none, I can do whatever I want with you." The smile melted, replaced by a curl of his lips and flaring of his nostrils, both of which reminded her how dangerous this man could be. "I can pull up your skirt, push you over my desk, and work my fingers into your pussy, one by one, until you're full of me. Until you come over and over and over and you're mindless and begging for me to stop. I can call five of my closest friends and order you to fuck each and every one of them. I can—"

"No," she whispered, her throat too dry to protest louder.

The kidnappers had submitted her application a month ago? How long had they planned this?

"No?" He folded his arms across his chest, accentuating his massive forearms. "Then why didn't you provide your limits on your questionnaire?"

She hadn't seen the application, but based on the research she'd done in the last few hours, there were numerous choices when it came to BDSM. "There must have been a computer error."

"A computer error. That is disheartening." He frowned. "Your application was approved based on your answers."

Her heart plummeted to her feet as she shot from her seat. "Does that mean you're going to reject my application? Because I dropped everything and flew across the country for this opportunity. I might lose my docent job at the Phoenix Art Museum. Doesn't that prove I'm serious?"

"It proves nothing." He slid off the desk and inched closer, towering over her. "Now tell me the truth." He softly gripped her chin between his thumb and forefinger. "Why are you here?"

The urge to tell him the truth about Tasha's kidnapping had her nearly spilling everything. But how could she trust the man who'd provided fabricated evidence of her father's embezzlement and security fraud to the FBI? The father she'd known and loved wouldn't have cheated his clients out of their money. For her, there was only one explanation: Cole DeMarco had set her father up for the crimes. He'd been her father's business partner in his wealth management firm, Walker Investment Securities, and yet he'd completely escaped liability.

No matter how much she'd pressed her father about the accusations against him, he'd remained silent on the subject, going as far as foolishly pleading guilty to all charges and accepting a life sentence in federal prison.

The last time she'd visited her father there, she'd begged him to hire the new attorney she'd found who believed he could overturn the plea deal, but he'd stubbornly refused.

Less than a week later, he'd committed suicide.

Any lingering teenage romantic feelings she'd had for Cole died along with him. From then on, all her fantasies of Cole DeMarco had revolved around revenge and finding the evidence to prove her father's innocence.

Which is why she didn't understand how she could still be attracted to him. Trapped both by his touch and the magnetic pull in his eyes, she had no choice but to answer as honestly as she could. "I want you to train me to be a slave."

A low hiss emitted from between his clenched teeth, and a pained expression pinched the corners of his eyes. "Do you even know what a slave is, Danielle?"

"Of course. I wouldn't be here otherwise."

Actually, she knew very little about slaves. Was he going to tell her what to wear and what to eat? Would every move be dictated by him for her entire stay?

He relinquished his grip on her and took a step back, but she could still feel the warmth of his fingers on her skin. "And why do you wish to become a slave?"

Sensing this was a trick question, she toyed with the bottom edge of the corset, resisting her usual habit of biting her nails. "Didn't I explain it in my application?"

"Your application was vague, to say the very least." His jaw tensed as he rounded his desk and took his seat behind it. Then he slapped down a file marked with her name. "I don't permit liars in my club or in my home. That's not what this lifestyle is about. Safe, Sane, Consensual. I need to ensure you meet those standards, or you'll find yourself on the next plane back to Arizona. Why are you here?" He didn't raise his voice, but it was tight, as if he was barely containing his anger.

Honestly, she'd prefer if he yelled. At least then she'd remember she was supposed to hate him.

"There's a man. A Dom…Dominant. He's asked me to marry him, but he has certain needs. He says he'll give up BDSM for me, but I worry I won't satisfy that part of him." When Roman had proposed marriage before leaving for his business trip, she'd been shocked. She loved him dearly, but as a friend, and she thought he'd felt the same. As for the part about him being a Dom, she'd learned that bit of information one night when the two of them had gotten drunk celebrating the New Year with a bottle of vodka. Pretending to gag but secretly curious about what that meant, she'd made him promise never to discuss his sex life with her again.

Cole ran his hand over his bald head. "This isn't a job like a cashier at McDonald's. This is a lifestyle. You don't just wake up one day and decide to become a submissive. It's in your blood, your head, your heart. It's a part of your identity, and without it, you're incomplete."

"That's me."

His lips twisted into a semblance of a smile. "Really? I'm so glad to hear it. I have my doubts about training you. If you really want this, you're going to have to convince me." He pressed the speaker on his desk phone and pressed a couple numbers. "Adrian. Please come into my office." He punched off the speaker with his fist and sat back in his chair, folding his arms across his chest, smirking as if he held the secrets to the world in his hands.

"What are you going to do?" she asked.

"Whatever I want. Isn't that what you agreed to?"

There was a double knock and the subtle groan of the door opening a moment before Adrian entered the room looking every bit as uncomfortable as he had when he left. He paused by the desk, his arms clasped behind him. "Master. How may I please you?"

Cole pushed back from his desk and swiveled his chair toward Adrian. "I'm afraid our new slave here is keeping secrets. That deserves a punishment, don't you agree?"

Adrian bowed his head. "Yes, Master."

Punishment? A chill passed through her, hardening her nipples and creating shivers down her arms. A heaviness settled in her chest, causing her to feel breathless. She was guessing punishment wouldn't be a time-out. Her own father had never laid a hand on her in reprimand. She'd never given him reason. Fifteen minutes in this house and she'd already earned one. How the heck would she survive however long it took to save Tasha?

The strangest part of it was her reaction was only based in part on fear. She hated that his words aroused her, and she had no idea why.

"What's your favorite color, Danielle?" Cole asked.

Shivering, she thought about home and the burning glow of the Arizona sun on Mt. McDowell at sunset, so different from the cold she'd found in Michigan. "I... uh...red."

Adrian chuckled but covered it with a cough and a hand to his full lips. Her stomach swooped and her body tingled as though she was on a roller coaster, balanced on the top of the largest hill, facing the inevitable drop.

"She's new to this, so I think we'll start gentle," Cole said to Adrian. "Let's try ten open-hand spankings."

Her mouth parted to protest, but the image in her mind of Tasha being blindfolded, bound, and gagged stopped her. Who knew what horrible things were happening to her right now?

The least Danielle could do was endure a harmless spanking. How badly could it hurt?

"Take off your panties and bend over my desk. Let's see if Adrian can turn your ass your favorite color."

She sucked in a large breath and slowly let it out, gathering the nerve to bare herself to these men. They'd already seen most of her, and she'd survived.

She sighed. "I should've said pink."

Adrian didn't suppress his laughter this time. Cole, on the other hand, didn't appear amused, his lips tightened into a straight line. "I'll pretend I didn't hear that, but in the future, back talk will result in additional punishment, brat."

A brat? Her? He really didn't know her at all. No one here did.

And that's when it hit her. Here at Benediction, she was a blank slate. She could be whomever she wanted. For the first time in her life, it was safe to surrender to her secret desires.

She rose from the chair and crossed to stand in front of the fireplace. As the fire warmed her skin, she slipped her fingers under the waistband of her panties and dragged them down her legs. Both men tracked her movements, making her feel as though she was on display.

Hanging the scrap of lace on her finger, she waved it back and forth before it fluttered to the carpet. Cole and Adrian stared at her hairless pussy with lust in their eyes.

Infused with a sense of power she'd never known, she stepped out of the shadows of the fireplace and moved to the desk. She laid her chest on the desk, the position making her hyperaware of the restrictive boning of the corset. With her ass to Adrian, she rested her cheek on the cool, smooth wood so she could still see Cole.

His gaze burned into her. "Danielle, I want you to count each spank out loud."

"Yes, sir," she said, hoping she wasn't supposed to call him Master.

Anticipating the first blow, she held her breath and closed her eyes. Adrian settled his hand low on her spine and pressed as if holding her in place. As soon as she realized that was exactly the point, he smacked her left bottom cheek, the force of it sliding her forward and the sting of it causing tears.

"One," she whispered, her voice cracking. No way could she take nine more of these without bursting into tears.

"Danielle," Cole said softly. "Look at me."

Compelled by the gentleness in his voice, she opened her eyes. Cole's pupils swallowed his brown irises, giving him the look of a man who was about to lose control. *Because of her.* She didn't know how or why. All she knew was she liked it.

Cole gestured to Adrian, and the slave slapped her again, this time on the right side.

"Two," she said, maintaining eye contact with Cole. For each subsequent blow, she counted, her voice steady and strong. It still hurt. Her ass and upper thighs stung like she'd sat on hot summer asphalt. Clearly, she wasn't a masochist. But rather than focus on it, she watched as Cole's eyes grew hooded. Watched as his breathing turned shallow and rapid and his throat worked over a swallow.

And in turn, he watched her equally as intently, as if he saw straight into her soul.

Her pussy throbbed, her vaginal muscles clenching and releasing, a pressure building low in her belly. By the time she counted to ten, her entire lower half pulsated with heat.

"Adrian, check if she's aroused," Cole said almost in a growl.

The slave slid his hand down her ass and all too briefly brushed his fingers through the folds of her pussy before removing his hands from her body altogether. "Yes, Master. She's extremely wet."

"Do you want an orgasm, Danielle?"

"Yes, sir. Please," she begged, her hips canting backward in a shameless attempt to cajole Adrian into touching her.

"Bring her to me," Cole ordered, the deep timbre of his voice almost bringing her to climax.

With a hand on her waist and one on her shoulder, Adrian led her to Cole.

He yanked her down to his lap, facing her outward, and then banded one arm above her breasts and one arm around her middle, securing her to him. "Spread your thighs and hook your feet behind my legs." Without a thought, she obeyed, exposing her pink, swollen folds to the blond slave who stared at her with sexual interest as he licked his lower lip. "Adrian, on your knees. Hands clasped behind your back. Use only your mouth. For every minute it takes to make her come, I'll tack on another minute to your cock torture."

Adrian dropped in front of her, his blue eyes narrowly focused on her sex. Her heart beat in tempo with a pounding between her thighs. She'd never felt so wanton. So alive. But it wasn't Adrian who made her feel that way. It was the man underneath her. The man whose rock hard thighs pressed into the softness of hers. The scent of him, as if he were fresh from the shower, surrounded her, making her mouth water for a taste of his skin.

She melted into his hold, becoming one with him, her body his puppet to command. Her darkest teenage fantasies brought to life by the man she'd dreamed of every time she'd rubbed her clitoris to orgasm. In none of them had Cole sat like a king on his throne, summoning his subjects to do his bidding. No, in her dreams, he'd touch her with his own callused fingers she'd imagined he got from spending hours in the gym lifting weights to maintain his muscular physique. He'd lick her with the tip of his tongue, circling her bud until her thighs shook from the impending orgasm. Then he'd pin her down with his weight and drive his cock into her again and again.

In her wildest fantasies, she couldn't have conjured this situation. Yet it was as if he knew her better than she knew herself, because something about Cole demanding Adrian to pleasure her made it a million degrees hotter than if he did it himself. The muscles of her pussy fluttered in a mini-orgasm, evidence of it trickling down her thigh.

She moaned, lost on a tumultuous sea of aching need that threatened to drown her. Cole's chest, pillowing the back of her head, rose and fell in rhythmic pulls of air, and she found herself synchronizing her breathing to his.

Adrian's face dipped closer to her pussy, his blond hair tickling the inside of her thighs. She silently pleaded for him to relieve her of the coiling spools of need before she lost her mind.

His tongue darted out to tease the hood of her clit, barely more than a whisper of contact, but it was enough to make her body tense and jump.

Cole grabbed her before she bolted, one arm settling under her breasts and the other on her collarbone. "Shh, pet. I'll keep you safe. Let Adrian make you feel good. Unless you'd rather rescind your application?"

It didn't matter what the application allowed him to do to her. She'd do it. For more reasons than she could name.

"I'll stay." She rested her head on his chest and turned herself over to his command, the heat from his hold searing into her. And that wasn't the only thing she felt. The hardness from his erection prodded her lower back.

Before she could regain control of her senses, Adrian resumed his position between her legs, lapping at her slit with the tip of his tongue. Mindless from pleasure, she ground her ass into Cole's cock, savoring the solid muscles beneath her back and the attentions of two men. But only one really mattered.

She twisted her neck to look up at Cole and froze at the heat in his eyes. Could he actually want her? Or was she just one more slave for him to command?

Adrian sucked her clitoris into his mouth. A moan she didn't recognize as her own tore from her chest. She'd never experienced anything like the pleasure that swarmed her. It burned, almost like standing too close to a flame. Her legs trembled. Every muscle coiled tight as she waited on the edge of the cliff for the final push that would make her unravel.

"Come," Cole mouthed silently to her.

And she did, the climax slamming into her with the force of a tsunami, the erotic wave starting from deep inside her core and flowing outward, washing away everything in its path. Bursts of colors blurred her vision, and she shut her eyes, powerless over the pulsations wracking her body.

Cole slipped his hand under her knees and pivoted her so she sat sideways on his lap. She rested her head on his shoulder, the adrenaline she'd been running on the last couple days depleted. "I'm not even sure how to count that, Adrian. I suppose it warrants an immediate removal of the cock ring."

"Thank you, Master," Adrian said.

She tried to thank him for the orgasm, but she was too tired to speak. Cole shifted his position in the chair and smoothed his hand over her hair. The door clicked shut, and she sighed, relaxed for the first time since she awoke to find the kidnappers in her room.

The scent of chocolate brought her back to reality, and she lifted her head, opening her eyes.

"Have a piece of candy and drink some water," Cole said, holding a bottle and a chocolate square in front of her face. "How do you feel, Danielle?"

She blinked, suddenly aware of the subtle ache of her naked behind, which was currently resting on Cole's legs. Her cheeks—the ones on her face—heated, and she dragged her fingers through her hair to cloak them.

How did she feel? Confused. Embarrassed. She'd never thought she was the type of woman who would enjoy a ménage à trois. But no way in hell was she going to tell him that. "Fine," she said, snatching the water, then slipping off his lap.

She scooped up her panties from the carpet and slid them on. Not that they'd do her much good.

"You have no reason to be ashamed," he said as if he'd plucked her thoughts from her head. Cole crossed to her, the animosity he'd displayed prior to her punishment completely gone, replaced with a softness she'd expect from a friend. "You're a passionate and sensual woman."

"Me? Sensual?" She laughed, placing her hands on her hips.

He moved closer and pushed the hair off her face, allowing it to glide though his fingers. "What about the man who wants to marry you? Surely he must know how hot you burn."

"He and I are waiting until marriage." The lie rolled off her tongue easily but left behind a bitter taste. She had no intention of ever marrying Roman.

Cole arched a brow. "He doesn't mind that you're here?"

She realized she was biting her nails again and dropped her hand to her side. "We're currently on a break."

His gaze landed on her lips. "A woman like you may appear reserved to those who don't see to the heart of you. I pity them, but their loss is Benediction's gain." He leaned closer, murmuring in her ear. "You don't fool me, Danielle. I won't confuse aloofness with shyness. I may not know your true reason for coming here, but I do know you're in the right place. While you're training, I'll make certain I fulfill all your sexual fantasies." He cupped her cheek. "Whatever they are."

Everything went still, even the air in her lungs. Unable to move, unable to breathe, unable to look away from his heated stare, she did nothing but wait. Wait for the world to start spinning again. For now, she understood why they called him "Master." He lured you with his deep, soothing voice, trapped you with his hypnotic eyes, and seduced you with barely a whisper of his touch. If she wasn't careful, he could easily make her forget her true reason for being here.

It didn't matter that she was as attracted to him as she'd been all those years ago. This is what he did. Convince you to trust him and then toss you to the lions, just like he'd done to her father. She wouldn't allow him to steal anything more from her. The time had come for Cole DeMarco to answer for his sins. She'd play the part of sex slave and, of course, enjoy the chance to broaden her sexual horizons. But never again—not for one second—would she allow this man to truly dominate her.

Breathing deep, she tore her gaze away and folded her arms over her chest. "So you'll train me?"

He pressed his lips together and paused before giving her a single nod. "We'll start tomorrow." He strode to a filing cabinet along the wall, flung open a drawer, and snatched a few papers. Then he picked up a couple of books off his desk and handed it all to her. "Here's another questionnaire to complete. This time, answer it honestly. Also, I'd like you to read these books tonight. There's a lot of crap out there on BDSM. Forget everything you think you know. These will give you a better understanding of what you're getting yourself into. For now, consider yourself to be on probation."

While Cole called someone named Gracie on his cell phone, she perused the questionnaire, baffled by its ten-page length. Slave auctions? Pony play? Water sports? Was that some kind of kinky surfboarding she didn't know about? And the kidnappers had agreed to all of it on her behalf? No wonder Cole didn't believe her story.

There was a brief knock on the door, and then a petite Asian woman wearing a shiny red minidress and six-inch red stilettos glided into the room.

"Gracie, please show Danielle to her bedroom." Cole lifted the mink off the back of the chair and brought it to Danielle, holding it open for her. She sighed in relief, not quite ready to brazenly walk through the mansion half-naked, and turned around, slipping her arms into the sleeves.

"You know," Cole said quietly behind her, "had you applied earlier, you would have been automatically denied based on the age requirement that slaves be at least twenty-five years old. Happy birthday, by the way." He wrapped his hands around the upper part of her mink-covered arms. "I still have my doubts, but I'm willing to give you some time to prove to me your sincerity. If I decide you're not being honest with me, I'll send you back home." He gently turned her to face him. "I don't care who your father was."

She gasped, his words causing her muscles to tense and her heart to race. "You know who I am." Why hadn't he mentioned it earlier?

His expression grew somber. "Of course. I wouldn't have permitted you here based on your ridiculous application. Consider this a favor." He took her hand in his and kissed the inside of her wrist, eliciting an involuntary shiver. "And, Danielle, you should know...I always collect on my favors."

Chapter Four

COLE REMEMBERS ME.

Danielle nervously toyed with her locket as she followed a very perky Gracie through the mansion. The woman chattered incessantly and pointed out each room with great detail. So far, she'd learned Cole's grandfather had built the family home after returning from World War Two and that Cole had turned it into a sex club when his parents had moved out fifteen years ago.

She tried to keep up, but her mind kept wandering back to the feel of Cole's arms around her and the way his eyes seemed to see straight into her soul.

He not only knew who she was, he'd approved her application because of it. What motivated his decision? Guilt because he'd knowingly allowed her father to go to prison for crimes he hadn't committed?

For too long, she'd carried around the guilt of causing her mother's death during childbirth. Saving Tasha, the only mother she'd ever known, would hopefully alleviate some of the guilt, but she also couldn't ignore the presented opportunity to learn the truth about her father's alleged crimes and clear his name. She owed it to him after the way she'd left things on her last prison visit. Eight years later, the cruelty of her final words still haunted her.

And yet she'd forgotten everything once that electric buzz filled her body just as it did the first time she'd set eyes on Cole DeMarco. She'd been seventeen when she'd spied him from the stairs of her home. He and her father had finished their meeting and were saying their good-byes.

He'd looked like a hero out of one of her historical romances about pirates, with a goatee and long black hair he wore in braids. He hadn't worn a business suit like the other men her father did business with, but instead wore jeans and a Detroit Tigers T-shirt. He'd been far younger too. Closer to her age than her father's forty-five years.

She'd willed him to turn his head. To see her. Just as she'd given up and had been about to go back upstairs, he'd looked directly at her. Their gazes locked for only a moment, but it had been enough to send her pulse skyrocketing and for an ache to settle between her legs.

Then he'd gone, leaving her wondering if she'd imagined it.

But in her fantasy, he'd crossed the foyer of the home and climbed the staircase to her. He'd taken her hand. Her dream fast-forwarded to the moment when he'd taken her virginity and vowed to love her for the rest of their lives.

Although he'd only visited the house a couple more times, she had always made sure to be there on the stairs when he'd arrived and when he'd left. Each time, she'd hold her breath, waiting for that brief moment when they'd make eye contact. He'd never once disappointed her.

How innocent she'd been. How silly. Who would've guessed eight years later she'd be living in that man's sex club?

If she'd known then that a few months later he would destroy her family and have her father sent to prison, she would've run back upstairs the minute she saw him and never waited for him on those stairs again.

Shaking her head to clear her mind, Danielle admired the vaulted ceilings, crown moldings, and dramatic archways of the home, overwhelmed by its intricate design. They passed two sets of stairs as well as a vast library she wanted to explore if she got the opportunity. Nothing revealed more about a person than their books.

Without pausing for a breath, Gracie switched from the history of the home to complaining about the snowy weather and then back to how each room was used when Benediction opened to the members at night. Something about a dungeon in the basement and fantasy rooms upstairs. From her description, the mansion sounded more like a castle.

As Gracie led her into the kitchen, Danielle's stomach cramped from nerves and hunger. Other than that chocolate, she hadn't eaten a bite since last night's dinner, too worried about Tasha and what to expect at a sex club.

Guess now that she'd experienced both pleasure and punishment, her appetite had returned.

She spotted a bowl of fruit, and while Gracie went over the open kitchen policy, Danielle nabbed a red apple to take up to her room. It wasn't much, but she didn't think she could manage anything more.

A silence befell the room.

Gracie stared at her expectantly. "You don't talk much, do you?" she asked. She didn't pause before answering her own question. "No, you're shy. I can tell. I'm a people person. An extrovert. I have a habit of talking too much and too fast, so I end up wearing a gag most of the time in the dungeon. Otherwise, the Masters will fill my mouth with their cocks. That works as well as a gag, and they seem to enjoy it more. Apparently, even in sub-space I can be quite chatty. Although I never shut up, I'm a surprisingly great secret-keeper. You could tickle torture me, and I still wouldn't give up a secret. You're obviously an introvert. I bet you like to read." She snatched a banana from the fruit bowl, peeled it, and took a bite. "What do you like to read?"

Danielle remained silent, unsure of whether Gracie actually wanted an answer. She did love to read, having spent most of her adolescence with her nose in a book and later, with her e-reader. Her novels took her away from the reality of being a painfully awkward, overweight child to the ballrooms of regency England, where the wallflowers married the handsome dukes, and to modern-day America, where tormented vampires fell in love with plain mortal women.

Sure enough, Gracie pursed her lips, then answered her own question. "Romance, right?" At Danielle's nod in confirmation, she continued. "I like the kinky books myself, especially the ménage ones. You know what I say: The more, the merrier." She giggled. "I'll let you in on a secret. Reality?" She grabbed Danielle's hand and squeezed as if they were best friends. "So much better than fiction."

To hide her shock, Danielle bit into her apple and took her time chewing as Gracie led her up a staircase at the back of the kitchen. Then again, who was she to judge? Hadn't she just allowed Adrian between her legs as Cole held her? Maybe it hadn't been a true ménage, but it certainly fell into what most people would consider kinky.

Besides, unlike the snobby girls she'd grown up with in Arizona, Gracie was refreshingly honest. She liked that about her. Regardless of Gracie's declaration about secret keeping, Danielle still couldn't completely trust her, but it would be nice to have someone to talk to—if Gracie would ever give her the chance.

The winding stairs took them to the second floor of the home, where mirrors of various shapes and sizes lined the walls of the carpeted hallway. "This is where we live," Gracie said as they passed several closed doors. "You can only access the living quarters through the kitchen. The other staircases lead to the club areas. Master has his private residence on the attic level of the house, but none of the slaves have ever seen it." Halfway down the hall, Gracie opened one of the doors and stepped inside a room.

Gracie crossed to the other side of the room and pulled back the drapes to bring sunlight in through the wall-sized window, showing off a four-poster walnut bed covered with a virginal white goose-down blanket and a matching walnut dresser, desk, and nightstand. For a moment, Danielle forgot where she was, captivated by the comfort of the room.

The sun's rays ricocheted off the beautiful pale pink crystal chandelier, which hung in the center of the room, creating slivers of dancing lights on the walls and frames behind the bed. The lights turned on, and her sight focused on the framed images.

Three Degas paintings.

Her Degas paintings.

Not the prints hanging on her walls now, but the originals, which had graced her walls before the government had confiscated almost everything in her home. The dainty dancers whom she'd envied as a child, knowing she'd never have the lithe body required for ballet. Despite that, she'd loved those paintings. To see them here, under Cole DeMarco's roof in the very room he'd assigned to her, reminded her of everything she'd lost.

Everything he'd taken from her.

When Gracie took a breath, Danielle cleared her throat and took the opportunity to prove she knew how to use her vocal cords. "How long have you been a trainee?"

"Oh, I'm not a trainee. I belong to Master Cole."

Danielle rubbed her chest where a raw ache had settled. "You're his…?"

"Slave. Yes. For two years."

"I thought he only trained." Of course he had slaves. He probably had a submissive or two at his beck and call at all times.

"He did. Until me. Now there's two of us who remain here permanently. Myself and Adrian."

Danielle smoothed her hand over the comforter. "Oh. Do you, um—"

"Fuck him? No." Gracie sighed. "Not that we haven't tried. He doesn't have sex with the slaves or trainees, although he has no problem getting us off through other ways. You'll understand after a few days. Somehow, Master knows us better than we know ourselves." She settled on the front edge of the bed and patted the spot next to her. "The man swears he's not a sadist, but he loves to watch his slaves squirm with desperation. I'd take a paddling over an orgasm denial any day. Right?"

Danielle sat beside her. "Um, right." Did all women speak so freely about sex? "Do you, um, get paid for being a slave?"

"Not officially, but the members' fees pay for my weekly stipend plus my living expenses, which remain low since my room and board are both covered. It's structured similarly to your trainee agreement." Gracie slid her a quizzical glance. "You did read your agreement, didn't you?"

"Of course. So what do you do for him?" Hating all the lies that were piling up, she nibbled on her thumbnail.

"Master tries to give me more of the social responsibilities in Benediction, like greeting the guests and taking their coats. Has he given you your first service requirement yet?"

Danielle ripped her thumb from her mouth and laced her fingers together to keep from biting on them. "I don't think so. What is that?"

"The trainees are responsible for cooking, cleaning, running errands, and anything else Master needs to run the house and club. It's kind of like working in the mailroom of a large corporation. You have to start at the bottom and work your way up."

"So I won't be expected to have sex?" Her stomach dropped, and she wasn't sure if the cause was relief or disappointment.

Gracie shrugged. "It depends. I was ready on my first day because I'd been coming to Benediction for seven years. A membership was the first thing I bought with the money I got from my trust fund on my eighteenth birthday."

"Eighteen?" On Danielle's eighteenth birthday, she'd had no idea what to register for in her first semester of college, much less know her sexual preferences. "How did you know you were…?"

"Submissive? Kinky? It's something I was born with. I've known since puberty. While other girls fantasized about kisses and getting felt up by thirteen-year-old boys, I was dreaming about adult men tying me up and spanking me. I never felt like I fit in with the rest of the vanilla world. It took a lot of energy to fake it. What about you?"

Although Danielle was here under deceptive circumstances, she'd felt as though she'd been a fraud her entire life. Being overweight and shy had prevented her from making a lot of friends, and other than Roman, when an occasional someone had broken through her shell and befriended her, she'd kept walls up, never allowing herself to grow close to anyone. "I've never fit in either."

"That's one of the things I love about kink," Gracie said, wrapping an arm around Danielle. "The community. We're all freaks in our own ways, and we don't pass judgment on one another. Okay, maybe a few of us do, like Cassandra, who unfortunately you'll meet soon." She patted Danielle's thigh as if reassuring her. "But you can finally be who you are inside without fear of recrimination."

Danielle exhaled. "What if I don't know who I am?"

"Don't worry your pretty head about it. Master will help you find out. Just enjoy the ride, and everything will fall into place. I take it you don't have a lot of experience in BDSM." At the knock of the door, Gracie jumped up from the bed and skipped across the floor. "That should be your new wardrobe!"

She flung open the door. Holding several hangers of clothing, a tall redhead strutted into the room like a model on a runway.

"I have the clothes Master ordered." The redhead stopped in front of the bed and glared at Danielle in disdain, pursing her lips as though she'd eaten a lemon. "Hm. I don't think Master gave me the correct size. I doubt any of these will fit you."

Although Gracie had warned her about Cassandra, the words still stung, and the bit of confidence she'd acquired from her short time here dissipated.

Gracie rolled her eyes. "Danielle, this is Cassandra. She's a bitch. Don't pay her any attention." She plucked the clothes from Cassandra's hands and gave Danielle a wink before hanging them up in the closet. "I think you'll look hot in these."

"Already hitting on the new girl?" Cassandra placed a perfectly manicured hand on her bony hip and smirked like a stereotypical high school bully.

Gracie twirled on her heels and stomped to the door, pointing her finger to the hallway. "Get out, Cassandra. You're just jealous because Master let me go to the freeway last night while Sir Logan used you in his *Shibari* demonstration and didn't get you off."

"Even without an orgasm, I'd rather have Logan Bradford's undivided attention than an orgy with a room full of strangers."

"Sir Logan isn't going to fall for your innocent act, Cassandra. Now, why don't you crawl back into the hole where you came from?"

Cassandra tossed her hair over her shoulder as she sashayed across the room and out the door. "One day I'm going to make you sorry. You can count on it."

"You can try." Gracie slammed the door, then rested her back against it. "Don't let her scare you. She thinks she's a lioness, but she's really a declawed alley cat. Lots of noise but totally harmless."

Danielle hoped her path wouldn't cross much with Cassandra's during her stay. She had enough to worry about. "I have to be honest. A lot of what you were talking about went over my head. It's like listening to a foreign language."

"I'll try and explain it in vanilla terms." Gracie pushed off the door and resumed her spot on the bed next to

Danielle. "Last night, Master assigned Cassandra to help one of the members with his demonstration. *Shibari* is a form of bondage, and one of its multitude of perks is the unique placement of the knots." She emphasized the word "unique," but Danielle still had no clue what it meant. "Master requested that Sir Logan leave Cassandra unsatisfied."

It may have been petty, but hearing it made Danielle smile. "Why would he do that?"

"Who knows?" Gracie shrugged. "Master always has his reasons. My guess is she needed a reminder we slaves are here to serve our Master. We're like nuns, only we wear less clothes and get to have sex." She skipped to the dresser and lifted a silver wristband with a key attached to it. "This is your trainee bracelet and your room key. Wear it at all times." She slipped it over Danielle's wrist. "It lets the patrons know to keep their hands off unless Master says otherwise. Your training classes begin at nine every morning, Monday through Friday, and the club opens nightly at eight."

"Classes?" Danielle swallowed hard, the subtle weight of the band around her wrist making everything more real. She was really going to train as a sex slave.

"First thing you've got to learn is safety. No one goes on the floor without that first class." Gracie's voice went from playful to serious before Danielle could blink. "You'd be surprised how much there is to learn about what makes up the requirements of 'Safe, Sane, Consensual.' You'll get enough tomorrow morning to enter the club tomorrow night, but the class runs through your three-month-long training program. Then you'll get classes on protocol, technique, and of course the labs, which are where you get to try out everything."

Danielle reached behind her, grabbing the items she'd acquired from Cole. "I'm supposed to redo my questionnaire, and to be honest, I don't know how I feel about some of these things." She motioned to the form. "There's a few obvious ones I know I won't try, but others…"

Gracie plucked the form from her hand. "The ones you refuse to do are your hard limits, and the ones you're not sure of are your soft limits. For example, fire play and anything to do with bodily fluids are a couple of my hard limits. Needles have always terrified me, but not enough to keep them off my list, so when I first got into the lifestyle, I checked them as a soft limit. Now needle play is a favorite of mine."

She winced at the idea. "Needle" and "play" were two words she never thought would go together. Definitely a hard limit. Perusing the rest of the questionnaire, she stopped on some of the more confusing items. She couldn't help lowering her voice to a whisper. "What about…same sex? How do I know?"

Gracie curled her hand around the back of Danielle's nape. "Only one way to find out." She leaned in and pressed her soft lips against Danielle's, giving her a moment to process before intensifying the kiss. Danielle found herself responding, parting her lips and sighing into Gracie's open mouth. She tasted like banana. And chocolate. Milk chocolate if she wasn't mistaken. Danielle wondered where she could find some more of that chocolate in this place, because the apple had done nothing to diminish her appetite.

Gracie abruptly ended the kiss. "Anything?"

No racing heart. No throb between her thighs. No desire to do it again. Kissing a woman hadn't nauseated her, but it did nothing for her other than make her crave a candy bar. "Not really. I mean, it's not that you're not attractive—"

"If your Master wanted you to do it, would you?" Still smiling, Gracie didn't seem to take offense. "I can't tell you how to answer, but it's something to think about as you complete your questionnaire. Remember, it's our role to serve our Master, but not at our own expense. It's like a mirror. Our happiness reflects on him, and his on us."

Danielle felt as though Gracie was talking in riddles. If kissing a woman didn't excite her sexually, why would she do it for her Master? "I don't understand."

"Don't worry. By the time you finish your training, you won't remember a time you didn't understand. Just keep an open mind and an open heart, and you'll find answers to questions you didn't even know you sought." Gracie hopped up from the bed. "I'll let you get settled, and then I'll come by later so we can have dinner together. If you need anything, press one on the phone to call my cell, two for Adrian, or zero for Master Cole." She threw her arms around Danielle and hugged her tight. "I'm glad you're here. I've been waiting to meet you—I mean, someone like you—for a long time. I have a feeling we're going to be good friends."

After Gracie left the room, Danielle removed her coat, lay back, and stared at the chandelier. Everything here was so confusing. She rubbed her temples. Her vision blurred from exhaustion, and her head ached slightly from lack of sleep, food, and the stress of knowing her stepmother's life was at risk.

In her purse, her cell phone rang. With dread, she retrieved it, then answered the unlisted number. Her stomach plummeted, and her pulse went into overdrive. "Hello?"

"You've been a good girl and followed my directions," said a voice she recognized as the man who'd been in her bedroom last night. "I can't wait to reward you. But first things first. You need to get into DeMarco's private residence. The only way to get to it is through a secret room, which is behind the bookcase in his office. The password to enter that room is 'benediction.' From there you'll need a key to get upstairs to his residence, and DeMarco is the only one who has it. Once you get in, you'll need to find a jewelry box. Your locket will open that box, and inside you'll find a trust document in your name, along with information on an offshore bank account. When you get it, you'll call me at 313-555-2468, and I'll give you further instructions. So far, Tasha is safe. It's up to you to keep her that way. *Tick-tock*, Danielle."

Chapter Five

SHE SHOT FROM the bed, her gaze darting around the room and the nape of her neck prickling. Despite Cole's assertion there were no cameras in the bedrooms, Danielle couldn't shake the feeling of being watched.

Nothing made sense. Why was there a trust in her name hidden in Cole's residence in a box that only her locket could open?

Danielle had very few items of her mother's, which was why the locket had meant so much to her when her father had given it to her on her thirteenth birthday. She'd worn her mother's locket every day since, only removing it to bathe.

Clutching the locket in her hand, she caught her reflection in the dresser mirror, ensnared by the image of her corseted body and the wildness of her brown eyes. In less than twenty-four hours, how did a woman like her go from the quiet solitude of her desert home to kissing a female slave in a sex club?

The reflection staring back at her wasn't someone she recognized. Sensuality radiated from her like a halo, from the flush of her cheeks to the unruly obsidian curls spilling down her shoulders. It was as if her arrival here had been a spark to kindling, igniting something in her she hadn't known existed. As if she'd been holding her breath, waiting for her life to begin, and it finally had.

Only she'd never imagined it would take her stepmother's kidnapping to do it.

Danielle had never been special. She didn't have a particularly outstanding singing voice. Her grades at school had been decent, but she'd been far from an A student. And although she'd loved art, she couldn't draw or paint anything worthy. She conceded she had a pretty face, but at a size sixteen, no one would ever call her beautiful.

Danielle's throat clogged with unshed tears, and she took a deep breath to keep them at bay. She'd spent her life being invisible, watching from the shadows, observing like a ghost. But with all the cameras set up in Benediction, slinking around wouldn't go unnoticed.

To get into his residence, she could either steal Cole's key or convince him to bring her there willingly. In both situations, she'd have to get close to him, and there was only one way do that with an owner of a sex club.

She'd have to *seduce* him.

It wasn't going to be easy. He already doubted her sincerity and questioned her motives. What would it take to get a man like him to lower his guard? Everything she'd read about BDSM in the last twenty-four hours stressed the importance of trust. Yet Cole had dozens of people literally bowing at his feet, and he still relied on cameras in almost every area of his club.

She shuffled across the room to the window and rested her forehead against the cold glass. Her room faced the back of the mansion, where Cole's property seemed to stretch for miles. As far as she could see, white snow blanketed everything. Still, she made out the pattern of a kidney-shaped swimming pool and a basketball court off to its left. In the distance, she spotted a gazebo.

The yard's brightness surprised her. Before today, she'd never experienced snow, having spent most of her days in the desert, except for trips to the ocean or Europe, which were always taken during summer vacation. She'd thought the sky would remain gray like when she'd arrived, but it was as blue and clear as the Mediterranean Sea in Nice, France.

She shivered. The beauty outside her window was all an illusion. She didn't dare forget the frigid temperature or the biting winds. It would prove as dangerous as the middle of the Arizona desert in August.

Sighing, she turned away and got to work unpacking. Other than her toiletries, the kidnappers had permitted only a pair of black pants and a light sweater, so it didn't take more than a minute before she'd emptied her suitcase.

Then she settled on the bed with her trainee application and books. The bed was as soft as it had looked, and she couldn't help but lay her head on the pillow. Her eyes fluttered shut and she blinked, making herself stay awake. Maybe reading about sex would help. She opened up the first book and started to read.

The room grew dim as the sun set, the light turning gray and snow falling from the sky. She attacked the application, checking off boxes and answering questions she'd never thought she'd ever have to answer. In fact, before today she hadn't known some of these kinks existed. A couple she had to look up on her cell phone's web browser.

She didn't get off on pain and doubted she could handle anything more intense than the spanking she'd received earlier. Still, she marked light beatings as a soft limit, figuring she may be able to tolerate items that didn't create too much pain.

Age play and humiliation were definitely hard limits for her, as well as anything to do with bodily fluids.

Then there were the other questions. The ones that made her heart beat a little faster and her breathing quicken. Bondage. Sensation play. Some of the role play. Multiple partners.

And most confusing, public sex.

It was difficult enough to wear lingerie and corsets in public, but nudity? Although she'd been fighting the urges to expose herself since as long as she could remember, she didn't even undress in a locker room. Too self-conscious about her weight, she preferred the privacy of the bathroom stall.

But she couldn't deny her pussy grew wet at the idea of others watching her have sex. Her entire body tightened, and, now lying on her stomach, she realized she was grinding her pelvis into the mattress. With a bit of apprehension, she checked "yes" to several of the items on the list, including multiple partners and public sex.

Chewing on the pencil's eraser, she continued answering the questions until there was a knock on her door. She quickly sat up and swallowed hard. "Come in."

Gracie sauntered into the room, this time wearing a white plastic-looking tube top and matching skirt that barely covered her ass. In fact, if she bent over, Danielle would see more than she wanted. She bounced on the balls of her feet, her long ponytail swishing back and forth. "Master Cole has asked me to bring you to the dungeon tonight."

"I thought I had to wait for my first safety class."

"Yes, that's generally the rule, but it's not my role to question Master Cole's orders. If you're hungry, we can join the other slaves in the dining room for dinner; otherwise, I brought a sandwich, candy bar, and bottled water for you." She held out a little brown lunch bag. "I'll help you get dressed, and we can go downstairs to the basement before it gets too crowded. The first time in a sex club can be a tad overwhelming."

Honestly, she'd hoped to have a quiet dinner and get a night's sleep before her first experience in the dungeon of Benediction, but she'd be lying if she said she wasn't curious. She snatched the bag from Gracie's outstretched hand. "What do I wear?"

Gracie squealed and jumped up and down, clapping. "What you're wearing now is perfect. I'll do your hair and makeup while you eat."

She sat on the edge of the bed. A strange feeling came over her, like she had a lump in her throat. Without her mom or close girlfriends, she hadn't had anyone to share these kinds of activities.

"We're going to have so much fun tonight." Gracie hopped on the bed, settling behind Danielle. "I'm not sure where to take you first."

As Gracie began brushing her hair, Danielle unwrapped the turkey sandwich and nibbled on it, watching Gracie in the mirror. "I was surprised when I got here. Benediction looks like any other home."

"For the most part, it is. Only we have safeguards to limit access. Members use key cards to pass through the gates, and we have a greeter at the front door—run by yours truly most of the time—where we check coats and verify member identification before allowing them beyond the entryway." Gracie took out a rubber band from only God knows where and pulled Danielle's hair off her face.

"What goes on upstairs?"

Apparently finished with Danielle's hair, Gracie leaped to stand in front of her, swiping Danielle's makeup bag off the bed. She pulled out some eye shadow and tipped Danielle's head up toward the light. Danielle shut her eyes, and Gracie swept the makeup across her lids. "Fantasy rooms. We have some downstairs in the dungeon, but those are mainly used for fire play, electrical play, and piercings. That's also where we do our demonstrations, like the *Shibari* Sir Logan did with Cassandra. Upstairs you'll find your fully equipped bedrooms, complete with built-in restraints and other amenities. Several of the rooms have themes. Medical, medieval, mirrors, and then of course, my favorite—the freeway."

Medical? Note to self: Stay out of the dungeon's fantasy rooms. "Why do you refer to Logan as 'Sir' and Cole as 'Master'?"

"Different clubs may have different rules, but in Benediction, while both refer to Dominants, the title of Master is earned after a certain amount of experience. Logan's fairly new to BDSM, which is why he's a 'Sir.' To make things even more confusing, a Dominant may prefer his submissive or slave to call him 'Master.' However, the rest of us would address him as 'Sir.' And of course if it's a woman, we'd use 'Ma'am' and 'Mistress.'"

"My head hurts from all these rules. What if I screw up and call someone the wrong name?" After Gracie applied mascara to Danielle's lashes, Danielle opened her eyes for the liner.

"It's understood you'll mess up protocol at first, and you may receive small punishments for correction, but nothing too severe. As long as you follow the 'Safe, Sane, Consensual' credo and don't interfere with a scene, you'll be fine." She rifled through the makeup bag.

"You mentioned the freeway earlier. What is it?"

Gracie puckered her lips, silently instructing Danielle to do the same, and she smoothed lipstick across Danielle's lips. "Simply put…it's an orgy in the dark. Well, not complete darkness, but dark enough that you can't make out a person's features. It's all about using your other senses and ridding yourself of societal constraints on sexual expression. For example, when I kissed you earlier, you knew it was me. But in the dark, a touch is a touch." Gracie stood to Danielle's side, allowing her to see the final results. "Ta-da!"

Gracie had worked magic, transforming Danielle's look from a bright-eyed innocent to a sultry siren, lining her eyes with black kohl and thickening and lengthening her lashes. She'd swept up Danielle's black hair into a high ponytail, curling a couple of tendrils to frame her face.

For the first time in years, Danielle actually liked her reflection. Her eyes misted, but she blinked back the tears of gratitude, no way willing to ruin all of Gracie's hard work. She grabbed Gracie's wrist. "Thank you."

Gracie smiled. "Anytime."

Arm in arm, they left the comfort of the bedroom and made their way through the house to the dungeon. Unlike earlier, the lights had been dimmed, sconces glowing on the walls and lighting their path. In only a couple of hours, the energy of the home had changed from innocent to sensual.

Danielle decided to take advantage of Gracie's eagerness to share her behind-the-scene knowledge of Benediction. "How many trainees are currently living here?"

Gracie stopped at the bottom of the kitchen stairs and nibbled on her lower lip. "Normally he only trains a dozen at a time."

"Normally?"

"Well, with you here, it's thirteen."

Why did the unlucky number feel like an omen? Cole had obviously made concessions to bring her into the trainee program. Was he telling the truth that it was because of her father? Or was there another reason?

"And where does Master DeMarco sleep?" Danielle asked.

Gracie stumbled over her feet, but quickly recovered. "Oh, um, Master Cole has a private residence upstairs on the other side of the house from the trainees' rooms."

"I must have missed the staircase to it."

Gracie stopped and whispered in Danielle's ear. "Master has a secret room behind the bookcase in his office. I've never seen so many screens outside of a television store. It's a voyeur's dream. A couple of the dungeon monitors sit in there during Benediction's business hours and watch what's going on in every room. There's not much privacy in this place, but privacy's overrated, don't you think? Anyways, the stairs to his residence are in there, although he's very protective of his private space. He doesn't let anyone up there and keeps it locked at all times. In fact, he's the only one with the key."

She nodded absently, wondering if she somehow managed to get the key, how in hell she'd ever get into his residence without being caught. "What are dungeon monitors?"

"Kind of like unpaid security guards. Several of the more experienced members volunteer a few hours every week to act as dungeon monitors and watch over the scenes to make sure everyone is safe. They're also given the responsibility of watching the club monitors."

Aware of the video cameras all around her, Danielle discreetly assessed the area near Cole's office. The hallway leading to it was empty. Maybe she didn't need to seduce Cole. If no one monitored in the secret room during the day, she could find the key, then sneak into his residence when he was busy somewhere else in the mansion.

Passing the den on the way to the staircases at the front of the home, Gracie waved to a group of people lounging on couches.

"Those are a few of our regular members," Gracie said. "They're here several times a week. We caught them on the early side of the evening. Check them out when you go back to your room later." She waggled her eyebrows. "Clothing is optional, but no sex is permitted. Fondling and petting, yes. Human tables, definitely." She pointed to a wet bar on the side of the room covered by bottles of wine, spirits, and liquors. "There's an open bar, but the rule is if you drink, you're not sanctioned to enter the dungeon or the upstairs rooms. People can't give consent if they're inebriated, and no one plays without giving consent."

Human tables? She couldn't imagine what that meant. Everything else sounded tolerable.

Danielle noticed they all wore wristbands of different colors, similar to the silver slave band she wore on her wrist. "What do the wristbands mean?"

"Benediction uses colored wristbands to identify people's kinks." Using her fingers, Gracie ticked off the kinks one by one. "You're most likely to see black for Dominant, white for submissive, yellow for switches, green for partner swapping, and blue for ménage. There are several others. Master Cole's aware of everyone's tastes. That's why he's so good at matching his slave trainees with dominant partners."

"Cole—I mean, Master Cole—plays matchmaker?"

"In a way. He's very good at determining what a member—and for that matter, a trainee—requires in a partner. Almost like a sixth sense. Every few months, he invites the available Dominants to a slave auction for those trainees looking to enter a contract after graduation from the program." Gracie's almond eyes widened, and her lips tipped up in a wistful grin. "It's a truly beautiful and thrilling event to watch."

At a loss for words, Danielle sputtered to a complete stop. A slave auction? Was that even legal?

Luckily for her, Gracie was still talking and didn't notice Danielle's shock or her inability to form words. "We have a choice of going upstairs or downstairs. The fantasy rooms have windows and audio for those who like to watch. Do you like to watch? I'm more of a doer myself. Downstairs you get more than the sights and sounds. You get the scent of lust and fear and pain and sex. It's intoxicating."

The more Danielle learned about Benediction and Cole DeMarco, the more questions she had. All of them jumbled in her mind, but Gracie was obviously so excited to show her the basement, she didn't have the heart to stop and ask them. If anything, seeing the dungeon first-hand should answer several of them. "Downstairs then."

Gracie threw her arms around Danielle and hugged her. "I promise you won't regret this. Your life will never be the same."

That was exactly what she was afraid of.

Chapter Six

HE GLANCED AT his watch and clutched the tree cutter in his hand.

Tick-tock. Tick-tock.

The end was so close he could almost taste it.

Despite the fact his dick throbbed, this act would give him no satisfaction. He loved the scent of fear. The sound of a defenseless woman crying for mercy. In the past, he'd been careful not to get caught, only killing the ones no one would miss. With the others, he'd inflicted just enough pain to bring him to climax. Those girls would never talk. Not if they wanted to stay breathing.

Tasha sat slumped in the chair, unconscious. He'd strapped her arm to the table next to the empty bottle of vodka.

They needed to send a strong message, one Danielle couldn't ignore. He'd tried to come up with something less permanent, but credibility was key.

In only a short few days, he'd make back their money. Then he'd spend hours torturing Danielle before he killed her. He'd bet she'd be hellfire to break, but it would make it all the sweeter to see the life ebb from her eyes.

And if he got caught…he'd use his contacts to get him out of it. As he'd learned from his family, everyone had a secret, and blackmail was a great way to keep someone in your pocket for a rainy day.

Too bad he couldn't keep Danielle. All that training, gone to waste. But he'd promised to kill her as soon as they transferred the money, and he was a man of his word.

He shook his head, clearing the arousing images of screaming women from his mind and focused on his task.

He lifted Tasha's limp hand off the table.

And cut off her finger.

Chapter Seven

DANIELLE AND GRACIE descended the wrought-iron staircase. The flickering lanterns on the dark walls gave it a true dungeon feel, as though she was walking from the present world into the past.

A low beat of a bass vibrated under her feet. Voices murmured underneath the various cries and moans and slaps and grunts. She hadn't understood what Gracie had meant by her description of the smells, but as she neared the bottom, it began to make sense. Leather, sweat, and musk greeted her as her gaze fell on the scenes in front of her.

An open floor plan lit by strategically placed replicas of old-fashioned candelabras and ceilings painted black further enhanced the dungeon environment. All the things she'd read about. The pictures she saw in those books Cole had given her and in her Internet research. It all existed live and in Technicolor. Leather and lace.

Latex and rubber. Various collars around necks. Men and women being led around on leashes, including a few who crawled. She saw plenty of lingerie and lots and lots of skin.

Men and women hung from the ceiling on some kind of harness made of rope. She pressed her thighs together, a rush of arousal so strong, she drenched her panties. Something about those bound people made her heart race.

She didn't understand. This wasn't her. Not that she believed there was anything wrong with exposing your body and expressing your sexuality in a safe environment, but it wasn't something she could ever imagine herself feeling comfortable enough to do. Even now, dressed in her panties and corset, she wore more than most of the submissives in the room, and still she wasn't comfortable in her own body. She envied these people.

Gracie led her by the hand and pointed out the different kinds of equipment. There were a few spanking benches littered around the room. All being used. She flinched as she watched a man hit another man's ass with a rectangular wooden paddle. The pain didn't tempt her, but she liked the way the bench was placed so everyone could see the ass turning red before their eyes.

There were a couple men with lanyards around their neck with a round silver medallion hanging from it. She nudged Gracie and discreetly pointed to them. "What's the significance of what those men are wearing?"

"That's Morgan and Ryder. They're both dungeon monitors. Come with me, and I'll introduce you to them.

If you're interested in a ménage, those are your guys." She winked. "Trust me."

"I'd prefer to stand here for a few minutes, if that's all right with you."

Gracie patted her on the back. "It's a lot to take in all at once. I understand. I was gonna let them know I'm available later, but I'll stay—"

"Go. I'll be fine on my own."

Gracie planted a kiss on Danielle's cheek. "I'll only be a minute." She vaulted off in the direction of the dungeon monitors, leaving Danielle to do what she did best.

Hide in the shadows and observe.

There were several scenes going on throughout the room. Her gaze darted around and stopped on one in the back. A man was locked into a stockade, his erect cock sticking through one of the holes. Another man was behind him, and although she couldn't see it, she guessed by the motion that he was fucking him. Yet another man was beating the man's cock with a thin reed of some sort and commanding him not to come. Judging by the locked man's expression of bliss, he wasn't going to last for long.

The dungeon was a feast for her senses. She'd watched porn before, but it had been simply a visual experience. Actors' moans and dirty talk had always come off as insincere and almost comical. The sounds in this room were real, and the pleasure was so palpable, she could almost taste it in the air.

A loud female cry coming from Danielle's left caught her attention. A young blonde was cuffed to an X-shaped piece of equipment, which Danielle had learned from her

reading was called a St. Andrew's cross, and a handsome man stood behind her with a whip in his hands. Sweat trickled down his face as he spoke to a man beside him.

Master Cole.

He'd changed from what he wore earlier into a pair of leather pants and a leather vest over a red T-shirt. A dungeon monitor medallion hung from his neck. Even as he answered the other man, Cole never took his gaze off the blonde on the cross.

The whip coiled so quickly Danielle barely saw it, but she couldn't miss the cracking noise it made as it struck the woman's back. The blonde's body jerked, and she groaned as the man did it once more.

Each time he struck, Danielle's pussy clenched. Her clitoris pulsed as if keeping a beat for the whip. Her fingers drifted between her legs, and she rubbed her swollen clitoris through her panties. She was two seconds away from plunging her fingers inside and getting herself off in front of these people.

Then the woman screamed. Her whole body writhed as she thrashed her head back and forth, crying the word "no" over and over.

Danielle waited for the man to stop—for Cole to stop him—but the whipping continued. A bubbling rage built and overflowed. She pushed off the wall and ran over to the scene. "Stop! Didn't your mother ever teach you 'no means no'? She's crying, for heaven's sake! Why are you just standing there? What kind of monsters are you?"

The room grew eerily quiet. Cole's body was stiff and his jaw rigid, as if he were angry with her.

Too bad. Since the dungeon monitors had failed to do their duty, someone had to step in and protect the woman.

Gracie suddenly appeared and grabbed Danielle by her arm. "I'm sorry, Master. I take full responsibility for Danielle's outburst and will take any punishment you believe I merit."

Cole's eyes narrowed on Danielle. "While I appreciate the defense of your new friend, I will deal with Danielle." He turned to the man. "Jaxon, please forgive me for the interruption. Feel free to use your choice of private room for Kate's after-care and keep it for the rest of the night." Jaxon went to the woman on the cross, where he proceeded to remove the cuffs from her ankles.

Danielle folded her arms over her chest. "She's not safe with him."

He splayed his hand on her lower back and led her through the club. "Come with me to my office."

Several of the people in the dungeon watched them with interest, but most of them had returned to their scenes.

"Do you know what 'Safe, Sane, Consensual' means?" Cole asked as they climbed the stairs. "It means the members of my club are held to a strict set of rules they must follow in order to sustain their membership. Let's start with 'consensual.' Everything that happens in this club is negotiated and agreed upon by the parties. Nothing will happen without consent. Every person in Benediction may utilize the club-recognized safe word, 'red,' to terminate a scene and face no repercussion. Kate and

Jaxon negotiated their scene prior to its commencement, whereby she consented to the whip."

She'd read about consent, and Gracie had mentioned it as well, but it was a difficult concept for her to understand. "How can someone give consent to being hurt? That's crazy."

"I assure you, it's not crazy. Only the sane can legally give consent, thus the 'sane' component to the standard. You may not get off on pain and I may not get off on giving it, but there are those like Kate and Jaxon who do. Benediction provides them a safe place to meet those with compatible sexual interests and indulge in the practices. It's not your place to judge or impose on others' sexual expression."

"She was screaming and crying. How was that sexual expression?"

"In some, pain enhances the pleasure. Whether she chooses the pain because she's a masochist or because she wishes to please her Master by taking the pain he wants to incur, it has nothing to do with you." He frowned at her as he unlocked the door to his office. "You obviously failed to read the books I provided to you."

"I read them, but reading about it and the reality of it are two different things."

He waved her into the room and followed, circling behind his desk, then taking a seat behind the computer screen. "Go on."

She twirled a piece of her hair around her finger and sat in the chair in front of his desk. "Before I interrupted, I couldn't tear my attention away."

"What did you feel as you watched?" he asked, softening his voice.

She thought about her body's response to the scene and how she'd been only seconds away from shoving her hand between her thighs to ease the ache. "Hot. Tingly. Breathless…" That wasn't all she'd felt. Her chest had tightened at the sight of Cole with Jaxon and Kate. "Jealous."

He shifted in his chair and ran his hand down his scalp. "Jealous?"

"Of Kate," she said, immediately kicking herself for admitting it. "All that attention focused solely on her. The way Jaxon looked at her as if she were the only person in the room."

"But she wasn't. Kate and Jaxon chose a public scene rather than a private room or their home so that anyone could watch." He rose from his chair and rounded the desk, stopping in front of her. Her pulse went crazy as he leaned forward, bracing his hands on the arms of the chair, effectively caging her in. "Tell me, Danielle. Has a man ever held your back against his front at a concert, slipped his hand under your short skirt, and fingered your hot pussy until you shook from climax?"

His face moved closer, almost as if he was going to kiss her, but at the last moment, he turned his head and he whispered into her ear, his hot breath causing her to shudder from the chills sweeping her body. "Have you ever kneeled on the floor and sucked off a man in the back of a dark movie theater? Does the idea of being caught get you wet? Did you wish to be in Kate's place and be watched?"

She swallowed hard and licked her suddenly dry lips. The images his words created spun like a carousel in her imagination. Her fantasies had never involved public sex, but she couldn't deny the ideas he'd painted aroused her. But she'd never feel comfortable enough in her skin to actually do those things. "I'm not into pain. Anything more than a spanking is at least a soft limit for me."

He pulled back with a frown. "That wasn't what I asked, and you know it." He removed his arms from her chair and casually perched himself on the corner of the desk, leaving one leg on the ground. "But that's okay for now. You're obviously not ready to accept it. I understand you've got societal rules about what's wrong and what's right guiding your thoughts and behaviors. However, Benediction doesn't follow those rules. We have our own. Rules you acknowledged to abide when you completed your application."

His expression darkened, and contrary to his relaxed posture, all signs of the flirtatious and mellow man vanished. "Because you interrupted a scene"—he folded his arms over his chest—"I must punish you."

Chapter Eight

POOR CINDERELLA MAY have had to do her chores in rags, but at least she didn't have to wear a corset and panties when she cleaned the bathroom. Even after losing her father and his millions, Tasha had continued paying a maid to clean their home. It wasn't as if Danielle had never cleaned before, but she'd never gotten on her knees and scrubbed the toilets.

Cole couldn't have chosen a better punishment. At this point, she would've rather been spanked again.

Unsurprisingly, Benediction's ladies' room was reminiscent of an upscale spa with a lounge area complete with full-sized lockers made from dark wood, cream-colored leather couches, and cushiony chairs. A long counter with a mirror above it spanned the length of the room, providing a space for women to do their hair and makeup, and beige and cream Italian marble floors and walls added to the ritzy ambiance.

Adjacent to the lounge was the bathroom. Decorated with marble and dark wood, it contained showers, toilets, and sinks each with a well-lit mirror over it. The mirrors were the last item she needed to clean to complete her punishment.

She blew an errant piece of hair off her face. So much for the makeup Gracie had applied and the hair she'd brushed. Danielle was a sweaty mess.

If Cole's purpose had been to shame her, it had worked. None of the members or trainees who had come into the ladies' room would talk to her. In fact, they completely ignored her. Even Gracie. Her lips had parted as if she had been about to speak, but then she covered her mouth with her hand and marched out of the room. Knowing Gracie's penchant for talking, that had been a punishment for her as well.

Danielle plunked the toilet brush into the plastic bucket and stood, her knees cracking. She rolled her shoulders and peeled off her rubber gloves. One more task on the list Cole had provided and then she could go back to her room to get some sleep. There was no way she had the energy to read tonight. She'd been up for twenty-four hours straight and had only gotten a few hours of sleep before the kidnappers had woken her in her bed, so it felt much, much longer. She'd set her alarm and get up in the morning to read before her first class.

She lifted a cloth and the glass cleaner out of the bucket and went to tackle the mirrors over the sinks. A glance in the glass brought her to laughter. Pieces of her hair stuck to the side of her face, and her eyeliner was so smudged, it appeared as though she had two black eyes. Good thing she wasn't vain, or she'd be in tears.

Spraying the mirror, Danielle heard the lounge door open with a swoosh. A couple of women chattered away, one voice she picked out as belonging to Cassandra. Bored out of her mind and within an earshot, she couldn't help but eavesdrop.

"He held me down and held a bullet vibrator on my clitoris until I thought I was going to come out of my skin, I was so sensitive," Cassandra said.

"You're such a lucky bitch."

"Too bad Master Cole went back to his office," Cassandra said on a sigh.

Danielle's chest burned, and her cheeks grew warm. Had Cole done a scene with Cassandra tonight?

She pictured Cole with a vibrator in his hands, holding it against *Danielle's* clitoris until she begged him to stop.

She snorted quietly. Nope, that would never happen. No way would she ever beg him not to bring her to climax.

She dropped the cloth and the glass cleaner back into the bucket and washed her hands. The thought of Cole with a vibrator made her tingly. It reminded her how close she'd been to coming before she'd interfered with Kate and Jaxon's scene.

She understood now she'd been wrong for interrupting, but she hadn't done it out of malice. She'd been trying to help. Couldn't Cole have let her off with a warning?

Instead, while she'd spent the last hour cleaning, he'd been forcing orgasms on Cassandra.

The lounge grew silent, and Danielle was once again alone. Exhausted, she slid the bucket into the cabinet underneath the sink and started to leave when her gaze landed on the couch. It looked so inviting, she was tempted to crash right then and there. Maybe she'd rest for a couple of minutes before going back to her room.

She lay on the couch and rested her head on a throw pillow. It wasn't very comfortable, but she relaxed anyway.

A red light blinked up in the corner of the room.

That's right. While Cole had mentioned there were no cameras in the bathrooms, he'd said nothing about the lounge area.

Was he watching her right now?

Someone had to be watching, and Danielle imagined it was Cole. That he sat behind his desk, staring at the monitor. He'd want to know she'd taken her time and completed her punishment.

Perhaps he'd unzipped his pants and freed his cock from the constraints of the tight leather. He'd wrapped his large brown hand around his shaft and slowly worked it up and down as he watched her, waiting for her to put on a show for him.

Looking at the camera, she ran her tongue across her bottom lip and moaned. She looked at the door. Would someone come in and catch her? If it were anywhere else, she'd stop and lock the door, but in Benediction, what she was about to do would probably be considered boring. She'd bet no one would blink if they caught her.

Her heart beat quicker, and she squeezed her thighs together. She brushed her hands down her breasts, coming to rest them on her middle abdomen. Her legs parted, and as one hand drifted south, the other released a breast from her corset. She licked her fingers, getting them nice and wet, then traced circles around her nipple.

In her mind, she saw Cole mirroring her actions, drawing his own thick fingers into his mouth and bringing the moisture to his cock, where he'd use the lubrication to bring himself off to the sight of her.

She dipped her hand below her panties and spread her labia apart with her fingers. Not surprisingly, she was already slippery from her arousal. She pinched her nipple and at the same time did what she'd been dying to do all night—slide two of her fingers inside her slick channel.

Keeping her eyes on the camera, she pumped her fingers in and out, pressing and rubbing her thumb against her clitoris. It wasn't close to what she wanted, but it was more than she needed.

What was Cole doing now? Was he slowing his motions, squeezing off the head of his cock, waiting to come with her? Or did the sight of her getting herself off prove too much and had he already spilled into his hand?

Her muscles tightened, and a storm gathered low in her belly. She thrust her fingers in as far as they could go and twisted as the pad of her thumb circled her clitoris. She hovered on the edge for a moment and then fell blissfully into the throes of climax, her pussy squeezing her fingers and her clitoris throbbing.

She lay there as the storm grew quiet, and her body melted into the couch cushions. With her eyes on the camera, she removed her hand from her panties and sucked her fingers into her mouth, one by one.

If he hadn't come by now, that should probably do it for him.

Ready for sleep, she stood from the couch and tucked her breast back into the corset. Then she barreled out of the locker room.

And straight into Cole.

"Finish cleaning so soon?" He panted, as if he'd been running.

She couldn't help but feel victorious. "Yes, Cole. I mean, Master."

He leaned to whisper in her ear. "I can smell you, you know."

"Smell me?"

"I can smell your pussy."

She gasped. "That's not possible."

"When it comes to me," he said, moving close enough she could feel his erection against her stomach, "anything is possible. What drove you to lie down on the couch and expose yourself to me? Anger because I punished you for breaking the rules? Or were you too turned on by the club to wait until you got to the privacy of your bedroom?"

All the confidence she'd felt earlier disappeared out the window, leaving only shame. "I just…"

"You knew I'd be watching."

She nodded, keeping her gaze lowered. "Yes."

"Is that what turns you on?" With two of his fingers under her chin, he tipped up her face. "To be watched?"

Would she have been as aroused without the camera? She'd masturbated plenty of times, but never had it felt like that. "Yes."

"Exhibitionism is nothing to be ashamed of, Danielle. Plenty of us find it sexy as hell." He motioned to the frames on the maroon wall. "What do you think of the photographs?"

She moved closer to study them. They were black and white photographs of naked men and women. Bound by rope. Tied by sashes to a bed. Chained to a wall. Each photo contained a single object in color. The ropes were yellow. The sashes red. Purple floggers. Pink rose petals.

They simply took her breath away with their passion and eroticism. "They're beautiful."

Dimples appeared in his cheeks, and his eyes twinkled. "Thank you."

Something in his expression spoke to her. It was pride. "They're yours? I mean, you're the photographer?"

"Yes," he said, nodding. He paused, staring at her intently. "I'd like to photograph you."

"Me?" Her stomach plummeted. He couldn't be serious. "I'm not model material."

"Why not?"

"Look at me."

"Believe me, I am." He cupped her face in his hands, swiping his thumb over her cheekbone. "And I'm not giving you an option. I'm telling you. You will model for me. Tomorrow. I'll come for you."

As he walked away with a hint of a grin on his lips, her stomach did a slow somersault, and she had to grip the wall so she didn't fall. Model for him? Was he insane?

Tonight's performance for the camera had been an aberration, no matter how much she'd enjoyed it. Even if she could relax in front of Cole to take the photographs, no one would want to see them. She could barely tolerate to see herself in pictures, most of the time shunning the camera at public events and avoiding family photos by being the one behind the lens. Mirrors and cameras had been her enemy for as long as she could remember, but it seemed as though she couldn't escape them in Benediction.

From across the room, she spotted Gracie speaking with the small blonde—Kate—whose scene Danielle had interrupted earlier. Both of them were looking straight at her, and her cheeks turned hot at the assumption they were talking about her.

Cole may have punished her for the mistake, but she still owed the woman an explanation for her outburst. Choking down her pride, she picked up a few pieces of chocolate from a bowl and sashayed her butt over for an apology. "I'm really sorry about interrupting your scene. I didn't realize you—"

"Enjoy getting beaten?" Kate said, accepting the candy from Danielle and unwrapping it. She laughed. "Yeah, I can see how it would look to an outsider. Don't worry about it. I assume you're new to the lifestyle?"

That was it? The girls Danielle had grown up with would never have accepted an apology so quickly. "Yeah.

Brand new." She popped a piece of chocolate into her mouth. "Like fresh out of the womb new."

"I'm relatively new as well," Kate said, "but I've got about a year and a half under my belt now. If you have any questions, I'm available. I don't know everything, but I'm happy to help in any way I can."

"And you know I will too," Gracie said. "But everyone has a different story. I've been in the lifestyle a long time and a staple at Benediction for years. In fact, I was here the first night Kate came here with Jaxon. You should have seen her. You think you were shocked, I think Kate wanted to sock me in the mouth for propositioning Master Jaxon in front of her. She's more of a masochist than a full-out kinky slut like me."

Danielle winced, uncomfortable with the disparaging term. "You're not a slut."

Gracie waved her hand in the air. "Yes, I am, and there's nothing wrong with that. I love sex, and I refuse to apologize for it. For years, men were not only expected to sleep around before marriage, they were applauded for it, while women were supposed to remain pure for their husbands and ignore their sexual urges. When they didn't, society shamed them and branded them a slut." She covered her heart with her palm. "BDSM is my scarlet letter, and I wear it proudly."

Danielle scanned the dungeon, taking in the scenes all around her. A wave of envy crashed over her. Everyone seemed so comfortable in their skin and free with their sexuality. She was nothing like them. Was she? "How do you know if you're submissive?"

"I'm not sure there's a list you can check off to tell you whether you're a submissive," Kate said, "and in my opinion, it's not something you can force. It's part of you, like your eye color."

She bit the inside of her cheek as she considered it. She knew without a doubt she wasn't dominant, but was she truly a submissive? "Is everyone in BDSM either a Dominant or submissive?"

Gracie animatedly bounced on her toes. "There are more ways to practice BDSM than I can count. You can be a masochist and not a submissive. You can be into bondage and nothing else. There are tops and bottoms and switches and baby girls and sluts. There are twenty-four/seven relationships and bedroom-only relationships. You can be married to your Master or married to a vanilla man and have a Master outside of the marriage—"

"What if a man is a Dominant, and his partner isn't submissive?" Danielle asked, thinking of Cole.

Kate tilted her head, her lips pressed together. "Well, that depends on whether the Dominant would be satisfied without having a submissive partner. If they're both okay with him satisfying that part of him outside their relationship, it may work. But to me, and I preface this by saying it's only my opinion, oftentimes Dominance and submission is like a sexual orientation. If you're straight, you're not going to be attracted to a member of the same sex, and even if you were, you wouldn't choose that person for a sexual relationship. I think in simple terms, if you're a submissive, you'll naturally be attracted to a Dominant, and vice versa."

She crossed her arms over her chest. "What's it like to be naked in front of so many people?"

"Honestly, I don't think about it," Kate said, snagging a cup of water from the high-top table behind her. "Even in a crowd, I only see Jaxon. No one else matters."

"But you're thin."

Kate gestured to the room. "Look around. Is everyone thin? No. We're normal people with normal jobs and normal problems. We've got cellulite and saggy breasts and gray hair. There's no judgment here." Her face lit up at the sight of Jaxon walking toward them. "I've got to go, but a couple of my friends and I go out every Thursday night for drinks. I'd love for you both to join us."

"I don't know how long I'll be in town, but if I get the chance, I'd like that."

A longing filled her chest as she watched Jaxon slip his arm around Kate and hold her to his side as if they were one. Only hours before, his whip had marked her skin and brought Kate to tears. Now his tender touch caused Kate to radiate with joy. Their connection was deep and powerful, and it shocked Danielle how much she envied Kate.

Yawning, she decided to go upstairs to get a couple hours of shut-eye.

Later tonight, she had work to do.

Chapter Nine

SHE JOLTED FROM the annoying beep of the alarm clock and quickly slammed her hand on the buzzer to stop it from waking anyone else on her floor. Three o'clock in the morning. The club was closed, and everyone should be asleep by now. A perfect time to explore Cole's office and check out that secret room.

Naked, she slipped on a silk robe and wondered how the kidnapper knew about the room behind Cole's bookcase and that Cole never brought anyone upstairs to his residence. It meant the kidnapper had to be someone at Benediction or had gotten the information from someone close to Cole—possibly even Cole himself.

In the dark, Danielle made her way to the door. She heard nothing but silence as she unlocked it, quietly turned the knob, and pulled the door open before sneaking into the hallway. She left it open a crack, so as to not make noise, padded down the hallway, and descended the stairs into the empty kitchen.

As quietly as she could, she tiptoed in the dark toward Cole's office, her heart thumping against her chest like a battering ram. When she got to the door, she pressed her ear to the wood; hearing nothing, she tried opening it.

Locked.

Frustrated, she sighed and rested her forehead against the door. How the hell was she going to get upstairs if she couldn't even get into his office?

Suddenly, the hallway lights came on.

Her heart in her throat, she twirled around, almost smacking into Cole. How had he snuck up on her?

His lips pressed together in a thin line. "What are you doing?"

He wore the same clothes as earlier, but something about him seemed different. When his eyes narrowed, she figured out what it was. "You're wearing glasses."

"Danielle, don't make me repeat myself."

She clutched her locket. "I couldn't sleep, and I thought maybe you'd be in your office to answer some questions."

His gaze dropped to her chest, and his nostrils flared, causing her to look down at herself. Realizing her black robe was sheer, she instinctively crossed her arms, even as a subtle throbbing began in her pussy. "You didn't provide me any pajamas, and I forgot to pack them."

He blinked and pulled his gaze up to her face. "If you'd like some, I'm sure Cassandra could—"

"No," she said firmly. "I don't need them."

He slid his hand into his pocket and removed a black braided keychain with at least a dozen keys hanging from it. Then he unlocked the door and waved her in.

"That's a lot of keys. What are they all for?" she asked as she stepped into his office, trying to sound casual.

He turned on the lights and closed the door behind them. "Danielle, it's late, and we both need to be up in a few hours. Why don't you just ask me what's really on your mind?"

"My father," she said before she could stop herself, the opportunity to learn more about the past too great to pass up. If she could get him to lower his defenses, maybe she could get him to reveal something that would help her prove her father's innocence. "How did you become his business partner?"

He tilted his head toward the ceiling and sighed before gesturing for her to take a seat in front of his desk. Instead of taking his chair behind the desk, he sat beside her. "About ten years ago, I met your father through a friend of mine, a venture capitalist named Jaxon Deveroux, who you met earlier tonight. Your father was looking for investors in his wealth management firm. He wanted to compete with the Wall Street bigwigs, and to do that, he needed additional capital, but he didn't have enough collateral to secure a loan from the banks, and the venture capitalists weren't interested because they'd make too small of a return on the investment. Jaxon was willing to broker a deal and contacted me, knowing that in anticipation of the rebound of the stock market and to diversify my portfolio, I'd been looking to heavily invest in businesses that relied on the market. I became a majority partner, not only investing capital but also providing a loan to the company."

"Wow. That must have been a lot of money." She flashed a smile, blatantly admiring the tribal tattoo winding around his sinewy biceps in an attempt to appear flirtatious. "Impressive for someone who must have been only…what…thirty at the time?"

He smiled in response, but his eyes remained guarded. "I was twenty-eight. And yes, it was quite a bit of money. I was fortunate to have been born to a rich family. Before he fought in World War Two, my grandfather patented a couple of inventions for the automotive industry, and while he fought in Germany, his attorney sold the rights to those patents to a couple of the largest car manufacturers in the United States. He came back from the war a hero and a multimillionaire. With the right investments, that money will last my family for generations."

"And you decided my father's business was the right investment. As a majority owner, you must have had access to all the files and records of the business, right?"

He shifted in his chair. "I was a silent partner, so I had very limited involvement in the day-to-day running of it."

Adrenaline shot through her body at the awareness that he'd sidestepped the question. He obviously didn't want to talk about those records. "Not so silent. You came all the way from Michigan to meet with my father right before—"

"I did." He paused. "You watched me from the stairs."

Caught off guard, she froze. "You remember?"

"The first time, I felt your presence before I spotted you watching from the staircase. Your father had mentioned he had a young daughter, but the beauty I saw on the stairs was not the child I expected."

She swallowed. "I was seventeen."

"I looked forward to those moments I'd see you. Too much." His gaze locked with hers. What did he mean by that? Had he experienced that same magnetic tug that she had whenever she'd seen him? "I was sorry to hear about your father's passing." Cole spoke softly, but the way the words sliced into her heart, he might as well have shouted.

The moment broken, she tore her gaze away and grimaced. "Passing. That's a nice way of phrasing it. Let's not pretend his death was anything natural."

She'd never forget the phone call from the prison informing her of her father's suicide. He'd paid another inmate to buy him peanuts from the commissary, and while alone in his cell, he had eaten the entire bag, knowing a severe allergic reaction to the nuts would kill him. And it had.

"No, I don't suppose it was," Cole said.

"Since you were his partner, you probably received all the documents and business property that the FBI had confiscated in their investigation, right? I'd love to go through it, you know, to make some sense of why my father stole from his clients."

He shook his head. "I wish I had for your sake, but since they were of no use to me, I had the government dispose of everything."

She didn't believe him. He must have kept something she could use. "But maybe—"

"Danielle," he said sharply, "you're going to have a long day tomorrow. I think it's time you return to your room and get some sleep."

"Of course." His dismissal gave no room for argument. This conversation was over. She might not have gotten the answers she wanted, but at least he hadn't suspected her real reason for coming to his office in the middle of the night. She rose from her chair. "Good night."

He stood and accompanied her to the door, his warm hand on the small of her back. "Don't forget you're going to pose for me tomorrow."

How could she possibly forget?

Chapter Ten

FOR THE HUNDREDTH time, Danielle glanced at the digital clock up on the wall and wondered when Cole would come get her for their modeling session. She and the other trainees sat on folding chairs in a circle along with Master Michael and Mistress Casey, who were coteaching the classes this morning.

Danielle had always regretted not going back to school and getting her degree, but she had to admit, classes had never been this much fun. No boring lectures for slave trainees. They got demonstrations and hands-on experience. So far this morning, she'd gotten to hold several floggers, feeling the difference between leather, nylon, and kangaroo. While she found it fascinating, she quickly determined she never wanted to be on the receiving side of a flogger.

At the beginning of class, Master Michael had taken her aside from the rest of the trainees and went over what he called BDSM 101. He'd not only given her the low-down on basic protocols and rules, he'd also explained Benediction's logistics.

Prior to membership approval, applicants required an endorsement from a current member and were thoroughly investigated, which involved submitting to medical tests and criminal background checks, as well as providing financial records. If they passed that stage, they paid a fifty-thousand-dollar fee, which went into a trust for the maintenance of the club for things such as condoms, computers, wrist bands, copying fees, and even food for the trainees. He went on to say Benediction was not formally a business, and Cole did not earn any money from running it.

Discretion was key, and everyone signed a confidentiality agreement. Not only were most of the members wealthy, many of them maintained high-profile careers in politics, sports, and entertainment.

She could understand the need for confidentiality. If anyone back in Arizona found out she'd spent time in a sex club, she'd…well, no one would believe it. But if they did, her reputation would be ruined.

After he'd finished her quick introduction to BDSM, he joined Mistress Casey, who was leading the trainees in a debate on what constituted consent, both in terms of the BDSM community and the law. Danielle was surprised to learn that although both parties may give consent, the state could still prosecute a person for assault.

Next, they moved on to more pertinent issues.

"Can anyone tell me why lubricant is so important in anal sex?" Mistress Casey asked the trainees. Twelve hands shot up in the air. Danielle's remained in her lap.

A firm knocking caused everyone's heads to swerve toward the door. Her breath stalled in her lungs at the sight of Cole in tight jeans and a black Henley shirt. A quick study of the other trainees' faces told her she wasn't the only one. Waiting for him to speak, she chewed on a fingernail.

Unlike the nervous wreck that she was, he leaned on the doorjamb, one leg crossed over the other, his posture casual and comfortable. Master Michael rose from his chair and crossed to Cole. They spoke in hushed tones, and Master Michael nodded.

Cole's cool gaze landed on her. "I'm going to borrow Danielle for a couple hours to help me out on a project."

Before she had the chance to move, Cassandra dropped from her seat to her knees and bowed her head. "Danielle really shouldn't miss her first day of classes. Whatever you require, I'd be happy—"

Cole folded his arms over his broad chest, causing his biceps to bulge. "Cassandra, is it your place to tell me how to manage my trainees? Think carefully before you answer."

A long silence was broken when Cassandra answered, "No, Master Cole."

It was like a train wreck. Painful to watch, but she couldn't look away. The other trainees smirked, obviously enjoying the show. There was no question Cassandra was a bitch, but Danielle's stomach twisted into pretzels over the woman's humiliation.

Of course, after her reading this morning and learning the rules from Master Michael, Danielle now understood the safety concerns that could come from distracting someone in a scene.

"Master Michael, please discipline Cassandra for me," Cole said. "Five minutes on the fucking machine without an orgasm and serving lunch to the other trainees should do the trick."

Cassandra snapped up her head. Her eyes blazed with fury before they softened and tears began to fall. Danielle recognized a manipulation when she saw one.

"Cassandra, who do you serve?" Cole asked.

"You, Master."

"We'll have a chat later today about whether you're serious enough to finish the trainee program."

"But—" Her jaw grew rigid, and she shot Danielle a murderous scowl, then quickly returned her attention back to Cole. "Yes, Master."

Cole beckoned Danielle with two of his fingers, his expression unreadable. "Danielle? Please come with me."

The other trainees shifted in their seats as Mistress Casey picked up where she'd left off. More excited about the photo shoot than learning the benefit of lubrication, Danielle hurried out of her seat, collecting her purse before following a stony Cole out the door. If she didn't know better, she'd think he was about to have her clean the bathrooms again, rather than pose nude for his photographs.

"I'm confused," she said once the door to the classroom shut. "We're here to serve you, correct?"

"As part of your training, yes." He splayed his hand on her lower back and led her down the hall, the heat of him seeping through her sheer black blouse. She swallowed hard and fisted her hands to keep from biting her nails. How could he remain so detached when only an innocent touch from him ignited a firestorm of need within her?

"Then why was Cassandra's offer to serve you punishable? Isn't that part of her job description?"

Holding a set of jangling keys in his hand, he unlocked a door. "While on the surface, it may sound as though Cassandra was offering to do something for me, in fact, her motives were quite selfish. First, she wanted to block you from spending time with me, and two, she wanted the perceived advantage in serving me. Not to mention, her offer was an attempt to maneuver into a position of power. It's what is commonly referred to as topping from the bottom, and it's a punishable offense, especially in light of the fact that Cassandra does it often."

Danielle had never considered a person's motives behind the good deeds. To her, it was irrelevant because in the real world, all that mattered was the end result. Before Tasha, Danielle's father had never placed value on receiving praise for his charity. He'd simply cut a substantial check and asked that his donation remain anonymous. But after he remarried, he spent nearly every weekend dressed in a tuxedo, leaving a teenaged Danielle home with Roman as he and Tasha mingled with Scottsdale's elite at one-thousand-dollar-a-plate dinners that Tasha insisted would bring him new accounts for his business.

"You call us slave trainees, but the difference between a slave and submissive wasn't very clear in the books."

He shrugged. "That's because there really is no clear answer."

"What do you believe?"

He leaned against the door. "For the ease of my training program, I use the term 'slave trainee,' but how you choose to perceive your role here is your own personal choice, and you may adapt what you learn here in any power-exchange relationship, no matter what you define yourself to be in the future. Many of those I've trained have entered relationships in the Dominant role."

"How did you wind up turning your family home into a sex club?"

"Believe it or not, the state has several laws on its books regulating sex. Even sodomy is still illegal in Michigan. About fifteen years ago, there was a crackdown on the local adult entertainment industry, and several of the clubs that catered to alternative lifestyles were closed for legal violations, including the BDSM club I'd belonged to. When my parents moved down to Florida, they deeded this house to me. I'd already been toying with the idea of investing in a new club, but instead, I decided to use my home. It's private property, making it much more difficult for the government to shut it down."

"Fifteen years ago..." He'd been in his early twenties. "You were already into the lifestyle?"

He nodded, his expression turning solemn. "There was a period right after college when my life spiraled out of control. A friend of mine brought me to a private play party and introduced me to a Domme. I was immediately intrigued by the lifestyle, but she wouldn't play with me until I agreed to stop drinking and submit to her for at least three months. Six months later, I began topping other women, and for the first time, I felt as though I was in the driver's seat of my own life." A breath shuddered through him. "If my friend hadn't introduced me to BDSM, I honestly believe I would have drank myself to death. Creating Benediction and training slaves is a way for me to pay it forward."

She bit down on her lower lip, wondering what could have possibly sent him spiraling out of control like that. "Do your parents know you turned the house into a sex club?"

"They know the basics. Understandably, they don't want to know about my sex life. But I didn't want them to come visit and walk into a sex club unaware."

"And they're cool with it?" If her father had lived, she couldn't imagine he'd accept her living in a sex club or training as a slave.

He chuckled. "They'd prefer I marry and raise a family in the home rather than train people in the art of Domination and submission, but they want me to be happy."

"What if you decide you want to get married and have kids? Would you move Benediction, or would you live somewhere else?"

He stiffened and a pregnant silence followed. "That's not a consideration. I'm not the family sort of man. It's a commitment I'm not willing to make with someone."

For some reason, she experienced a pang of disappointment. "'Til death do us part too much for you?"

He moved closer. "Tell me, Danielle. You've indicated you're here for your potential fiancé. What role do you see yourself playing? Do you imagine waiting for him on your knees, naked and open, as he walks through the front door every night? Or is it something you wish to remain in the bedroom? A little bondage with some scarves? An occasional slap on your luscious bottom as he takes you from behind?"

She'd never imagined any of those things, but his words created vivid images she knew she'd picture later in her bed. "Isn't that why I'm here? For you to teach me, so I can determine what I want in a power-exchange relationship?"

Suspicion banked in his eyes. "I don't know. Why are you here?"

Rather than wait for her answer, Cole unlocked the door and pushed it open. She stepped inside and gasped at the sight.

The dark hardwood floors, exposed pipes in the ceiling, and track lighting gave the room a warehouse feel, and framed black and white photographs like the ones she'd seen in the dungeon lined the cream-colored walls. Interspersed were paintings of nudes done in oils and drawings in chalk.

In awe of his talent, she turned to him. "Is this your art gallery? Oh my God. You did all this?"

"Self-indulgent, I know, but yes." His eyes twinkled, and a light blush stained his cheeks. "All the artwork was created by me throughout the years."

She toured the space, mesmerized by the subtle details he'd captured in each piece of art. His paintings and drawings were every bit as lifelike as his photographs, down to a small mole on the side of a woman's lips and the curve of a hip. While the photos all included some form of kink or sex toy and were often limited to a single body part, his drawings and paintings focused solely on the person as a whole.

One wall contained only mirrors, cut into shapes such as stars and lightning bolts. Had he designed these as well? "I noticed the mirrors throughout the house. You use them here too. I've never considered a mirror as art before."

He shrugged and strode to her. "I like mirrors."

"I don't."

"Why not?

"Mirrors tell the truth. Without them, I can pretend to be someone else. I can forget what I look like."

Creases in his forehead appeared. "Why the hell would you want to do that?"

"I don't know if you remember, but I used to be a lot heavier than I am now. But even now, I'm not thin." She scrutinized her reflection in the jagged mirror. "I'm not beautiful."

He gripped her shoulders and twirled her toward him. "Who says?"

"No one has to say it to my face." She motioned to the wall of mirrors. "It's very clear every time I'm forced to see my reflection."

With two of his fingers under her chin, he turned her head away from the mirrors to stare into his warm eyes.

"Then you're looking in the wrong ones. You're beautiful. You've always been beautiful." He tucked a strand of her hair behind her ears, his tender touch eliciting a shiver. "And I'll prove it to you. Let my photos be your mirror. See yourself as I see you."

Always been beautiful? Was that a line to make her feel better or did he mean it? And if he did, how would he know?

She didn't doubt his talent, but the models in the photos must have had perfect bodies, something she'd never have even if she lost another forty pounds. Her thighs were too thick and her butt too round. Sure, she had big, firm breasts, but without her bra, gravity kicked in. He'd need to use some photo-editing software to make her appear beautiful.

His eyes narrowed. "I see those negative thoughts floating around in your mind. Trust me to erase them all for you. Can you do that, darling?"

She exhaled loudly, nodding her assent while her inner critic scoffed at his promise. "I'll try."

"Come with me." He laced his fingers in hers and directed her toward the back of the room to an adjacent alcove. He'd transformed the small space into a studio with several cameras on tripods, gigantic lights, and a white backdrop that extended onto the floor.

"Take off your clothes and then lay down on the middle of the sheet." He fiddled with the cameras, aiming them all toward the center, where he expected her to lie. Naked.

While Cole seemed indifferent to her presence, her own heart sprinted a marathon as she began to undress.

Her hands shook so much, she had a difficult time unbuttoning her blouse, and it took several tries before she could get the first one through the hole.

She shook her head at herself. Dozens of naked women strut around Benediction every night. Hers was just one more naked body. Cole probably wouldn't bat an eyelash, especially since he'd already seen her without her clothes. He was an artist. She was his model. And his slave. One who he had to train, and part of that training must entail building self-esteem. After all, what kind of slave would she make if she feared getting naked?

She peeled off her blouse and unhooked her bra, letting it fall to the floor, then she slid down her skirt. Her mouth went as dry as Scottsdale in the summer as she folded her clothes and left them in a neat pile. Blowing out a breath, she settled where he'd directed, lying flat on her back with her arms over her head so her breasts would appear perkier, a trick she'd learned from one of her women's magazines.

She waited for what felt like forever, watching Cole in action as he concentrated on tipping the lights and shifting the cameras while he sucked his bottom lip into his mouth. Finally, he finished fiddling with the equipment and turned his attention to her.

He froze.

A muscle jumped in his cheek, and his jaw grew rigid.

Had she done something wrong?

Moments later, he snapped out of his odd stupor and kneeled beside her. His hands seemed to tremble as he set her head on her folded arms. "I'm going to take a few photos of you just like this." He kept his gaze trained on her face like a total professional.

"Should I smile?"

He stood and stomped to the cameras. "Do whatever feels natural."

Right. Natural. Because she always posed naked for an owner of a sex club.

One by one, he moved behind each camera, shooting a photo before adjusting the aim. "Have you ever seen the *Mona Lisa*?"

She blinked, thrown by the question. "Yes. I've been to the Louvre a few times. Why?"

"Ever wonder about her expression? Scholars have debated it for years. The Italian title of the painting is *La Gioconda,* which means—"

"Lighthearted." She'd studied Da Vinci in college in her beginning art history class. His artwork wasn't particularly her favorite, but like millions of other people, she was intrigued by the *Mona Lisa*. She'd even written her final paper on it.

"To many, it's a portrait of a happy woman." He snatched a camera off its stand and stalked closer to her, his gaze no longer contained to her face. "But is she truly content, or is she simply showing the world what they expect to see?"

Heat rushed through her body, hardening her nipples and moistening her pussy. "Perhaps the smile has nothing to do with the subject and everything to do with the artist."

Only inches away from her now, he dropped to his knees and snapped a photo. "What do you mean?"

"A man like that was too incredibly talented to simply paint what everyone else would paint if they held the brush. True artists see differently. They use all their senses in their creation." She squeezed her thighs together, his nearness sending her heart into overdrive, a quickening beat she felt not only in her chest but between her legs. "Maybe Da Vinci saw beneath the surface and painted what lay inside Mona Lisa," she said.

"You may be right. Did you know Da Vinci was obsessed with mirrors? He believed if you stood in front of a six-way mirror, you could see all the different facets of a person." He inched forward and planted his hands on her thighs, then spread her wide open. "I think it's possible to achieve the same with a camera. Let's find out all of yours."

A small gasp popped out of her as he bent her knees and crawled between them, wearing a grin rivaling the *Mona Lisa*.

"All we'll need is some hot wax."

Chapter Eleven

DANIELLE TRIED TO keep calm despite having Cole between her naked thighs. "Hot wax? Does it hurt?"

He absentmindedly caressed her kneecaps. "I promise it's not my intention to inflict any pain. They're special candles specifically designed and marketed for wax play. As you've seen, my photographs are in black and white with a hint of color. To keep my hands free, I've set the cameras on timers. I'm going to drip different colors of hot wax on your body as the cameras shoot. If the wax hurts, tell me and I'll stop."

He left her spread open as he collected a few colored candles from a table in the corner of the alcove. All the reservations she'd carried about baring her body had disappeared. Although she was the one exposed and on display, a sense of strength and power filled her. She wasn't embarrassed.

But she was embarrassingly wet.

She loved being on this side of the camera. Loved the way Cole's eyes had darkened and his gaze locked on her damp pussy. And as he turned from the table and sauntered toward her, his arms loaded up with candles, her own gaze flew to the outline of his erection through his jeans.

She'd caused it.

He kneeled beside her and set the candles on the floor, eying her hungrily. "I had no intention of touching you today, other than what was necessary for the photographs. But the way you're laid out for me with that glistening pussy and those pebbled nipples...I'm not that strong. Say yes, Danielle. Tell me I can touch you and taste you."

"Yes," she said without hesitation, not wanting him to change his mind.

Then his hands were on her, one caressing the curve of her collarbone while the other swept from her neck to her breastbone. "Softest skin." He bent to her breast, taking his time to lick around the areola before pulling the tip into his mouth and sucking on it. Nibbling on it. Setting her body on fire. She couldn't imagine the wax making her skin any hotter.

She watched his eyes close as he seemed to concentrate on her breast, his facial hair abrading her skin.

Her hands clenched with a need to spear her fingers into his hair and hold him to her chest. This felt like love-making. Not art. For a moment, she permitted herself the fantasy that Cole wanted her as more than his slave. That his mouth was on her breasts not because of the photographs or because he was her Master, but because he was falling in love with her.

Her imagination ran wild with the fantasy of him sliding his cock between her breasts and climaxing on her skin. She wanted him to brand her with his teeth. Claim her with his cock.

He growled against her chest. "You taste so fucking good." He moved to her other breast and dragged his teeth from the lower swell of her breast over her nipple.

Since she first saw him when she was a seventeen-year-old virgin, she'd felt a connection to him. An invisible tether drawing her to him. When they shared the same air, her other senses were enhanced. Everything became clearer when she was with him, almost as though she'd been living her life looking through distorted glass.

But right now, she didn't care. Nothing else mattered but the feel of him playfully tugging on her nipple.

With a muttered curse, he released her nipple and picked up a candle.

Her heart drummed a staccato beat, and her hips arched as her arousal built. She felt feverish, her skin tight. Her breasts ached, and her juices dripped down her thighs.

On display, she was naked, completely bared to him with her knees spread wide enough for him to witness her extreme arousal.

It was wanton and dirty. And she loved it.

With a match in hand, Cole lit a green candle and held it over her.

She held her breath, afraid to move.

The first drop of hot wax hit her stomach, right above her belly button. Her body bowed, the shock of it drawing a soft cry from her lips. The wax's heat quickly dissipated but left her aware of her sensitive skin.

"Too hot, darlin'?" he asked. "If it is, say the word, and I'll stop."

She shook her head. "No. Don't stop."

He licked his lips as he tipped the candle over her breastbone, dripping the wax between her breasts and lower, down her belly. Her legs. Her arms. He blew out the candle and lifted another one over her, trailing the wax in what seemed like circular patterns.

The heat in his eyes created a hunger in her she'd never known. For his lips. His touch. His cock. His heart. Every. Single. Piece.

She knew she was playing with fire in more ways than one. Cole DeMarco was a dangerous man. Her enemy. A man who had sentenced her father to death and left her alone in this world. No matter what he did to her body, no matter how much she wanted to surrender, she couldn't forget what she was here to do. She had to get the bank account information and save Tasha. And maybe, just maybe, she'd find the evidence to prove her father had been innocent.

This was role play. A consensual game between two adults. He didn't truly want her. She was simply a canvas for his art, no more than a prop for him to use in his photographs. For all she knew, he photographed all his trainees. Made them feel special. Made them feel beautiful. Made them want to submit to his commands.

Cole's expression turned feral, his eyes darkening, narrowing, and his lips flattening into a straight line. "Let's turn those red nipples a deeper shade, shall we?" Wax dripped on the sensitive skin, lighting up the nerves and sending shockwaves deep within her pussy.

She threw her head back and moaned, the fine line between role play and reality blurring.

He dropped to his knees, his face hovering only inches over hers. His thumb swiped across her bottom lip and plunged past, brushing her tongue before sliding back out again. "Your lips...I wonder what they'd look like after sucking on my cock. They're already so plump. So fuckable. I can't resist them anymore."

And then his mouth was on hers in a bruising crash of passion and aggression that made her heart sing and her body soar. He tasted sweet, like red licorice and cola. His tongue teased hers, touching and retreating, teasing and promising.

All too soon, he pulled away. She breathed heavy, her mind and body at war with one another, and her body winning. Why did he kiss her?

He picked up the candle again and held it directly over her pussy, so close she could feel the heat of the flame. He stared at her between her legs and licked his lips.

The hot wax hit her labia. Her pulse raced. Then those lips that had been on hers curled into a feral smile.

Heat enveloped her clit as the wax made contact. She shuddered. A throbbing began in her clit, and the muscles in her abdomen tightened, her arousal spiking to an all-time high. She needed more. Needed him.

"Tell me, baby. Tell me what you want," he said, his voice raspy.

She gazed into his eyes. "Please make me come, Master Cole."

His nostrils flared, and his pupils dilated, making his rich cocoa eyes turn ever darker. A muscle jumped in his jaw, and his lips pressed into a straight line.

He scooted down her body and settled himself between her legs, but he didn't undress. Using his thumbs, he spread the lips of her pussy apart and examined her as if it held the key to ending world hunger. The cameras continued to flash and snap, recording every moment. It was dirty. Wanton. Sinful.

He blew a stream of air over her clitoris, and the small breeze caused her pussy to throb. His thumb brushed over the bundle of nerves as lightly as the previous air. Apparently, he wasn't done torturing her.

Torture had never felt so good.

He dipped his fingers lower, gathering her wetness, and slid those fingers back up to her clitoris, squeezing it between his forefinger and thumb. A throaty moan passed through her lips.

She wanted to grind herself against his fingers, but even without him stating it, she instinctively knew he wouldn't allow it. She'd begged him to make her come, and unless he requested her to do something, she was to lie here and permit him complete access to her body. He'd take care of her on his own time table, and there was nothing she could do to change his mind.

Her firsthand knowledge of sex was limited to experimentation with one man, Davis, her TA in art history 101. Lost after her father's arrest, she was desperate for companionship. And Davis had been desperate to pretend he wasn't gay. The sex had been painful and awkward. Their brief affair ended when he'd entered into a committed relationship with his male roommate.

He sunk a finger inside of her. "You're drenched. Is this all for me, Danielle?" He added another, stretching her.

"Yes," she admitted honestly. "I've been wet since the moment I stepped into your office yesterday."

"I promise I'm going to take care of you, baby, and as I told you, I never break a promise. But right now, I want to play with you a little bit more. See how hard I can make you come. You've got to hold back until I say you can let go, yeah? Because I don't want you simply to come. I want to watch you shatter."

Hold back? Was he kidding? How the hell could she stop herself from coming? It was on the tip of her tongue to tell him it was impossible, but instead, she answered, "Yes, Master."

A growl erupted from his throat, and then he was on her. He peeled some wax from her clitoris before sucking it between his lips. His fingers slid high inside of her and rubbed. It was as if someone had plugged her into an electrical outlet. Her thighs shook, and her heart hammered so loudly and so quickly, she felt as though she'd pass out. Heat built in her pussy. Growing hotter and hotter until it boiled. Every muscle in her body clenched with the need for release.

His tongue worked its magic on her clit. Flicking it over and over in time with his fingers, which continued to massage the sensitive spot inside of her. With soft reverence like a prayer, his name spilled from her lips, her subtle way of begging him to push her over the edge.

He buried his face into her pussy, groaning as he ate at her.

She couldn't hold on much longer. The dual sensations caused by his fingers and tongue, not to mention the sounds of his licks and his moans, were pushing her closer and closer to climax. It didn't seem possible she'd held out this long. That she hadn't already come and come hard. She should've known he'd get his way. He wouldn't be satisfied until she shattered.

He hooked his pinky around the bottom of her pussy and dipped it between her bottom cheeks, exploring the sensitive skin. She jerked, the touch short-circuiting her brain and making her crazed for more. Even though she didn't use the words, he answered her anyway. It penetrated her, creating a slight burning and awakening a whole lot of nerves she'd never known existed.

It was too much. She couldn't take anymore.

He lifted his face. "Come, Danielle." When he licked her clit hard with the flat of his tongue, she had no choice but to comply. She felt the orgasm from the tip of her toes to the top of her head and everywhere in between. Her entire body pulsed and quaked. Her toes curled, her hands clenched, and her eyes rolled in the back of her head. It was that good.

She didn't come. She exploded. Broke apart.

Just as he'd promised.

She shattered.

Chapter Twelve

COLE REMOVED HIMSELF from between her legs and stood. "Stay there while I clean the wax off you."

The cameras had stopped their snapping of pictures. Cole turned off the studio lights, dimming the space. Her eyes fluttered shut. She wanted to escape and go back to her room for a shower, but she didn't have the energy. Breathing deep, she listened to the sounds Cole made as he moved around the room.

She felt his presence beside her moments before he brushed something across her lips. "Open up." He popped a piece of chocolate into her mouth. "How are you feeling?"

She sighed. "Tired."

He chuckled and fed her another piece. "Eat a little more candy."

An orgasm and chocolate. No wonder people came here for slave training.

"I'm going to rub some baby oil on your skin to help soften the wax and then scrape it off with a comb." He kneaded the top of her breasts with his oiled hands.

"I get a massage too?"

"How's that?"

"Heaven." As his hands inched lower and stroked the area that included her nipples, she opened her eyes to an up-close view of Cole's covered erection. "Do you need me to take care of it?"

He stopped for a brief moment and hissed out a breath. "I'm good. Let's get you cleaned up, and I'll take you back to your room."

Her heart slammed against her breastbone. "Or you could take me to yours," she offered, guilt and hope snaking together as she seized the opportunity to access his residence.

He avoided her eyes. "I don't allow any slaves in my private residence."

The words sliced through her like a machete. He'd reverted to his Master voice, speaking as if this was a rule he'd had to repeat a thousand times. Silly of her to think for a moment she meant more to him than a slave. "Right. Of course."

"If I could, I would." Using the comb, he removed pieces of wax from her chest. "I have to have clear boundaries, or I'd never have any space to myself."

"It's fine, I get it." She gritted her teeth and lay as still as possible, trying her best to dissociate from her body as she would in a doctor's exam. Cole worked in silence, completing the process of removing wax from her skin.

When he got to her pussy, she clamped her legs together. "I'll get that off myself. If you don't mind, I'd prefer to return to my room for a shower." A warm one that would erase the chill that had settled in her bones.

"Danielle..." His lips flattened into a firm line. "I hope today helped you feel beautiful."

For a short time, she'd almost believed it was true. "You certainly did your best to make me feel that way."

As she sat up, he reached behind him and grabbed a plastic bottle, then held it out to her. "Drink some water before you stand."

"I'm not thirsty." She hated that she sounded like a petulant child, but she couldn't help it.

"I'm not asking, Danielle. Drink the water."

Sighing, she uncapped the bottle. "Yes, Master."

After she'd taken a couple sips, he slipped his arm around her back. "Up you go."

She squirmed away from him. Why did he have to act as if he cared? "I don't need your help."

"Too bad you don't have a choice. This is what we call 'after-care.' After a scene, it's the Master's responsibility to attend to the slave's needs. Blood sugar drops, and you can experience dehydration."

Embarrassment heated her cheeks. "Chocolate and water."

"Yeah. Chocolate and water. A blanket. A hug. A ride home or assistance to a room. Whatever's necessary to ensure the health and welfare of the slave or in this case, you." He picked up her clothes off the floor. "Turn around."

Her breathing hitched as he encircled her chest and slipped her arms into the straps of her bra before hooking it in the back. Her skin felt tender, as if she'd spent too much time in the sun. Finding after-care to be far too intimate for her taste, she shivered when he helped her into her skirt and blouse.

He slowly spun her to face him and took her hands in his, interlacing their fingers. "Tomorrow, I'd like to show you the photographs."

"Of course."

He steered her through the gallery, a painful reminder of her status in his world, then past the jagged mirrors, where she discovered her disappointment was etched on her face. She didn't understand why she cared so much about Cole's intentions. They both had a job to do and a role to play. If anything, today had served as a reminder that everything that happened here may have looked, smelled, and felt real, but it was simply a mirage. As long as she remembered it, her heart would remain intact.

After Cole locked the gallery door, he splayed a hand on her lower spine and directed her to the kitchen, so he could take her upstairs to her room. A glance at the grandfather clock at the end of the hallway and the people littered around the main floor told her it was night-time. She rubbed her eyes with the back of her hand. Had they really been in the studio all afternoon? No wonder she was so tired.

As they passed the foyer, a harried Gracie ran up the stairs from the dungeon, taking two at a time. Strips of black leather-looking material crossed in an X over her breasts, barely concealing her nipples, and ran down her sides until it merged with a piece that covered the juncture between her thighs. "Master Cole, we have a problem. Anthony Rinaldi has asked Cassandra to join him for electrical play."

Cole stiffened and removed his hand from her back, his jaw tightening and eyes narrowing. "He knows he has to go through me or a dungeon monitor to scene with a trainee."

"Yes, Master, but he refuses to listen," Gracie said. "Not to mention Cassandra is arguing with the dungeon monitors as well."

It figured Cassandra was at the root of the problem. The woman was literally a glutton for punishment.

Cole yanked his cell from his pocket and dialed, then raised it to his ear. "Michael, will you please have Anthony Rinaldi and Cassandra brought upstairs to my office?" He disconnected and frowned, his anger morphing into concern. "She wants to try electrical play with him? Have you explained he's a sadist?"

"Oh, she knows." Gracie folded her arms over her chest. "I'm certain this is one of her ploys for attention. She's a brat, not a pain slut."

Danielle admired how Cole immediately took charge of the situation, but it was clear he didn't have time to worry about her well-being at the moment. She pasted on a fake smile and stepped back from him. "You obviously have your hands full with the club, and I'm fine to get myself to my room, so I'm going to go—"

"You'll wait for me," he said firmly. "This will only take a moment."

Gracie glanced between them and seemed to pick up on the tension. "I'd be happy to take her upstairs, Master."

He hesitated. "Thank you for your offer, but I'll see to her myself."

Danielle didn't know much about after-care, but to her, his behavior reminded her of someone insisting he walk his date to the door. At this point, she didn't see why Gracie couldn't fulfill his Master obligations toward her.

Dressed in a see-through black mesh dress, Cassandra sauntered up the stairs with what appeared to Danielle to be a triumphant grin. As soon as the troublemaker caught sight of Master Cole, she schooled her expression into one of remorse. As she had earlier in class, she dropped to her knees in front of him. "Master Cole, I'd like permission to scene with Anthony Rinaldi."

"Permission denied. Please stand."

She tossed her long red hair over her shoulder as she complied. "May I ask why?"

Cole remained calm, calmer than Danielle would be in the same position. She didn't understand why he indulged her behavior. "As your Master, I don't have to explain my decision to you, but since you're a trainee and this is a learning experience, I will. Rinaldi is a sadist and not the kind you read about in your BDSM romances."

She raised a brow. "Then why is he a member?"

From the dungeon, two men climbed the stairs, Michael trailing behind them. The taller of the men wore a black business suit and was built like a football player, while the other, an older man with graying brown hair, was dressed casually in jeans and a Polo shirt. Which one was the sadist?

Answering Cassandra, Cole didn't seem to notice Rinaldi's approach. "I've known him for a number of years, and he's been a member of Benediction since day one. So long as he follows the rules, a sadist has just as much of a right to membership as any other person. However, unless you're a masochist with a high pain tolerance, this is not a man to tango with."

"Cole," the older man said smoothly, offering a hand. "I wasn't aware you were running a dance studio."

Michael's phone rang, and he answered, motioning to Cole with his hands that he was needed elsewhere. At Cole's nod, he headed toward the kitchen.

Cole eyed Rinaldi's outstretched hand but didn't shake it. "Anthony. I'm told you tried to negotiate a scene with my slave trainee. You're aware you need to obtain prior approval, yes?"

Undeterred by Cole's rejection, Rinaldi winked as he dropped his hand to his side. "You and me, we go back a long time. I figured by now, you'd trust me."

Danielle sensed an undercurrent of animosity in Rinaldi's words. Cole remained calm, but his hands twitched as if he was keeping himself from saying what he really felt.

If Rinaldi didn't follow the rules, why wouldn't Cole terminate his membership?

"My decision has nothing to do with trust," Cole said in much the same way he'd told her he didn't bring slaves to his bedroom. "Everyone, including Benediction's original members, must adhere to our policies. Cassandra is not a masochist, and as her Master, it is my role not only to see that her limits are honored, but to know when to add limits for her own protection."

Rinaldi tilted his head and ruminated for a moment. "Fair enough." Then to her horror, he turned to her. "I don't recognize you." His assessing gaze slid down the length of her body. "I don't suppose there's any hope this one's a masochist? What's her name, Cole?"

Cole shoved him. "You will never fucking touch her. Don't talk to her. Don't even look at her. You're not worthy to breathe the same air as her, and you're certainly not worthy of learning her name."

Danielle froze. Why was he so protective of her?

A sick grin turned Rinaldi's otherwise unremarkable face into one of a psychotic. "No worries. I can see the girl means something to you." He smacked his cohort on the back. "Let's go find us a masochist. I'm itching to cause some pain."

Although they could access the stairs if they went right, Rinaldi swaggered left. "Welcome to Benediction, Danielle Walker."

An icy chill swept through her. Why had he asked Cole for her name if he already knew it?

Cole tensed, and his eyes darkened as he watched Rinaldi leave. Gracie laid a gentle hand on his arm and shook her head. "He's not worth it, Master. Let him go."

Rinaldi disappeared from sight before Cole moved a single muscle. Then he turned to Cassandra. "We'll need to speak tonight about whether you're committed to Benediction and your training as a slave. Until then, you're to return to your room. You're excused." Swallowing hard, Cassandra wisely kept her mouth shut and ambled toward the kitchen. "Gracie, thank you for your assistance. As a reward, I'll set up a scene for you with Ryder and Morgan." As if nothing had occurred, he returned his hand to the small of Danielle's back.

Gracie beamed. "Of course, Master." She caught Danielle's gaze and wiggled her eyebrow before galloping off to the basement.

With everyone now gone, Cole made good on his word and escorted Danielle to her room, his touch even more confusing now that she'd witnessed his attack on Rinaldi. "How did Rinaldi know my name?" she asked.

The fingers of his hand curled into her waist. "Word gets around when Benediction gets a beautiful new slave trainee."

She didn't believe him, but why would he lie? Now at her room, she pivoted so her back rested against the wooden door and searched his eyes for the truth. "I thought you were going to hurt him."

"I wanted to."

Her heart skipped a beat. "Because of me?

He leaned forward, bracing his hands on either side of her head. "Because Rinaldi and I have a complicated history, and it's my responsibility to protect"—his gaze dropped to her lips—"all my slaves. You're safe here."

She held her breath as his mouth inched closer and closer. At the last second, he stopped, brushing his thumb against her cheek. "Get some rest. You're going to need it."

Leaving her wanting and confused, he turned and walked away, as if she'd imagined the entire moment. And although she was flooded with the urge to confront him on it, she let him go, knowing it was for the best.

Chapter Thirteen

A RECTANGULAR, LIGHT blue Tiffany box with a white bow tied around it sat on her bed as though it was her birthday.

She fingered the Tiffany locket around her neck and shivered, goose bumps developing up and down her arms. The sensation of being watched returned.

Could Cole have left her a present?

She couldn't remember the last time she'd received a gift. Tasha wrote her checks, and Roman took her shopping to pick out something she wanted, but a surprise gift? It must have been more than eight years ago. Before her father had been imprisoned.

This box looked innocent enough, but for some reason, it felt...ominous. She sat on her bed, picked it up, and shook it. The box was light, and she didn't hear anything.

She carefully untied the bow and slid it off the box.

Footsteps sounded in the hallway, and then the noise disappeared, almost as if someone had stopped in front of her door. Was it the person who'd left her the gift? Were they waiting for her reaction?

Her hands trembled as she slowly lifted the top off the box. Gasping, she dropped its bloody contents on the floor. Nausea choked her.

A finger.

Discolored and gray, with dry, crusted, black blood coating the bottom where it had been severed from the hand, there was no mistaking the finger's identity.

The long red polished nail.

The faded scar underneath the knuckle.

The platinum and diamond wedding band.

The finger belonged to Tasha. *Had* belonged to Tasha.

Her belly churned, and she gagged. Rushing to the bathroom, she barely made it to the toilet before emptying all the contents of her stomach.

Why? She'd done everything they had asked. Gotten on a plane and left her life in Arizona behind. Convinced Cole to let her train as a sex slave.

How had the box gotten to her room? She'd locked the door.

Maybe one of the trainees knew something about how it had arrived. But what if it came from one of the other trainees? Was one of them working for the kidnappers? It would certainly make sense. Any one of them could be watching her and reporting back.

But what had she done to warrant Tasha losing her finger?

Her poor stepmother. She didn't deserve this. No one deserved this.

Danielle flushed the toilet and cleaned up at the sink, brushing her teeth and rinsing her mouth out with mouthwash. She couldn't fall apart. Not when Tasha's life was on the line.

Now she had to figure out what to do with the finger. She couldn't keep it here. But she couldn't bear to throw it away in the garbage either. What if she needed it later as evidence? Surely when Tasha came home, they could contact the police and start an investigation.

Her breathing calmed, and her hands steadied. She could do this. She'd take the box outside and find a safe place to hide it.

She stepped out of the bathroom and into her bedroom just as the door to her room clicked shut. Frozen, she scanned the room, immediately noticing the package and the finger were gone.

They'd been in her room while she was in the bathroom, oblivious, only feet away.

The nausea returned as she raced to the door and flung it open. She stepped into the hall and found it empty. It had to be one of the trainees. There was no way anyone else could've gotten away so quickly. She scanned all the closed doors. Which one hid the trespasser? Did they know what they had delivered?

The door across her hall creaked open, and looking polished as ever, her red hair flowing over her shoulders, out came Cassandra. She smirked as she noticed

Danielle. "Need help packing your suitcase? If you need a ride, I'd be happy to call a taxi for you."

There was no mistaking the fact that Cassandra was a class-A bitch, but had she left the box in her room? Could she be working with the kidnappers?

"I'm not the one who Master Cole is planning on speaking to about her commitment," Danielle said, curling her shaking hands into fists at her hips.

Surprise registered in Cassandra's eyes before she concealed it. "Oh, that? You obviously don't know how things work around here. I'm what's known in the BDSM community as a 'brat.' I make trouble because the Masters get off on punishing me. If you knew anything about BDSM, you'd get it." She raked her gaze down Danielle's body. "You're a poser. I don't understand why Master Cole allowed you to train."

Danielle took a steadying breath. "I don't have to explain myself to you, nor do I answer to you." Instead of retreating, Danielle stalked closer to her, lowering her voice and speaking nonchalantly. "And you're not a brat. You're a selfish little girl playing adult games. Those Masters who you believe get off on your behavior? They see right through you." She twirled around and went back into her room, shutting the door.

Standing with her back against it, she spied a pill bottle halfway under the bed. Had that been there before?

She scooped it up. There was no label, but it was definitely a prescription pill bottle. She held it up to the light and saw two pills inside.

Her cell phone rang.

Trembling, she went to the nightstand and lifted her phone, not surprised to see the call was from an unlisted number. "Hello?"

"They're sleeping pills. You need to get DeMarco to bring you to his bed, and then you can drug him in order to search his residence for the box."

"Where am I supposed to hide the pills when I'm walking around half-naked all the time?"

He laughed. "A Tiffany box for a Tiffany girl. Hide them in your locket."

She wiped the tears from her cheek. "Why did you cut off Tasha's finger? I've done everything you've asked."

He hesitated. "*Tick-tock*. We thought we'd remind you of the seriousness of the situation. Don't get too comfortable with DeMarco. He wouldn't help you even if he knew."

"I need assurances that Tasha's okay."

"Well, you're not going to get it. Just be grateful we didn't send her whole hand."

The call went dead before she could say another word.

Pacing the room, she dumped the tiny oval pills in her hand. She checked the identifying markings and looked it up on her phone's web browser.

The results popped up immediately. It was a sedative used to treat insomnia and dissolved in water. She read over the information, including the dosage instructions. Two pills were more than generally prescribed, but it wouldn't cause any lasting health issues.

She breathed a sigh of relief. Her stepmother had taken sleeping aids for years without any problems.

The message from the kidnappers had made it clear. Time was running out.

After checking that the door was locked and turning out the lights, she quickly undressed and padded naked to her bed, then slid beneath the sheets, drawing the blanket up to her chin. She closed her eyes and tried to relax, but as exhausted as she was, sleep eluded her.

She didn't feel safe. How could she when the lock on the door couldn't prevent someone from breaking into her room?

Hours passed, and the sound of the voices of the trainees returning to their rooms ceased. Eventually, her limbs grew heavy, and she closed her eyes.

The next thing she knew, warm breath fanned her face and a hand brushed over her breast. She arched into it, her nipple pebbling under the touch, heat suffusing her body. As she woke, her fuzzy mind tried to remember who was touching her. The last thing she remembered was being in her bed. Alone.

Her eyes shot open. The room was completely dark, but she sensed someone beside her. Felt a hand on her breast and the cold, sharp press of a blade against her throat.

Panic filled her, sending her heart racing. "Who's there?"

The hand stilled, followed by a long pause.

"I'm your secret admirer," the unknown man whispered. "Shh. You don't want to alert anyone I'm in here. After all, you can't tell DeMarco why you're really here."

Stifling a cry for help, she swallowed, her throat dry with fear. His voice didn't sound familiar, but she couldn't be sure between him whispering and the whir of her pulse in her ears. "Are you the one who left me the box?"

"I'm sorry if it frightened you. That wasn't my intent."

"You're frightening me now."

"I'm not here to hurt you."

"Then why are you here? Why do you have a knife?"

His hand drifted down her abdomen. "The knife is just a precaution. I'm not a monster."

She grabbed his wrist, halting him from going any farther. "If you don't remove your hand, I'll scream. I don't care who comes running. If you want me to get that account information, then you can't kill me. You can't even hurt me. So get the hell out of my room, and don't come back."

He pulled away and got up from the bed. "You're braver than I thought. I'll go…for now. But remember, the longer it takes for you to find that bank account, the more opportunities I'll have to come back. You understand?"

She swallowed thickly. "Yes."

She waited until he was gone before jumping out of bed and pushing her nightstand in front of the door. Then she dropped to the floor, wrapped her arms around her knees, and cried.

Chapter Fourteen

DANIELLE HAD BARELY slept.

That was the third night in a row she'd gone without sleep. With the knowledge that she wouldn't be safe even behind a locked door, she didn't think she'd be able to sleep until this was all over.

While having breakfast with the trainees, she'd fallen asleep midbite, the chocolate donut still in her mouth when Gracie had shaken her by the shoulder. After, she'd scarfed down the rest of it and two cups of black coffee so she'd have enough energy to make it through the day.

She and the trainees were brought to the dungeon for a flogging demonstration.

With a duffel bag at his feet, Master Michael stood in front of a steel frame that reminded Danielle of a horizontal bar used in gymnastics, with a trapeze-like contraption hanging from it. Leather restraints dangled from the trapeze and were also attached to the bottom sides of the frame.

All the trainees, including Danielle, gathered in a semicircle in front of the structure. Completely drained despite the sugar and caffeine, she swayed on her feet, knocking into Lily.

Michael held a black flogger in his hands. "Today I'm going to demonstrate some different flogging techniques. Although the majority of you will remain slaves after you leave here, a few of you may take the Dominant role at some point in the future. Either way, it's important that you be familiar with proper technique." His eyes searched the trainees until they landed on her. "I need a volunteer. Danielle, since you're new and haven't had the chance to play much in the dungeon, why don't you help me today?"

Though his expression hadn't changed, she swore she saw lust in his eyes. She didn't know how to feel about that. While he was striking with his dark wavy hair and gray eyes, she wasn't attracted to him. But this wasn't about sex. He was just doing his job.

Taking a deep breath, she moved to stand beside him, facing the trainees.

"Remove your clothes," Master Michael said casually.

Okay, now she was wide awake. There was nothing casual about taking her clothes off in front of a room of people. Her pulse skyrocketed as she looked out at the trainees. Part of her still rebelled at the idea of exposing her body, worried about the trainees' reactions. What if they laughed or were disgusted by her?

As she slowly peeled off her top, she thought of Cole calling her beautiful. She could do this. In fact, she wanted to do this. Being naked in front of an audience was her fantasy brought to life, and while her mind was conflicted, her body was on board with the idea, her nipples tightening and her pussy dampening as she slid her skirt down her legs and bared herself completely.

Michael continued his tutorial. "There are several pieces of equipment that can be used to support a slave during a flogging, the most popular of which are the spanking bench and the St. Andrew cross. But using this bondage frame is perfect when you want to have access to both front and back. Face, neck, and head are three obvious areas to avoid. But you should also avoid fingers, toes, the kidneys, and the spine." He ran his hand down her back and guided her beneath the frame, then brought her arms over her head. "Grip the bar with both hands, and spread your legs apart about two feet."

Her heart beat wildly as he secured her wrists with the leather bindings, then bent and did the same to her ankles. "Are they too tight?" he asked.

She shook her head. "No. They're fine, Master Michael."

He moved behind her, so she could no longer see what he was doing. She concentrated on breathing and listening to his lecture.

"Floggings work best on fleshier areas that are supported by strong bones and muscles. In the back, those are the thighs, ass, and lower shoulders, and in the front, you've got the breasts and, depending on the amount of pain your sub can handle, the cunt or cock."

She gasped before she could stop herself. Master Michael patted her butt. "Don't worry. I've reviewed your file and I'm aware of your limits."

"Mind if I stay and watch?" asked a smooth voice she recognized as Cole's.

She craned her head and saw him as he approached from the entrance of the dungeon. She nearly whimpered from the urge to cry and divulge what had happened to her last night in her room. What good were all the locks and security cameras if they couldn't prevent someone from coming into her room uninvited? As evidenced by the kidnappers breaking into her house and then in her room at Benediction, this week had taught her that she could only rely on herself for protection. From now on, she'd shove furniture in front of the door while she slept and would check her room for hidden intruders whenever she returned to it.

"Of course you're welcome to watch," Master Michael said. "I was just about to demonstrate some of the ways to use a flogger, but since you're here, would you like to do the honors?"

Cole was going to flog her? She despised her reaction to that thought, feeling as though a whole swarm of butterflies fluttered in her abdomen. *Enemy. Enemy. Enemy.*

"You have the deer skin?" Cole asked.

She tried to remember what Master Michael had said about the deer skin floggers. Would it cause a lot of pain?

Master Michael searched through his bag and handed Cole a different black flogger. "Right here."

Breathless, she tugged at her restraints, the butterflies in her stomach multiplying with each passing moment.

Cole's hot body pressed against her naked back. "Danielle, what's your safe word?"

She took a deep breath at the reminder she could stop this at any time. "Red, Master Cole."

He squeezed her shoulder and stepped away from her. "For the purpose of this demonstration, I'd like to utilize the stoplight system. You're aware that red will immediately stop the scene, but yellow will indicate you'd like to pause and discuss, and green is continue. What color are you at now?"

Her uneasiness over the flogging had lessened to an acceptable degree at the knowledge that she retained some control by having her safe word. "Green, Master."

"Danielle is new to the flogger and has a low tolerance for pain. I like to begin with the buttocks. You start light to warm up the skin."

She tensed as the first strike fell on her right butt cheek, the sensation part thud and part sting, but neither painful. Waiting for his next strike, she closed her eyes and relaxed her muscles.

"Because the buttocks are a small, rounded area, you need to be careful not to wrap the falls of the flogger onto the hips or hit the tailbone," Cole said.

He continued to flog her lower body, pausing in between strikes, giving her just enough time to process the heat of it before moving on to another part of her body. "Once I've warmed up my slave's skin, I prefer to use a more cyclic style of flogging, which means one stroke flows into the next. You can do this either with a circular or a figure-eight motion."

The blows rained constantly and rhythmically on her skin until she could no longer anticipate his next strike or differentiate one from the other. She felt as though she was weightless, floating in space and being pulled deeper and deeper into a hypnotic state where nothing else existed but her and the flogger. Her brain shut down, and all her worries disappeared, nothing in her mind except how good she felt and how she never wanted it to stop.

"What color are you at?" Cole said in her ear, his hand rubbing her back.

Color? She didn't know what he meant, but somehow, she heard herself respond, "Green."

His hand was gone, and then the flogger hit the front of her thighs. The thud of it traveled up her legs, causing a deep pulsating to begin in her pussy. She rocked her pelvis forward, desperate for more. Each blow on the lower half of her body sent a vibration straight to her clitoris. There was no pain, just mindless pleasure and an ache for something to fill her empty pussy.

The pulsating spread throughout her body, and she shook from the need to come. She heard Cole and Master Michael talking, but she no longer understood what they were saying. A delicious sting radiated from her nipples throughout her breasts as Cole whipped them over and over. Her body shaking, she pulled at her restraints, desperate to touch her throbbing clit.

All of a sudden, the flogging ceased, and Cole was right behind her, his clothes rubbing across her sensitive skin and his erection pressing into her lower back. Her pussy was so wet, all he had to do was lower his zipper and in a single thrust, he could be inside her. "Danielle, you pleased me very much."

She whimpered as he pushed his fingers inside her pussy and began to fuck her with them. Awareness of their environment crept into her consciousness, and her pussy clenched around his fingers at the thought of others watching. Scorching tension wound in her lower belly, and all her muscles tightened as the inferno inside of her grew and grew and grew until Cole rubbed his thumb on her clitoris.

"Here's your reward for being such a good girl," Cole murmured in her ear. "Come for me now."

Another few seconds of direct stimulation on her exposed clitoris combined with the forceful thrusting of his fingers in her sent her soaring into climax. A rush of liquid heat zinged through her body as pleasurable contractions filled her pussy, and all her tension melted away like butter.

Moments passed. Her head hanging to her chest, she sighed, completely relaxed. An arm snaked around her waist as her wrists were released from the restraints. She dropped her heavy arms to her side and rested her weight against whoever was holding her. She heard the rip of the Velcro, and then her ankles were free, although she didn't have the strength to move her legs.

She opened her eyes and looked up to see Cole was the one with his arm around her. His brows furrowed. "Are you all right?" he asked, sounding concerned.

The world tilted and spun, shiny spots distorting her vision. His face disappeared.

She heard him say her name.

Then…

Nothing.

Chapter Fifteen

SHE WAS HOT.

Too hot.

Had she fallen asleep by the pool? It wouldn't be the first time. She loved to lie out on the lounge chair and read, but usually the maid or Tasha would wake her up before she burned.

Tasha.

Her heart thumped violently, and panic squeezed her throat.

She opened her eyes to complete darkness and tried to move, but there was a foreign weight on her legs.

"Shh. It's okay. Go back to sleep," Cole whispered from behind her.

She felt the mattress beneath her hip and realized she was in Cole's arms, one of them below her head and the other spread over her waist. He'd also thrown a leg over hers, effectively holding her captive.

Cole DeMarco was spooning her. And she was naked.

How the hell did they get here?

"What happened?" she asked, her voice raspy.

His hand brushed over her hip bone, back and forth, soothing her. "You fainted after the flogging, so I carried you upstairs. You woke up, mumbled it wasn't time to get out of bed yet, and passed out again. I didn't want to leave you, in case there was something medically wrong. If I didn't know better, I'd think you hadn't slept in days."

She hadn't. "How long did I sleep?"

"Six hours."

Peering over her shoulder, she covered his hand with hers. "You stayed here the whole time?" Her mind was alert and her muscles relaxed, as if she'd slept much longer.

On a sigh, he removed his leg and tipped her hip toward him, propelling her onto her other side to face him. "I didn't mind. It's been years since I've gotten to take a nap."

"But you have so many other things to do." She didn't know what to do with her hands. The intimacy of their positions on the bed would suggest she place them on his chest or shoulders or…lower. His own hand had returned to her waist, his fingers subtly sinking into her flesh. She could move closer, throw her leg around his thigh as he had done, only from this side, she could level his hardness between her thighs and bump her tingling clit against it. Her mouth grew dryer as her pussy grew wetter, and she fought against the urge to squeeze her thighs together, knowing Cole would guess his effect on her.

"Nothing was more important than staying with you." He brushed his knuckles down her cheek. "Now, are you going to tell me the truth?"

Feeling as though the room was suddenly devoid of air, she sat up and brought the sheet with her to cover her chest. "The truth? What do you mean?"

He stared at her for a moment, a notch forming between his brows. "You were exhausted. Aren't you sleeping at night?"

Relieved that's all he'd meant, she waved her hand. "You know what it's like. New state. New bed. Loads of new information running through my mind."

"You had a nightmare while you slept today." He came up on his forearm, and the hand of his other arm skimmed her knee. "You kept calling for Tasha."

"I don't remember it." She looked down at the bedspread, hoping she hadn't said anything else.

"Tasha's your stepmother, isn't she? Does she know you're here?"

She gave a halfhearted laugh. No doubt the kidnappers had informed Tasha about what Danielle had to do to save her. "Yes. She knows."

"Why would you be crying out for her?"

"It was just a nightmare. It doesn't mean anything."

"Dreams are the mind's way of processing events and feelings." He sat up and took her hand in his. "You know, if anything is wrong, you can tell me. I can help you."

She closed her eyes to ward off the threatening tears. God, it was so tempting to take him up on his offer. Although she'd gotten some sleep, she was so damned tired of carrying this burden all alone. But if it got back to the kidnapper and she lost Tasha as a result, she'd never forgive herself.

"There's nothing wrong," she said. "Thank you for staying and watching me this afternoon, but right now, I'd like to get ready for the club."

For a moment, she thought he'd call her out on her brisk dismissal. Instead, he planted a chaste kiss on her forehead and slid off her bed. "Get some dinner. You'll need the strength. You're on water duty tonight."

With a wicked smile promising a night filled with sensual surprises, the infuriating man strode out her door. The second he left, she blew out an exasperated breath and jumped off the bed.

Her fevered body and her guilty mind waged war against one another as she attempted to decipher what he could possibly have planned for her tonight in the club. She couldn't imagine anything sexy about serving cups of water to the members. It didn't matter what he had planned, as long as they ended the night in his bedroom, so she could drug him and find that box.

After applying some mascara, she threw on a black Lycra minidress, quickly pulled her hair into a pony-tail, and checked herself in the mirror. She sighed. She didn't look half as good as she had when Gracie had made her over, but frankly, she wasn't going to the dungeon to pick up a Dom. There was only one man she needed to impress and only one man to whom she had to answer. And he didn't seem to care if she wore makeup at all.

After dinner with the other slave trainees, she went downstairs, eager to learn what Cole had planned for her service.

The dungeon pulsed with energy, a sensual beat of music heightening the erotic atmosphere. She no longer blinked at the sexual acts going on around her, but she wasn't immune to it either. Instead, she became a part of it, a proud cog in the wheel of the club. Her hips swayed as she glided across the floor to serve the members their drinks, and a euphoric sense of belonging placed a lightness in her soul. In only a couple of days, she'd gone from an outsider to an interloper to a…slave.

Before she'd experienced it, she would've never believed a slave in the BDSM world would mean anything more than a twenty-four/seven sexual object. But she enjoyed serving the members under Cole's direction. Bringing water to them seemed like such a little thing when he'd assigned her the task earlier tonight, but after two hours, she truly felt as though she belonged here.

Every member she'd served had shown her gratitude for her service, not only in their words of thanks, but in the tone of their voices and the kindness in their eyes. Most of them were Dominants—Masters, Sadists, Tops, and Daddies. She would've thought they'd see her as something lesser, but they made her feel worshipped. The exhilaration of pleasing so many people brought her a sense of peace and happiness she hadn't experienced since before her father had gone to prison.

Wearing the dungeon monitor medallion around his neck, Cole leaned against the wall, his feet crossed at his ankles and his arms folded over his chest. His stance said casual, but the sharpness of his eyes told her he was in tune to everything going on around him. After handing off cups of water to a Domme and her baby girl, Danielle took a moment to observe Cole in his natural habitat.

He always exuded confidence, but here in the dungeon, he reminded her of a lion. Powerful. Graceful. Dangerous. In a room full of alphas, he was the king, and everyone acknowledged it in their subtle mannerisms when they were around him. Gazes lowered. Heads nodded in recognition. Spines straightened. And in turn, he acknowledged them with a smile, a handshake, or a comforting touch on their shoulders.

Tonight, he was dressed in black leather pants and a vest over his bare chest. Her mouth watered as she drank in his six-pack, the muscles of his abdomen rippling with each inhalation, and the triangle of hair between his pecs that thinned into a line and disappeared below his waistband. Her fingers itched to delve into the hair and follow the trail down over those sharp muscles. She'd never found tattoos attractive, but his black tribal armband tattoos sent a delicious shiver down her spine. Her nipples tightened and her pussy moistened at the thought of tracing them with her tongue.

She shook her head, clearing her thoughts. She was on a mission to seduce Cole, but sex with him would only be a means to an end.

She brought her gaze to his face and found him staring at her with a knowing glint in his eyes. Her cheeks heated from him catching her ogling him. He crooked his finger at her, silently commanding her to join him.

Tossing her ponytail over her shoulder, she crossed the room, her sole focus on him. "Yes, Master. How may I please you?"

His lips tilted up in a grin. "Oh, let me count the ways." He pushed off the wall and took her hands, yanking her closer. "You already please me. Now it's your turn." He pulled her over to a row of cabinets bolted to the wall, then opened one and took out a pink box. He removed two silver balls, each the size of a Ping-Pong ball, and placed them in her sweaty palms. "Go to the ladies' lounge and slip these both inside you. You may need to clench around them to keep them from falling out. When you're done, you may resume serving the waters."

All sorts of questions popped into her head. What were these things, and why would she want to put them inside her? Since she wasn't wearing panties, if the balls fell out of her, others would notice. Yes, it was a sex club, so it wasn't the worst thing in the world if it happened, but she didn't want to disappoint Cole. If he wanted her to prove to him she could do this, she would. And he did say it was for her pleasure...

She stomped inside the locker room, almost running into Cassandra, who was gathering towels from the floor by the door. Expecting a sarcastic barb, Cassandra shocked her by remaining silent and ignoring her. Danielle wouldn't have thought the woman was capable of following through with her punishment. Cassandra's slumped shoulders and her bloodshot eyes, which could only have come from crying, almost made Danielle feel sorry for her. *Almost.*

After shutting the bathroom stall door, Danielle tried to figure out the best way to get these balls in her pussy. Deciding to remain standing, she ripped off some toilet paper and covered the seat, then placed one foot on it. She took a deep breath and relaxed her muscles before pushing one ball inside her.

It didn't hurt, but it wasn't pleasurable either. Still, she followed Cole's directions and slid the second ball inside, clamping down to keep it from popping back out. She lowered her leg to the floor and felt the ball go deeper into her channel. Her pelvic muscles tightened, and a pulse of arousal swirled in her belly.

Cassandra had disappeared by the time she left the ladies' lounge, but a couple of members she'd never met sat on the same couch where she'd masturbated for the camera. They both stared at her, and her heart immediately started to race. Could they notice she had the balls inside her? Did it matter to her if they could?

It did matter, but not because it embarrassed her. She wanted them to know. It aroused her to think everyone knew Cole had ordered her to insert the metal balls into her pussy and she had followed his orders. The thought made her so slippery, she had to clench her muscles harder, which resulted in another flutter of arousal.

Cole waited for her outside the lounge. "I've decided to add another requirement to your task. Don't spill any of the water."

"And if I do spill, or if I release the balls?"

"Punishment, of course. Perhaps a few minutes with your nose to the wall."

The image of standing in a corner with her nose pressed against the wall filled her with a sense of shame. He was right. Punishments inducing shame would always work on her.

"I won't fail, Master."

His eyes dilated, and his nostrils flared. "We'll see. Better get going. We've got a lot of thirsty members looking for their water."

"Yes, Master." She twirled on her bare feet and padded over to the table with the cups and pitcher of water. Each step caused the balls to rub against the inside of her pussy, stimulating her, but it wasn't enough to cause her to lose the balls.

She poured ten cups of water and grabbed the tray, balancing it on one hand like a waitress. As she passed Cole, she threw him a little smile to let him know she was doing well. Something in the way he smirked hinted maybe she wasn't seeing the whole picture.

Only a few minutes later, that missing piece of the puzzle became clearer when a low buzzing began inside of her and she nearly tripped over her own feet. She snapped her head around and glared at Cole to find him laughing, shaking his head, and pointing to the cups. A mix of fear and arousal sent her pulse skyrocketing and her libido into overdrive. The balls vibrated, and Cole held the controls. No way could she hold the balls in or keep from spilling if he brought her to a full orgasm.

She sighed and forged ahead, figuring at least she'd get an orgasm out of it before he punished her. Determined to last a little longer, she held her head high and her pussy clenched tight as she served a couple more members their water. Every minute or so, the vibrations grew stronger, creating a buzzing in both her pussy and her ass, a sensation so strong she had to grit her teeth to keep from crying out. Even with the music playing in the background and people's grunts, moans, and shouts, Danielle could still hear the sound of the balls, and by the sympathetic smiles of the submissives, everyone close to her could hear it too. Cole wanted them to know and wanted her aware of it.

Like Gracie had sworn, Cole knew the slaves better than they knew themselves.

Cole didn't just see her. He'd figured out what made her tick.

Service gave her pride and a sense of belonging, but exhibitionism aroused her.

Having delivered all the cups, she returned to the table and filled more, her hands shaking. She refused to look over at Cole, biting her lip and taking steady breaths to keep herself from losing control of her body.

Sweat beaded on her forehead, and her clit pulsated in time with her heart. Very carefully, she hefted the tray into the air and set off to finish her task.

With his head in the lap of Mistress Casey, Adrian rested on a plush area rug, his eyes closed as the Domme sifted her fingers through his thick blond hair. Thin red lines marred his arms and his thighs as a result of his beating, but he appeared so peaceful. So content. Danielle almost didn't want to disturb them, but both of them required water. Trying to ignore the fluttering in her pussy, she tiptoed over to them and handed over a cup to Mistress Casey, who then lovingly brought the water to his lips. Witnessing after-care from the outside, Danielle found it was so much more than simply a responsible person taking care of another after a scene. Mistress Casey didn't seem eager to rid herself of Adrian anytime soon. She got as much from taking care of him as he did.

But what did it mean? Was there anything more to Mistress Casey and Adrian's relationship?

Was there more to her and Cole's?

Her body lit up like a firecracker when she caught him staring at her from across the room with his cell to his ear. He hung up, then slid the phone into his pocket, exchanging the device for another. She had no doubt he'd palmed the remote for the balls inside her. As he mouthed the word "come," he cranked up the vibration to what had to be full blast, and she lost control.

Waves and waves of contractions bloomed outward from her core like hot lava flowing from a volcano, blazing upward to her chest and outward to her fingers. She moaned, loud enough and strong enough that everyone around her would know she was in the midst of a climax. Tremors rocked her legs, weakening her knees, and before she could catch herself, the tray tipped, spilling water over the rims of the cups. The buzzing stopped, but as the orgasm's aftershocks pulsed, she wasn't certain if it was due to Cole turning off the vibrators or them slipping out.

To check, she squeezed her thighs together and clenched her pelvic muscles, gasping when it set off another climax, this one small in comparison, but stronger than any she'd ever given herself.

The tray suddenly left her hand, and Cole's hand encircled her waist, steadying her. His scent tantalized her, and she burrowed into his side, accepting his comfort and care as Adrian had with Mistress Casey.

"You did very well, Danielle."

She peeked up at him. "I spilled the water. Did the balls stay inside?"

"What do you think?" The hand at her waist revealed two silver balls. "Was the game worth the punishment?"

The satisfaction of exhibition plus two amazing orgasms? "Um…I'm going with yes. Totally worth it."

"I'm glad." He kissed her forehead. "I have to go upstairs. Go to the corner and touch your nose against the wall. Count to one thousand, and then you can finish up your night's assignment."

"Will you be back down tonight?" she asked. If he left for the night, she'd lose her chance to convince him to take her upstairs to his residence.

"I'm not sure." He swept some stray hairs off her face, and a slight frown etched lines on his forehead. "I've got a meeting, and I'm not sure how long it will take. That doesn't mean you get out of your punishment. I trust you."

Guilt over lying to him and panic that she'd miss an opportunity to seduce him slammed into her, causing her stomach to churn and her chest to constrict. After she finished her service for the night, she'd search him out.

It wasn't as if she wanted to go back alone to her room, where she didn't feel safe.

Unable to form a reply, she simply nodded and padded off to stand in the corner. As she silently counted to one thousand, her breathing stabilized and her body relaxed. By the time she finished, she felt reenergized.

Danielle handed a good-looking man working with ropes a cup of water and headed back to pour additional drinks for the members. Waitressing sure beat cleaning bathrooms.

Bending to retrieve ice from a small cooler, she felt a shift in the club's energy, and her body shivered as if she'd submerged herself in ice. She sensed someone watching her, and she intuitively knew it wasn't Cole. She slammed the cooler shut and twirled on her bare feet, scanning the room for the threat.

At first glance, there was nothing out of the ordinary. A Domme pegged her sub while another man slapped his face with his cock. From her front and her back, Ryder and Morgan flogged a blissed-out looking Gracie, who was clearly floating in sub-space from the beating. A woman dressed as a cat licked a man's feet. There were several other scenes, but none of the individuals paid Danielle any attention.

A large man led a skinny blonde by a leash that was attached to her metal chain collar. She crawled across the floor, red welts and perfectly round bruises covering most of her body. Recognition slammed into her as he steered the woman toward a hallway. This was Rinaldi's bodyguard. That meant…

Rinaldi stepped out of the shadow, his gaze planted on Danielle.

Even as the naked blonde passed him on her knees and he spoke to the bodyguard who then took the slave inside a private room, he never took his eyes off Danielle.

He smiled at her, a smile filled with promises of pain and suffering.

He obviously wanted her to know he was watching her, but why? It was as if he was waving a red cape to entice the bull, but who was the bull?

Cole had warned Rinaldi to stay away from her, and though he'd brushed it off when she'd pressed, she couldn't help thinking Cole knew more than he'd said about the sadistic man. Although it was possible she was overacting, her instincts encouraged her to tell Cole about…what exactly? That he'd stared and smiled at her? It sounded so silly in her head, but then she remembered how enraged Cole had become when Rinaldi had spoken to her. Besides, this gave her the excuse she needed to go upstairs and see him.

She scoped out the room and spotted Master Michael by the women's lounge. Requiring approval of a dungeon monitor, she sidled up to him. "May I be excused from my duties for a few minutes while I go upstairs? I need to speak with Master Cole." When he frowned, she added, "It's urgent."

He glanced at his watch. "Fifteen minutes. You're to go to his office, and if he's not there, you must immediately return to the dungeon. No running around Benediction looking for him."

"Thank you. I'll be right back." She headed for the stairs. Unease slid down her spine as the feeling of being watched continued. But when she looked over her shoulder to where Rinaldi had been standing, he was gone.

Chapter Sixteen

NIBBLING ON HER thumbnail, Danielle passed the full den of mingling members and headed toward Cole's office. She rounded the corner of the hallway and stopped short at the sight of Cole hugging and kissing the cheek of a woman she didn't recognize. A heaviness settled in Danielle's chest, and her stomach burned as if she'd swallowed acid.

Like a spy, Danielle hid her body behind the wall and peeked to ascertain the stranger's identity. She was a knockout dressed in a modest off-white pant suit that accentuated her flawless mocha skin and feminine curves. Around her neck, she wore a stunning triple-stranded diamond choker. In her hand was a black duffel bag, similar to the ones the Doms carried with their toys and equipment.

Cole ushered the woman into his office and spoke on his cell as he shut the door. "Elena and I will be upstairs in my residence. Please ensure I'm not disturbed for any reason."

The engagement of the lock on his door sounded like a boulder dropped from a mountain.

She stopped short at the recognition that she was jealous. So jealous she wanted to storm into his office and lay claim to him. Which of course would be ridiculous and foolhardy, since not only did she not have a claim on him, he belonged to everyone and no one. He could have almost any submissive in Benediction, but they could never have him. His boundaries had assured him of that. But then who was the woman?

Someone poked her in the back. "Gorgeous, isn't she?"

Startled, Danielle flipped around and found Sedona and Cassandra standing behind her.

Had they been there the whole time? "Who is she?"

Cassandra rolled her eyes. "She's Master Cole's collared submissive, of course."

Although Danielle didn't trust a word out of Cassandra's mouth, she couldn't help the doubt from creeping into her thoughts. "He doesn't have a collared submissive."

"And you know that for a fact?" Cassandra asked. The redhead's eyes softened. "They have somewhat of an open relationship, at least on his end. After all, he's the owner of Benediction, and not only can he have whatever slave he wants, he has."

With every word Cassandra uttered, the vise on Danielle's heart tightened. "He doesn't have sex with the slaves."

"True," Cassandra said. "He mostly gets off on watching us. Matching us up with Dominants or sometimes other slaves. That's when he becomes the director. He sets up a scene for the slaves and tells us what to do. He's done scenes with slaves, but he refuses to penetrate. That's because of her." She pointed to Cole's closed door. "Right, Sedona?"

Sedona gave Danielle an apologetic shrug. "I can't confirm it, but she is a member of the club, and she's the only woman who he takes to his private residence. Why else would she go upstairs with him?"

"Listen," Cassandra said, throwing an arm over Danielle's shoulders. "I know you think I'm a bitch, and well, yeah, I guess I am, but I'm going to be straight with you. Everything that happens here is make-believe. When he's touching you and saying how wonderful you are, how beautiful, how special. When you're vulnerable and in the arms of a Dom, receiving after-care, you begin to think maybe you mean more to him than just sex. Maybe it's the real deal. Maybe we could have something permanent. Then the next night, he's playing with another sub and you hear him saying those same words."

Although the words certainly applied to Danielle's situation, she had a suspicion that Cassandra was speaking from personal experience. Could that be why she disliked her? Was it possible she had fallen for Cole as well?

Danielle toyed with her locket. Feelings were irrelevant. The only thing she should be concerned about was whether Cole had a collared slave, because if he did, he'd be much more difficult to seduce.

Cassandra removed her arm and turned Danielle to face her, gripping her by her shoulders. "Cole DeMarco doesn't only train, he remolds his trainees into individuals with self-esteem and self-worth. Just remember that."

Sedona shoved Cassandra. "Cassandra, how's she supposed to have any self-worth if you implied Master Cole is lying to her?"

Cassandra took her usual haughty stance and tossed her hair over her back. "Not my problem if she needs a man to bolster her self-esteem. I have it, and I know the truth. Same as you." She turned to Danielle. "Enjoy your time here. Enjoy Master Cole. But don't hang your heart on a happy-ever-after with the man, because you don't mean anything more to him than I do."

"Have you played with anyone but Master Cole yet?" Sedona asked.

To her, Adrian didn't count, since he was a slave acting on Cole's orders. "No. He hasn't let me." Not that she'd wanted to play with anyone else.

Cassandra and Sedona shared a look, then Sedona grinned at Danielle. "Are you finished with your assigned service?"

Her cheeks flushed as she thought about how Cole had made good on his promise to change service into sexy play. But Cassandra was right. That was Cole's job as her Master and owner of Benediction. He would do it for any slave trainee. "I took a break, but I'm supposed to deliver waters to the members."

Sedona linked their arms together and pulled her toward the stairs leading to the dungeon. "The rule is you can play so long as you've finished your assignment for the day. I'll take over for you, and you can play."

"I don't know…"

Cassandra joined her other side. "How's this then? You learn firsthand how to negotiate a scene, and then if you want, you can follow through."

Danielle didn't trust her, but what was the worst that would happen? Cole would punish her? If she didn't mean anything to him, he wouldn't care. Besides he was busy with the perfect pantsuit. "Okay."

Was she crazy? The minute she saw Cole with that woman she must have lost her mind, because she was actually taking Cassandra's advice and accompanying her and Sedona into the dungeon. Could she allow another man to touch her? She knew if Cole had ordered it, she could, but without his knowledge? She wasn't even sure she wanted to find out.

As they advanced toward the good-looking man she'd served water to earlier, she told herself it didn't matter what Cole thought because right now, he was with another woman.

"Sir Logan," Cassandra said. "This is Danielle. She's a new trainee."

He smiled and offered his free hand, a beige loop of rope in his other. "Nice to officially meet you, Danielle. What can I do for you?"

Logan's face lit up from his smile, light laugh lines appearing at the corners of his lips, but his eyes remained intensely serious. Too serious for someone so young. With brown hair worn in a buzz cut, he towered over her five-foot-seven-inch frame, and his simple white wife beater enhanced his firm, lean physique. But despite his attractiveness, her heart didn't thump any faster.

Sedona slid her arm around Danielle's waist. "As part of her training, she needs to practice the skill of negotiating a scene, and we thought you'd be able to help."

"Just negotiate?" He stepped closer. "Or will I get the privilege of playing with you as well?"

She averted her eyes and checked out the floor instead. "I'm not sure. I haven't…that is…Master Cole has been present for my previous scenes, and I'm not sure how I feel doing one without him."

He gently tipped up her chin with two of his fingers, forcing her to look at him. "Do you have permission to do a scene?"

"Sir Logan, you know she can scene so long as she has a dungeon monitor's approval, and since you are a dungeon monitor, she doesn't have to worry," Cassandra said.

"I'll tell you what," Logan said softly as if he and Danielle were the only two people in the room, "why don't we just talk and see where it goes?"

"Have fun. Don't do anything I wouldn't do," Cassandra said.

Sedona grabbed Cassandra by the arm and yanked her away, both of them in hysterics. "Come with me, slut."

Logan dropped his fingers and stepped back, keeping his gaze locked on her.

Danielle waited until the women were out of earshot. "May I ask you a question, Sir?"

"Of course. I don't follow a lot of protocol." He gestured to the nearby loveseat, and they went to sit on it. "You can call me Logan. What's up?"

"Should I be concerned that Cassandra is being nice to me?"

He frowned. "I'm not sure. She was acting unusually supportive tonight."

"Yeah." At least she wasn't the only one noticing it. She scanned the room and didn't see either of the trainees. "I wouldn't put it past her to be setting me up for something."

"Listen, if you're worried, I can call him and ask his permission first."

"No. He's busy," she said a little too forcibly. She couldn't bear it if Cole gave Logan permission to scene with her. It was better not to know. Besides, she hadn't decided to do a scene yet. Surely she didn't need permission to talk to Logan. "I don't want to disturb him. It's fine."

"Right. I almost believe you." Logan leaned into her. "Why don't you tell me what brought you to Benediction, Danielle?"

Wringing her hands together, she took a deep breath and prepared herself to lie again. "There's a man. My fiancé. Well, not really my fiancé because I haven't accepted, but he's a Dominant. No, I guess that's not really true. He's dominant but he's not a Dom. And he said it wasn't important to him that I…I'm here to learn more about submission."

"That was a nice story." He reclined and crossed his arms. "Complete bullshit, and your acting job wouldn't win any Academy Awards, but I can see why Cole would accept your application."

She had to hand it to him. His laid-back demeanor and gentle teasing made it impossible not to like him. "Oh yeah? And why is that?"

"To peel back your layers and discover what's hidden in your core."

"Are you comparing me to an onion?"

He shook his head. "You smell too good to be an onion. You're more like the Internet. Everyone takes it for granted. What you see is what you get. What people don't realize is how complex it really is or how many layers there are to it. The deeper you go, the more secrets you find—secrets that are right there for everyone to see if they only knew where to look. People can attack it, do some damage, but the core is strong. It survives."

She didn't know how to respond to something so insightful without revealing anything more about herself. Since the best defense was an offense, she turned the tables on him. "Are you a computer engineer or something?"

"A criminal defense attorney with a side business in software design."

With a hobby of tying women up with rope. Busy guy.

"Sounds as though you're the one with the layers," she said.

"We're not here to discuss me." He sat up straight and turned his body toward hers, creating the illusion of intimacy. "So you've had a few days at Benediction. Is there anything you've seen or heard about that you'd like to try?"

Suddenly feeling shy, she shrugged. "I don't know."

"You do know. You just don't want to say. Communication is essential in BDSM, especially in the negotiating of a scene. You can't be afraid to ask for what you want or to say no. We can go over your soft and hard limits, but that still leaves too many acts and items to discuss."

How could she articulate what she wanted to try when she could barely admit it to herself? The checklist of items she'd completed for Cole when she'd arrived at Benediction had opened her eyes to a new world filled with sexual possibilities.

"Stand up," Logan said, taking her hand and bringing them both to their feet. "I'm going to try a verbal exercise with you. Don't speak until we're all done or do any of the things I order, all right?"

She swallowed the knot of apprehension in her throat. What good was a verbal exercise if she couldn't speak? "Okay."

He moved closer. "You're a dirty slut."

Really? Was that supposed to turn her on? Because all it did was make her want to slap him.

"You've been bad and deserve to be punished." After a beat, he continued, giving time for her mind to process the words before saying more. "I can't wait to turn your ass red."

He kept his gaze on her, the intensity of his stare burning into her. "Take my dick out right now, and with your mouth, show everyone how much you love it." Her pulse skittered, but she didn't move a muscle.

"I want to hurt you." He didn't pause and wait for a reaction. "Remove all your clothes, go to the stage, and make yourself come three times." She bit her lip, and her pussy clenched, the image blossoming before her eyes.

His nostrils flared, and his voice dropped to a husky whisper. "I'd love to see my ropes decorating your naked body." His throat worked over a swallow, and if her eyes didn't deceive her, his words had affected him as well, judging by the outline of his erection through his jeans. "I'm going to tie you to my bed and do whatever I want to your body."

He reached out his hand as if he was going to touch her. She held her breath. Did she want him to?

Before he made contact, he dropped his arm to his side. "I'm going to share you with my friend." Her nipples hardened, rubbing painfully against her dress. "Crawl over to the stage." She winced.

His sexy smile returned, and this time, he did touch her, taking her hand and returning them to the loveseat. "Good job. Do you want to know what I just learned from you?"

"Yes. Please do tell." She folded her arms across her chest, although she had no doubt he saw her body's reaction to his words. Still, he was a man, and men, in her opinion, weren't usually that astute.

One by one, he ticked off his fingers. "You're definitely not a masochist, although you wouldn't mind the occasional spanking, especially if it was in front of a crowd. You're not into humiliation. You're interested in bondage and multiple partners. You're submissive, but only for the right man, because that's not your kink. Interestingly, you are an exhibitionist."

Her jaw went slack. "Why is that interesting? I'm sure there are plenty of exhibitionists at Benediction."

There was no way he got all that by her nipples. She didn't know how he'd figured it all out simply by asking her those questions, but it was uncanny in its accuracy. Did they have a training program for the Doms where they taught them how to read body language, or was it something innate to people like Logan and Cole?

"True. But not one of them has held Cole's attention as you have."

And that's why he left her in the dungeon while he went upstairs to his residence with his collared submissive. She turned away, catching Sedona by the stairs talking animatedly with a few of the trainees. "I don't want to talk about him."

"Look at me. Same exercise, only I want you to answer my questions." He didn't stand this time, but he held her hand and rested it on his thigh, his thumb brushing the inside of her wrist.

"Do you want to play with Adrian?"

She sighed, thinking about how Adrian had carried out Cole's orders between her thighs. But would she have enjoyed it without Cole's arms around her?

"Do you want to play with Gracie?" She pressed her lips together and held back a laugh. Thanks to Gracie's kiss, she knew same-sex scenes were not for her.

"Do you want to play with Master Cole?" Her body instantly heated. The few days with Cole had already trained her body to respond to the thought of how easily he could bring it pleasure. But her body needed to catch up with her brain. It didn't matter how he'd made her body come alive. Because all of it meant nothing. She was just another slave to him. And once she seduced him and drugged him to get access to the account information, he'd likely hate her.

"Danielle, do you want to play with me?" Her gaze dropped to his lips. They were definitely kissable. In fact, there wasn't a single part of him she found unattractive. But no, she didn't want to scene with him. At least not without Cole.

"I think we have the answer." He kept her hand in his but removed his thumb from her wrist making her suspect he'd used her pulse to derive his conclusions. "Regardless of what brought you here, you've got feelings for Master Cole, and from what I can tell, he's got feelings for you as well."

She huffed. "You're wrong. He doesn't feel anything more for me than any of his other trainees. We don't have a future."

"You can't know that. The future's irrelevant if you don't live in the present."

"Attorney, software designer, and philosopher, huh?"

He laughed. "I'm well-rounded, what can I say?" He squeezed her hand, then released it, standing. "If you decide Cole doesn't do it for you, come find me. I'd love to see you in my ropes." He winked at her before he picked up his rope off the floor and trekked toward the back rooms.

A larger crowd had congregated by the stairs, a mix of trainees and members. Curious, she went over and cut through the gathering to tap Sedona on the back of her shoulder. "Sedona, what's going on?"

Sedona twirled around, her eyes wide. "Apparently, Master Cole has decided to redecorate the gallery with a baseball bat."

Chapter Seventeen

DANIELLE ELBOWED HER way through the cluster of people, not caring whom she had to mow down to get to Cole. From the corner of her eye, she caught Cassandra with Anthony Rinaldi. She ran up the stairs to the main floor, and as she neared the gallery, she heard crashing and the shattering of glass.

What would've caused Cole to lose his control? Had the woman broken up with him? Had he loved her? Her chest burned at the thought of Cole in a rage over the loss of another woman.

Several members stood outside the door, watching the commotion. Cole would hate that. She made her way through the group to the inside of the gallery and shut the door behind her, cutting off their ringside view of Cole's breakdown.

Master Michael and Gracie each had a hand on Cole's arm, obviously attempting to stop him from creating further damage. With eyes as black as the night without the moon, a struggling Cole clutched a baseball bat in one hand and a photograph in the other.

"Let me go," he demanded in a voice similar to the one he used on his slaves, only laced with desperation. "If I want to destroy my artwork, it's my right."

"Well as your friend," Gracie said, "I forbid you."

Cole raised a brow. "How are you going to stop me?"

"Like this." In a blur, Gracie swept out her leg, hooking it around Cole's ankle and knocking him off his feet on to his back. Then, before he had the opportunity to recover, she jumped on his chest, seized the bat out of his hands, and threw it to the side.

Michael swore under his breath and rubbed his hand over his face. "How the hell do you know how to do that?"

"Oh, did I forget to mention I'm a third-degree black belt in karate?" Gracie asked nonchalantly.

Cole's eyes were closed, and his breathing was slow, but Danielle still sensed his distress. It hurt her too, unshed tears clogging her throat and stinging her eyes.

She kneeled beside him and caressed his cheek. "Gracie. Master Michael. I'd like to be alone with Master Cole."

Master Michael's jaw twitched. Gracie slapped her hands together, lifted herself off Cole, and turned to Michael. "Come on. Let's go do some damage control out in the club. I'm sure the gossip has already made its rounds."

Master Michael rocked on his heels as he considered the situation. "If you'd like me to stay, Cole, just say the word."

Sitting up, Cole shook his head. "No. Go with Gracie. Danielle will be safe with me. I promise my theatrics are over." As Gracie and Master Michael headed toward the door, Cole called out, "Make sure you lock it."

Now that they were alone, she didn't know what to do for him. How could she ease his pain?

She could seduce him, here and now, while his guard was down. Once he broke his rule against fucking a trainee, it would only be a matter of time before he brought her up to his bed. She might be taking advantage of the situation, but she'd be giving him comfort in return.

She'd be a vessel for him to slake his lusts. There'd be no expectations of a relationship or promises of forever. Only a temporary fix for his broken heart.

His head hung to his chest as she stood and unzipped her dress. She tugged it down her legs and when it dropped to the floor, she kicked it out of the way and kneeled in front of Cole. Trying to copy what she'd seen around the club, she spread her thighs and bowed her head.

She swallowed thickly, shivering with both apprehension and arousal. Her body warmed, a flush breaking out on her chest and a subtle pounding in her clit. She'd never been more aware of her position as his slave. Although it sliced her in half to think of serving him as he thought of another woman, she'd do it. Not out of guilt or because she expected anything in return, but because he needed her.

"Master Cole, how may I be of service?"

He snapped up his head and leveled his gaze on Danielle, capturing her with the blatant heat in his eyes. The fury and pain from his eyes melted away, replaced by sexual awareness and desire. Her nipples jutted out, drawing his attention to them.

He shifted himself closer to her and cupped a breast in his hand, brushing his thumb across the center and licking his lower lip. "You really want to serve me?" At her nod, Cole squeezed her flesh, his nostrils flaring and his pupils dilating. He placed his hands on her waist and tugged her toward him, then lying on his back, lifted her so she straddled his chest. "I'm going to sink my cock inside of that addictive pussy of yours and lose myself in you."

"No." She shook her head even as she grinded her pussy against him, painting his skin with her glistening arousal. "You don't fuck the trainees. I won't be your regret."

He tucked two fingers high inside her pussy and worked her clit with his thumb. "My only regret is not doing it sooner." With his other hand securing the back of her neck, he pushed her face closer. "But if you don't want me...if you want to use the safe word—"

"Use me." She couldn't deny him. Didn't want to. "Whatever you need from me, it's yours. I belong to you."

He growled. "Not yet, you don't. But you will. I'm going to fuck you so hard and so deep, you'll never doubt who your Master is." He hoisted her over his face and began to devour her, spreading her wide and probing her entrance with his tongue.

She threw back her head and surrendered, overwhelmed by his fevered and voracious appetite for her. The whiskers on his cheeks rubbed against her thighs, sensitizing the skin and setting it on fire. His mouth fit over her labia as if he was trying to suck her entire pussy at once. His tongue swept from her channel to her clitoris, which he flicked again and again. Like lightning, it scorched her flesh, making her thighs tremble and her pussy quiver. Her muscles clenched, an electrical current igniting her cells with pulses and throbs.

It was too much. Too intense. She tried to lift herself off him, move away, but he caught her by her thighs and yanked her down so hard, she worried she'd smother him.

He didn't complain. Just kept on working her and working her hard, adding his fingers, first one, then two, then three inside her tight passage, rubbing the elusive spot only he could find. His hungry groans vibrated against her clitoris, adding another layer to her sweet torture.

Every part of her coiled tight, the heat in her lower belly blazing like a fire. "I'm going to come."

Rather than answer her with words, a rumble tore from his chest, and he pressed his fingers harder as he massaged the bundle of nerves high inside her pussy.

The raging fire grew higher and higher, larger and larger, until it consumed her. Her eyes squeezed shut, the force of the orgasm drowning her in pleasure, and an unfamiliar wail tore from her chest.

Before her climax had finished, he pulled his fingers from her contracting pussy and rolled her over so she was under him. "Forgive me." He scrambled to release his cock from his pants. "I can't be gentle."

She didn't know how he'd managed it so quickly, but he sunk his cock in one swift motion, the force so strong, she slid a few inches across the hardwood floor. "Oh, God."

He stilled and cupped her face in his hands. "You were fucking made for me." He kissed her gently. "Take me away, my beautiful Danielle. Make me forget."

His words were like a benediction to her ears. For a few brief beautiful moments in time, she could pretend he meant those words and that she truly belonged to him.

She returned his kiss, lightly at first, then more passionate, showing him with her lips, her mouth, and her tongue just how much she wanted him. He pumped inside of her, his stroke long and slow, as their kiss grew violent and bruising in its intensity.

Suddenly, he sat up, taking her with him, his cock still buried inside her. She became aware that while she was naked, he'd remained fully clothed. Needing to feel his bare skin against hers, she peeled off his leather vest and rubbed her pebbled nipples on his chest. She dragged her fingers down the length of his arms, relishing the strength of his muscles and the intricate design of his tattoos.

"Tell me what it feels like to have my cock inside of you." He palmed her breasts and bent to her chest, sucking a nipple into his mouth.

Chills raced down her spine, and pleasure darted from her nipples to her pussy. "I…can't."

He wrapped his arms around her, holding her so close, she didn't know where she began and he ended. "You can. You will." He thrust upward, grinding against her clitoris.

"I feel electrified. Alive." She whimpered and bit the soft spot between his neck and shoulder. "You're stretching me. It burns. I've never had anything as long and thick inside of me. It's as if you're touching a part of me I never knew existed."

He plunged his fingers into her hair and tugged her head back, a ferocious expression on his face. "It didn't, and you know why? Because it's mine. Your pussy was designed to squeeze my cock. Not your fingers or a toy. No one else's cock. Just mine." He lifted her off him and placed her on her hands and knees, shoving her legs apart. Without mercy, he drove himself into her pussy again and again, his testicles slapping against her clit.

She'd never felt anything like it before. His cock completely filled her, almost as if it had swelled and lengthened. Sweat dripped down her spine, and her breasts swayed beneath her. Deep in her pussy, a sharp pleasurable tension developed, making her writhe and moan. "You've got to stop. It's too intense."

"It's my cock hitting your G-spot," he said breathlessly. "You think you've climaxed before? That was minor league compared to what I'm about to do to you. Let go, baby. Let go, and I'll make you fly."

As if he'd fucked her a hundred times and had trained her body to respond to his commands, her body listened, shattering like glass. She screamed and cried as wave after wave of contractions wracked her pussy, making her breathless and her heart accelerate. Cole pounded faster and then stilled, his cock twitching inside of her and a rush of warmth bathing her swollen tissues. He collapsed on top of her, breathing heavy and kissing her neck.

He dragged her with him to the floor, and she rested her head on his outstretched arm. It wasn't comfortable, but she didn't care. Her body still buzzed from the high of her orgasm. Right now, there was no place she'd rather be than in Cole DeMarco's arms.

Danielle turned on her side to look into Cole's now peaceful caramel eyes. "Who is she?"

He frowned, and the hand that had been caressing her stilled. "She?"

"The beautiful collared woman you took upstairs to your private residence. The woman who obviously upset you." She brushed her hand over his chest. "Is she your lover? The slaves believe she's your collared submissive. The one woman with whom you have sex." She flinched. "At least until me."

Staring at her, he didn't respond. A dozen different expressions passed over his face as he seemed to process her question. Was he wondering the best way to admit the truth? She preferred he say it quickly, as if he was ripping away a Band-Aid from her skin.

She held her breath, waiting to hear the words.

He bent his head and kissed her softly on the lips. "The woman is a submissive. But she's not my submissive. Her name is Ariana Ivanoff. And she's my ophthalmologist."

Ophthalmologist? Stunned into silence, she waited for him to continue. He sat them both up and dragged his hand down his face.

"I'm going blind."

Chapter Eighteen

DANIELLE HAD PREPARED herself to hear several explanations as to the identity of the mystery woman, but nothing could have prepared her for Cole's shocking words.

"Every day I lose more of my sight. My ability to differentiate between colors. To see at night. Someday soon, it will all disappear. I'll live in complete blackness. Just like my father and his father before him."

Cole blind? She couldn't imagine it. "Just because your father—"

"It's genetic, but I'd hoped the symptoms would start later in life or not at all." He stared at the remaining mirrors, bitterness evident in the twist of his lips and the wrinkles around his eyes. "Seems fate had a different design for me. Ariana has confirmed the disease is progressing rapidly now."

She laid her palm on his cheek. "I'm sorry. I can't imagine what it would be like to be in your situation. But it's not a death warrant. Plenty of people live full lives without sight."

He turned to her. "You're right. You don't know what it's like," he said with enough venom to make her flinch. He rose from the floor, his body taut and sweaty, and motioned to the art on the walls. "Without my sight, who am I? I'm a voyeur, Danielle. I stand behind my camera and sit behind my desk of video feeds, just watching. If I don't have those pleasures, what's the point?"

Uncomfortable having this conversation without wearing clothes, she snatched her dress off the floor and pulled it over her body. Then, although she was at a loss as to how, she went to try and soothe him. "There's more to you than the voyeur, and it doesn't take a pair of working eyes to see it."

He huffed. "Right. I'm also an artist. A photographer. What kind of pictures can I take when I can't see the subject? When I can't manipulate the lights and shadows or play with the colors?"

Pain and sorrow had replaced the bitterness in his eyes, and it finally hit her that Cole considered his loss of sight as an equivalent to death. Everything in his life revolved around his ability to use his sight. If he hadn't known losing his sight was a possibility, would he still have become a voyeur and a photographer?

She gathered him in her arms and laid her head against his chest. "You can hire an assistant who can help you."

He sighed into her, resting his chin on top of her head. "What would be the point if I couldn't enjoy the art with my own eyes?"

She pulled back to peer up at him. "Is that why you took my photographs? For your own enjoyment?"

"No." He cupped her face in his hands. "I wanted to show you how I see you and prove to you that you're beautiful."

"What you proved is that you—the artist—believe I'm beautiful. Would you find me any less beautiful if I gained a hundred pounds or I was disfigured in an accident?"

His thumb stroked her cheekbone. "No, of course not, because your beauty is more than skin deep."

"And you can't see that, can you?"

He paused. "No."

"You've taught me so much since I've gotten here. Let me return the favor. I'll show you you're more than a voyeur." She stood on tiptoe and kissed his neck, sucking and nibbling. "I'll teach you how to see with your other senses."

He pulled her away and held her head immobile. "And what do I have left to teach you, my lovely Danielle?"

"Teach me how to please you."

His grip tightened. "Me? Don't you mean your soon-to-be fiancé?"

Was he…jealous? She wished she could tell him the truth about her relationship with Roman, but if she did, the house of cards she'd built on a foundation of lies would fall apart.

Deflecting, she asked, "Why don't you want to get married or have kids, Cole? It has nothing to do with Benediction, does it?"

He searched her eyes. "When my grandfather went blind, my grandmother put him in a home. They didn't know what caused it or that it was genetic." He relinquished his hold on her as he spoke with a flatness that sent chills down her arms. "My parents married at nineteen. My father had no idea that he'd someday lose his sight as his father had or that he'd pass the disease on to me. My mother didn't sign up to be a full-time nurse to her husband. I would never put a woman in that position. I'd never have a child knowing I'd possibly condemn him to a life with a disability."

She thought of her own parents. Would her mother have remained pregnant if her doctor had told her there was a possibility she'd lose her life in the delivery room? Would her father have married her mother if he'd known she would die in childbirth? What sacrifices would they have made for one another if they'd had advanced knowledge of what their future held? She no longer had the ability to ask them, but unlike her, Cole had that luxury.

"Have you ever discussed this with your parents? Do you really think if they knew then what they know now they'd have gone their separate ways?"

He shook his head. "My parents have always maintained they'd do it again even knowing the future."

"Because they love each other. When you love someone, you take the good with the bad." She blinked back the burning in her eyes and pinched her nose to ward off the tears. "My father lost my mother in childbirth. Don't you think it weighs on me? If I hadn't been born, my mother would've lived. My parents would've had years of happiness together."

As a child, she'd worried that if she reminded her father that she was responsible for her mother's death, he'd stop loving her and would send her away. When she'd grown older, she'd known her father would never have done that. He'd loved her. Eventually, she'd shared her thoughts with Roman, who'd convinced her she wasn't responsible. Who did Cole have to confide in?

He stalked to her. "I don't have to know your mother to know she would've gladly sacrificed her life for yours and she would've never regretted it. And I know how much your father loved you. He never blamed you. He never blamed anyone for her death." He clutched her shoulders and leaned toward her. "It was a terrible tragedy, but he got something so precious out of it. *You*. You aren't responsible for her death, Danielle."

"Then how can you believe your parents feel any different? When you love someone, you accept the good, the bad, and the ugly. You take someone in sickness and in health because it's better to spend your days with someone you love than endure a lifetime of loneliness. Miracles happen every day. To live your life in fear and without love is as great a tragedy as my mother's death."

He wiped his hand across his lips and once again moved away from her, this time picking up his vest off the floor. "Do you want to know why I named this club Benediction? Because when I learned I inherited the disease, I lost my faith, and without it, I lost my reason for waking up each morning. BDSM gave me back some semblance of control in my life. When a woman submits to me, she places her trust in me, and I become her higher power.

To me, that's a blessing. It's as close to believing in God as I'm ever going to get. I believe the tangible truth of science, and that says it's only a matter of time before I go completely blind."

"Are you sure it's genetic?"

"With Stargardt disease, if both parents carry the gene—"

"Then there's a chance you won't pass the disease on to a child." Why would he deny himself the chance of love and happiness based on a possibility?

He rested his back against the wall, the ruins of his beautiful art at his feet. "What am I going to do? Test every woman I want to date and only follow through on the ones who don't carry the marker? Somehow I don't think it would go over well. Besides, it will never get that far because I refuse to place the burden of caring for me on anyone I love."

Suddenly, it all made sense to her. She understood why Cole thought he couldn't get married or have children and why he'd found solace in BDSM.

He was scared.

She marched to him and poked him in the chest. "You won't burden your family, but it's acceptable to ask for help from a slave. That's your plan, isn't it? Rather than depend on those who love and care about you, you'll settle for those who find pleasure in service to you. People like Gracie and Adrian. Is that why you started this training program? Are you auditioning slaves?"

"No," he whispered, his voice raspy.

She didn't believe him. She had no doubt he'd told her the truth when he'd said his main purpose in forming Benediction had been to give back and provide service to the BDSM community. But it also couldn't be a coincidence he chose to train slaves as part of it.

"Why wouldn't you hire a nurse?" She snorted. "Hell, you probably could afford your own hospital."

"I'm not sick. Nurses are for those with an illness."

"I don't disagree," she said softly. "I'm sure there's a world of options for someone like you who can afford it. What does your father do?"

"He and my mom bought a small condo near the beach, and he's got one of those dogs for the blind. A golden retriever." He laughed. "My whole childhood I wanted a dog, and they refused because Mom's allergic."

She took his hands in hers. "We make sacrifices for the ones we love. But because of your fear, you're making a sacrifice no one expects from you."

His brows furrowed. "Fear? Me?"

"Yes, the great and powerful Master Cole is human just like the rest of us. Asking for help doesn't make you weak."

"I realize that."

"No, I don't think you do." She laid her hands on his hips and looked up at him. "Putting your faith in the hands of those you love takes strength, but giving up your dreams of having a family is cowardly."

His face hardened. At once, she realized she'd made a detrimental mistake by accusing him of being a coward.

"I'm sorry to disappoint you, but my dreams have never included marriage and kids. You being here doesn't change that."

Like a pointed arrow, his words pierced her heart. Tears sprung to her eyes, and she immediately stepped back. "Wow. Thanks."

He reached for her, but she sidestepped him. "Don't be like that. Stay with me—"

"Will you take me upstairs to your bed?"

"No."

"So nothing's changed. I'm good enough to break your rules and fuck, but not enough to share who you are outside of Benediction. Then why should I bother staying? So you can fuck me once more before you send me to my room?"

Looking sheepish, he shoved his hands into his pockets. "Let me take you."

She shook her head and put up her hands in front of her as a barrier. "I can find my own way, thank you. And if not, I'll ask a slave for help. That's what they're here for, right?"

She pivoted on the balls of her bare feet and stormed out of the gallery, carefully avoiding any of the broken glass or debris from Cole's meltdown. She honestly didn't know why she bothered.

The shattered mirrors and frames' jagged edges couldn't hurt her any worse because making love to him tonight had nothing do with saving Tasha. At some unknown moment between arriving at Benediction and now, she'd fallen for him. Not the silly teenage idea of him, but the real man. But even now, after she'd given him her body and, sadly, a piece of her heart, he wouldn't take her to his residence. Her plot to seduce Cole in order to gain entrance into his private residence had backfired in more ways than one.

She only prayed that Tasha wouldn't pay for her failure.

Chapter Nineteen

HE SCRUBBED THE blood off his hands in the bathroom
sink, still high from his climax.

The bitch hadn't cried or screamed like he preferred,
but the fear in her eyes as he told her his plans for her had
set him off like a grenade. This was just the stress reliever
he'd needed.

No one understood what it was like for him. His wife
didn't care what he did as long as he continued to pay
for her glamorous lifestyle and went to church with her
and the kids on Sunday morning. He loved his family
so much that he'd made a pact with the devil to protect
them. He'd never lay a hand on them, but a guy had to get
his releases in some way, and no one missed the whores
he recruited.

He'd kept his sadistic desires to a minimum over the
years, but lately he'd required more. More pain. More
blood. He spent hours inventing and trying out new ways

to torture his sluts with electricity and especially liked using his defibrillators. Unfortunately, some of them died before he could truly enjoy them.

As he dried his hands with a towel, he wondered if there was a woman out there who would last beyond twenty-four hours of torture. Danielle's curvy body sprung to mind. All the ones he'd played with previously were thin. Perhaps someone plump like Danielle, with ample flesh over her bones, would withstand his type of play. She'd surprised him by taking to the BDSM lifestyle with enthusiasm. He'd watched the footage of her over and over, his dick getting harder each and every time.

His mouth watered. He bit into his cheek until he tasted the coppery flavor of his blood. How would Danielle taste as tears rolled down her cheeks?

It was because of Danielle that he'd been indebted to the Russian *Bratva* for eight years. Her father, James Walker, had fucked him over good. Eight years of having that psycho breathing down his neck as he tried everything in his power to get his hands on the money that James and Cole had hidden in a trust for Danielle in an offshore account. It had taken months to track down which bank he'd used and one dead bank manager to learn that the terms of the trust were ironclad. Only Danielle could claim the money, and even then, she had to be married or at least twenty-five years old. If she died before either of those conditions were met, the funds would be disbursed to charity.

All those lies James had told about losing all his clients' money. Had James and Cole really believed no one would know they'd hidden the *Bratva's* money or what lengths they'd go to get it? She didn't know it, but she owed him.

The least she could do was provide him some pleasure before he killed her.

Chapter Twenty

THANK GOODNESS THE hallways were empty as Danielle headed upstairs. A few members congregated in the den, but Master Michael and Gracie had obviously cleared the area outside the gallery after Cole's breakdown.

Cole's refusal to bring Danielle to his residence after making love to her had left her feeling confused. What she felt for him was no longer a simple crush based on some chemical attraction. In only a few days, she'd grown to care for him. It made what she had to do that much harder. But even if she was here under different circumstances, the issue remained that he may have framed her father or at least let him take the fall for the crimes. Since she'd been here, he'd had plenty of chances to tell her about the box and the account. The fact that he hadn't told her she wasn't the only one keeping secrets.

The dungeon's music vibrated under her feet, and what she now recognized as the scent of sex hit her nose.

The club would still be open for a few hours, and for a moment, she considered going up to check out the fantasy rooms. She wanted to lose herself in someone else's life like she did when she read a book. But instead, she let her feet take her upstairs to her room.

Danielle unlocked her door, stepped inside, and flipped on the lights.

A note rested on her pillow.

Her heart raced as she scanned the room for anything else that was out of place. Spotting nothing, she checked inside the closet, in the bathroom, and under her bed to ensure no one was hiding. Once she was satisfied she was alone, she picked up the typewritten note.

She lifted her nose to the paper. Someone had sprayed her perfume on it.

For some reason, it felt like an even greater violation than having her room broken into.

Her hands trembled as she read the note. *There's always a risk to love, and now you have two lives to save. You have twenty-four hours to get us the account information or not only will you lose your stepmother, we'll kill your lover, Cole DeMarco. Remember, we have eyes and ears everywhere at Benediction. If you tell anyone about this, they'll both die.*

How did they know Cole and she had become lovers tonight? Her stomach sank. Cole hadn't turned off the video cameras inside the gallery. Any of the dungeon monitors viewing the screens would have witnessed their lovemaking. As she'd suspected, that meant whoever was working with the kidnappers was someone Cole trusted completely.

What was she going to do now that he still wouldn't bring her to his residence? She'd have to drug him while they were in the club, steal his keys, and hope the dungeon monitors sitting in the screening room wouldn't stop her from going upstairs. It was a terrible plan, but what other choice did she have?

She startled as her cell phone blared.

The note wasn't enough for them? They had to make certain she was thoroughly threatened?

She checked the cell's screen and sighed in relief at the sight of Roman's phone number. She answered, trying to sound relaxed. "Roman. How are you?"

"I'm good. Listen, I've been trying to get ahold of Mother for the last couple of days. Have you seen her?"

"No, I've been out of the house." She cringed. No way would he believe that. He knew her better than anyone.

Luckily, he didn't seem to notice. "I'm worried. She missed our weekly phone call, and that's not like her."

She waved her hand even though he couldn't see her. "Maybe she's busy planning one of her fundraisers. You know how she gets. I'm sure she'll get around to calling you when she gets a free moment."

"I suppose. When she gets home, will you tell her to phone me to put my mind at ease?"

Her throat grew thick. "I…"

"Danielle, what are you not saying? And don't lie to me."

She buried her face in her hand. She'd have to come clean, at least enough to explain why she hadn't seen Tasha. "I'm not at home."

"You mean right now?"

She blew out a breath, knowing what her words would do to Roman. "Right now and…I'm in Michigan."

"Michigan?" His voice rose. "What the hell for?" He sighed when she didn't answer. "Tell me you're not trying to prove Cole DeMarco framed your father."

Of course that's what he believed. How many nights had she spent with Roman, cursing Cole and vowing revenge against him? Roman had finally convinced her that without evidence, she had to move on with her life.

Telling Roman about his mother would put them all in danger. "I have to do this. I have no choice."

"We all have choices, Danielle. And you've obviously made yours. I suppose this means you've also made your decision regarding us?"

Even if her feelings for Cole hadn't developed, she'd never feel anything romantic toward Roman. "You know I love you, but as a friend. That's never going to change."

He sighed. "I understand. Truth be told, I feel the same." A pregnant silence followed. "You said you're in Michigan. Where are you staying?"

Damn the man for being so intuitive.

"I'm staying at Cole's."

"At a sex club, you mean. An innocent like you does not belong in a place like that. What are you thinking? Do you know what happens there?"

She almost laughed at his brotherly concern for her innocence. "Roman, I wish I could explain, but I can't. This is something I need to do, and someday I'll tell you why, but for now, you have to trust me."

"Are you…?"

"I'm learning about BDSM," she admitted, flinching over the discussion of her sex life. "Pretend I'm going back to school."

"Cole DeMarco is a dangerous man. There are things you don't know about him."

Shock coursed through her. "How would you know anything about him that I don't?"

"After your father's death, I had him investigated." He waited a beat. "DeMarco's got ties to the mafia."

She couldn't believe it. She didn't believe it. "Just because he's wealthy and partly from Italian descent doesn't mean—"

"One of his club members, Anthony Rinaldi, is a notorious crime boss who's under investigation for money laundering, prostitution, drugs, and murder."

That she *could* believe. With only a look, Rinaldi had made her skin crawl. He was the only person she'd met at Benediction who didn't seem as if he belonged. He clearly refused to follow the rules, and there was definitely animosity between him and Cole. As before, she questioned why Cole allowed him to remain a member. She knew there was a reason, but she'd never believe Cole would willingly have anything to do with the mafia.

"That's horrible, but it has nothing to do with Cole," she said, unable to prevent her voice from shaking.

"Rinaldi was one of your father's clients. You don't find that an awful coincidence? The man who turns over evidence to the feds just happens to be friendly with one of the people who your father allegedly stole from? All I'm saying is to be careful. I realize you're a grown woman, but I think you're in over your head. Why don't you go home and, if it's still important to you when I get back, we'll talk about how to work together to bring down DeMarco. Sound good?"

She closed her eyes. "Sure."

"Shit, I've known you long enough to know it means you're not gonna listen. Just promise me you'll stay safe, yeah?"

"I promise, Roman."

Thank goodness he was in Russia. For some reason, the kidnappers had never mentioned him. They must have waited for him to go out of town as part of their plan. She was never as grateful as now for the job that took him away from her for weeks at a time.

"You call me if anything comes up you can't handle, and I'll fly back in a heartbeat," he said. "And, Danielle, if you speak with Mom, tell her to pick up the damned phone and call me before I call the National Guard on her ass."

A twinge of guilt panged in her chest. "You got it."

"Love you."

"Love you too." She disconnected the call and stared at the note on her lap.

"Not five minutes after we make love, and you're sending your love to your fiancé," Cole said from the doorway.

How long had he been listening, and how had she not heard him enter?

She crumbled the letter in her hand and shoved it under her pillow. "I've told you. He's not my fiancé. And don't ever come into my room again without knocking first."

"It doesn't matter what title you give him," he said, ignoring her request. "You're here for him. Because you love him."

She got up from the bed. "I do. I've loved him for years. Roman is my stepbrother, or rather, he was before my father died."

Cole appeared taken aback. "You're in love with your stepbrother?"

"No." She shrugged, moving closer to Cole but keeping enough distance to keep her feeling safe. "And he's not in love with me either. Not really. It's true he asked me to marry him, but our relationship is based on friendship, not passion. Honestly, I don't know why he asked."

"So your reason for being here…to learn how to please him, you made that up?"

The lies upon lies she had to tell were giving her a headache. "I don't know the details, but he's confided in the past that he's dabbled with BDSM. So I didn't lie to you, per se. It's just I have no intention of ever sleeping with him. Why do you even care?" Or for that matter, what was he doing here in her room?

"I don't know. I just do." He stalked nearer. "Cassandra came my office to tell me you did a scene with Logan."

So her instincts had been right. Cassandra had been nice to her just to get her into trouble. "We didn't—"

"I know. I spoke with Logan. Even though you were only practicing negotiating a scene, I still don't like it." He stopped in front of her and slipped his arms around her waist.

Her body arched into his, and she steadied herself by gripping his arms. "Why?"

"Because when I think of you, only one word comes to mind."

She couldn't catch her breath. "What word?"

"Mine," he growled, crashing his mouth against hers in a claim of possession.

Her head spun as she tried to catch up with her body. His hands cradled her ass, and as he lifted her off the ground, she wound her arms and legs around him, furiously accepting everything he had to give. He ate at her mouth with an intensity fueled with desperation. She didn't know what had changed from the time she'd left the art gallery, but she didn't want to stop to question it and lose her chance to make love with him one more time.

Why worry about the future when she had this moment? She'd cherish each experience as if it were a precious gift. And maybe when they left each other's lives for good, they'd leave a little of themselves behind.

Without breaking the seal of their lips, he staggered to the window and pressed her back against the cold glass. She rocked her naked pussy against him, back and forth, to create the friction her swelling clitoris craved. A thousand tiny sparks danced down her spine and through her pussy.

How many times would it take until her body was satisfied? She'd already climaxed tonight both in the dungeon and the gallery, and still she hungered for more.

He set her to her feet and yanked her dress over her head, his scorching gaze raking over her, pebbling her nipples and making goose bumps pop up on her arms. He swiped his long finger into her pussy and pulled it out, bringing it to her lips. "Taste us."

She sucked his finger into her mouth. The mixed salty tang of his come and her juices were sharp on her tongue. She moaned, her body quivering from the eroticism.

"Turn around, put your hands on the glass, and stick that ass out for me."

Her body on fire, she followed his commands. Anyone in the backyard could look up and see her. It was unlikely, but the idea of it caused her pussy to clench. Standing right beside her, he gripped the back of her neck, holding her in place. He gave her no warning before his other hand smacked her ass. Heat quickly bloomed as she surrendered to the pain. Again and again, he spanked her, each blow sending vibrations through her pussy and to her clitoris.

Unknowingly, she'd removed one hand from the window and covered her breast with it. She caressed the heavy flesh and plucked at her nipple, sending shards of heat down to her needy clit.

"Fuck, that's hot," Cole said. "Pinch that nipple hard for me."

Her legs shook, and she cried out as she squeezed her nipple as hard as she could and then pulled.

"You like pain with your pleasure," Cole said as he spanked her once again. "Now that we know that, we'll have to readdress your soft and hard limits." He kneaded the fiery cheeks of her ass, then drifted his fingers up and down her crack. Unsure of what he'd do next, she clenched her ass. "No, baby. You can't keep me out. I'm going to claim that ass. Not now, but soon."

He squatted behind her, and his tongue traced her crack before he spread her cheeks and pressed his tongue deeper. Heat filled her belly and spread outward, sending her heart into triple time and curling her toes. What he was doing was dirty and sinful, but it felt too damn good to stop him.

His tongue disappeared, and she sucked in a breath when he pushed the tip of one finger inside. "You're so tight. I wouldn't fit inside without hurting you. We'll have to work up to it. Start you wearing a plug to stretch you to take me."

Her throat grew dry. "Will the plug hurt?" She didn't like the idea of sticking something cold and foreign inside her bottom. But she couldn't deny she wanted him to claim her every way he could.

He slipped his finger in farther, and she gasped at the burning fullness. If that's how it felt with one finger, how could she handle anything more? "It might feel uncomfortable, or you might love it. But it shouldn't hurt." Slowly, he moved his finger in and out, igniting all the nerves along its path.

She crooked her head over her shoulder and licked her lips as she watched him fucking her ass with his finger.

Heat flared in his eyes. He stood, ripping off his vest and swiftly removing his pants. "I need to fuck you." One hand yanked her hair as the other snaked around her waist and brought her to a standing position. Then he forced her up against the cold glass of the window, holding her arms over her head, his hot erection digging into the small of her back. "Beg for my cock."

She didn't hesitate. "Please, Master, fill me with your cock. I need you."

Gripping both her wrists in one of his hands, he used his other to line up his cock with her drenched entrance, and in one thrust, his entire length was seated inside her pussy. He plunged in and out of her slippery channel, pressing her overheated body into the cool glass of the window.

He commanded her body and its responses as though he was its true master, bringing her to the brink of orgasm before backing off, keeping her teetering on the edge. Each time, her muscles clamped harder around his cock, greedy for release. Knowing full well what he was doing to her, he laughed, and she felt the rumble of it vibrate through her straight to her pussy.

"You want to come?" he crooned. "You need permission. Ask me."

"Please, Master, may I come?"

He released her arms and pinched her nipple. "Not yet."

She grumbled indignantly. If he wasn't going to give her permission, why the hell did he make her ask for it? "Please?"

"You need to ask louder. I want everyone on this floor—everyone in the entire mansion—to know who's fucking you."

Her pussy rippled with a mini-orgasm, her arousal dripping out of her from his words.

"Let's hear you," he said loudly.

"Please, Master Cole, may I come?" she shouted. She threw her head back and groaned. "Please?"

"Yes, Danielle. Come with me. Now." His hand drifted down from her breast to her pussy where he flicked her swollen clitoris and pounded into her once. Twice. Then froze.

His cock twitched and pulsed inside her, his hot release jetting against her walls, setting off her own climax. Her pussy gripped him, milking him as it clenched over and over again, sending pulsing waves of liquid heat through her body. "I'm coming. Oh, God, I'm coming so hard." She shook from the force, and it if wasn't for Cole's body still pressing her into the glass, she would've fallen. "I think you killed me."

Chuckling, he dragged her with him to the bed, and they both fell onto it, resting their heads on the pillow. His fingers played with the ends of her hair as he rained kisses down her cheek.

Her hand curled into his chest. "Does this mean we're going steady?"

He kissed the tip of her nose. "It means for as long as you're here, I'm your Master. You don't negotiate with anyone other than me unless it's in class, and no one touches you without my permission. It's not the traditional type of relationship you're seeking, but it's the only one I can offer."

She tried not to think about tomorrow. "I want it. Whatever you can give, for however long you choose to give it, I accept. I belong to you and only you." She leaned in and kissed him on the lips, sweeping her tongue into his mouth and reigniting her arousal.

He inched closer, slipping his hand under her pillow. She heard a rustling before he removed his hand, bringing with it the note left by the kidnapper. He frowned and started to flatten out the paper. "What's this?"

She seized it from his hand and jumped out of bed. "Oh, it's nothing. Just something I was working on. It's garbage." She crumpled it up into a tighter ball and dropped it in the trash. "Nothing to worry about."

She slid back into bed with him.

Nothing at all.

Chapter Twenty-One

MUCH MORE REFRESHED after having slept with Cole in her bed last night, Danielle locked her bedroom door behind her, a delicious soreness between her thighs to remind her she'd spent half the night making love. She turned around and smacked into Cassandra.

Cassandra wore a huge smile and little else, her silver mesh dress barely covering the tops of her thighs. "So rumor has it you and Master Cole got it on in the gallery. And then later in your room. In fact, half the floor heard you last night." The smile slid away as if it had melted. "Just remember what we talked about. I don't want to see you hurt."

Gracie stomped down the hall from the stairs and got in Cassandra's face. "What about hurting her?"

"Drop dead, Gracie." Cassandra shoved Gracie backward. "I'm sick of you treating me like something you scraped off the bottom of your shoe. You're not the goddamn queen, and I'm sick of you acting like it." She waved at Danielle. "I'll catch up with you later."

It was sweet of Gracie to stick up for her. She was like an ankle-biting Chihuahua going after a Doberman pinscher.

Danielle threw her arms around Gracie's shoulders and led her down the hall. "She wasn't really threatening me. When I was upset last night, Cassandra gave me some advice. Of course, immediately after, she convinced me to negotiate a scene with Logan and then tried to get me in trouble with Cole."

"Sounds like something she'd do. Whatever advice she gave you, I hope you did the opposite, because that girl only thinks about herself. The fact that he's falling for you hard has got to be eating her up inside." Gracie began walking down the steps.

Danielle hurried behind her. "Falling for me. Why do you think that? Did he say anything to you?"

Laugher spilled from Gracie's lips. "Master Cole's different around you. He's more…attached. I've lived with him for years, and never has he spent so much time with one slave. I've got my money on you two."

At the bottom of the stairs, she pulled Gracie in close to whisper into her ear. "I can't tell you everything, but I will say, he broke his rule with me. Several times."

"You mean you and him…?" Gracie's eyebrows rose. "That's huge. And speaking of huge, you are so frickin' lucky." She spread her hands a foot a part from each other. "I bet he needs magnum-sized, am I right?"

Her stomach twisted, and nausea hit.

"Danielle? Are you okay?" Gracie asked.

Her mind raced. "Yes, I just remembered something. No big deal."

In all the chaos, she'd forgotten her birth control pills in Arizona.

One would think that would've been the first thing on her mind when she discovered she'd be infiltrating a sex club, but Tasha's kidnapping had driven all rational thought from her head. She counted back and figured she had only missed a handful of pills.

It would be fine. She'd simply make sure they used condoms in the future.

"Danielle," Cole said from behind her.

Breathless, she flipped around. "Good morning." Noticing the trainees watching their interaction, she added, "Master."

He leaned in as if he was going to kiss her but stopped before he made contact, sliding a glance at the trainees. "It is. I never got to show you how your pictures turned out. Since you have a few minutes before class begins, why don't we go to my office and I'll show you now?"

As the folds of her sex dampened, she shoved her concerns about the lack of condoms to the back of her mind. It had only been six hours since he was inside of her, and she could still feel him. Yet as sore as she was, she couldn't wait for him to fill her with his cock once again.

The trainees whispered to each other as Cole led her by the hand through the kitchen. She shrugged it off. Between having her shout out his name last night and this display of ownership, Cole obviously wanted everyone to know she belonged to him.

He brought her to his office and closed the door behind them. Then he crossed the room and reclined in his chair behind his desk, looking devilishly pleased with himself. "Pull up your skirt and sit on my lap."

Her jaw dropped, and heat climbed her nape. "But I'll get your pants wet."

He patted his leg. "They'll dry. But I'll have your pussy's scent on me all day to keep me company while I go downtown to see my banker."

She glided to him, slowly lifting her skirt and revealing her bare skin underneath. "People are talking about us." With her skirt around her waist, she settled sideways on his lap. "Cassandra mentioned something, and Gracie—"

He covered her lips with two of his fingers. "You're not my dirty little secret. I want everyone to know. For as long as you are here, you belong to me and no one else. No hands-on training for you unless I'm present."

She thought about arguing with him, but it wasn't worth it. She didn't want to play with anyone other than Cole, even if it was pretend. Besides, she really didn't need to learn much more, as she wouldn't be in the lifestyle once she got her stepmother home safe.

His hand covered the mouse, and he clicked on the screen, bringing up dozens of pictures. Most of them were limited to a single body part. Similar to the ones on the dungeon wall, they were in black and white with a pop of color. But instead of coloring an object such as a flogger, he'd used the wax. The mounds of her breasts were tipped with nipples the color of raspberries. The folds of her sex—her labia, her vulva, even the pearl of her clitoris—were colored pink and looked like the petals of a rose. He'd performed magic, turning her body into a work of art.

"Wow. The pictures are amazing, Cole. I can't believe how incredible my pussy looks." She didn't understand why reviewing pictures of her most intimate body parts didn't embarrass her but speaking about them did. Squirming on his lap, she flushed and felt her cheeks turn red. She buried her face in the crook of his neck.

"I love when you talk dirty." His hand caressed her inner thigh, and he nipped her earlobe. "There's more. Check the screen."

She angled her head toward the computer. These photos were different. They were still done in black and white, but they were full body shots. The curvy model was clearly in the throes of climax, her torso arched and her head thrown back in abandon. Cole had left her lips in color in addition to the wax. They were red, as if they'd been thoroughly ravaged by her lover. Each picture was a testament to the model's beauty.

"That's not me," she said, confused.

"It is."

She leaned into the screen to study them. The model wasn't fat. Sure, she wasn't skin and bones, but her heavy breasts, rounded stomach, and wide hips were soft and inviting. "You must have altered these images."

"The only thing I did was adjust the photos to black and white. The rest is you." He buried his fingers in her hair, cradling her scalp, and turned her to face him. "Has anyone at Benediction said anything about your weight or made you feel anything less than beautiful?"

She thought back to the last few days. "No."

His hand slipped down to cup her cheek. "The only one who doesn't believe you're beautiful is you. Yes, this club caters to the wealthy, and that means an unusually high amount of bodies manipulated through plastic surgery, but is everyone thin? Is everyone good-looking? No, of course not." He rested his temple against hers. "But you won't find judgment here, Danielle. Only acceptance. I won't allow you to leave your training without at least helping you find acceptance of yourself."

Her throat tightened. For so long, she'd blamed others for her low self-esteem, but Cole was right. The only opinion that mattered was her own. He'd started her on the journey of discovering who she really was, removing the barriers she'd created to protect herself. Even when she left here, she would always cherish being part of a community that had accepted her in every way.

She kissed his cheek. "And I won't leave without doing the same for you."

"I accepted who I am a long time ago."

She echoed her sentiments from last night, hoping it wouldn't anger him again. "Resigning yourself to a life without love isn't acceptance. It's fear."

He brushed his lips over hers. "I'm going to teach you how to embrace your exhibitionist nature."

She glided her tongue across his bottom lip. "And I'm going to teach you how to be a voyeur without your sight."

He gripped her nape and pushed her mouth against his, leisurely tasting and sampling. "It sounds as though we've both got a lot of work to do. Are you sure you're up to it?"

She rocked back and forth on his lap. "Oh, I'm definitely up to it, and from what I feel poking into me, so are you."

He jutted his chin toward the screen. "I haven't decided which one to frame for the dungeon. The rest I'm going to hang on the walls of my bedroom, so even when you're not there, I can masturbate to the image of your pink pussy."

Her breathing stuttered. "Do you do that a lot?"

"Since you've been here?" His lips curved upward. "Constantly. I'm going to need to see a doctor for carpal tunnel."

Growing wetter by the second, she wanted to play. "Not anymore. Now you can have my pussy whenever you want, Master." His cock twitched under her ass. "But maybe you could masturbate one last time. For me."

He raised a brow. "You want to see how I touch myself when I think of you?"

More than anything. "Yes, please."

He lifted her off his lap. "Sit on my desk." She situated herself in front of him, the smooth wood cool under her hot skin. Leaning forward, he slid his hands between her thighs and pushed them open. "Keep them spread." He inhaled and groaned. "God, you smell so good."

He fell back into his seat and unzipped his pants. Now free from confinement, his cock sprung forth, a bead of semen already pooled at the tip. His gaze remained on her pussy as he swiped his thumb over his glans and drew the moisture around his cockhead in a circular motion before gripping his shaft in his fist and sliding his hand up to the corona, then down to his heavy sac and back up again, pulling the satiny skin tight enough for her to see the bulging veins.

She licked her lips. "I fantasized about you doing that when I masturbated in the ladies' lounge."

He worked his shaft roughly and hissed through his teeth. "You have no idea what that did to me. I was as hard as a rock, and it took every ounce of resistance, but since I was inside the screening room with two of the dungeon monitors, I had to keep my pants zipped. When you slammed into me as you came out of the lounge, I thought I'd lose it and take you then and there against the wall. After you left, it took two pumps before I came all over my hand."

She would've never believed she could have such power over a man like Cole DeMarco. It was a heady feeling to be wanted that badly. With a surprising desperation, she wanted to take his cock in her mouth. "Forgive me if it's not my place to ask, but may I finish you off, Master?"

His hand stilled. "I don't think I'll last very long, but by all means, be my guest."

She slid off the desk and fell to her knees in front of him. He squeezed his shaft up to the bulbous head, bringing forth a few more drops of his essence.

He pushed his cock toward her lips. "Lick it."

Her tongue gathered the moisture and curled back into her mouth. His semen was a combination of bitter and salty, like a shot of tequila followed by the lime and salt.

She licked her way around the head, then dragged her tongue down his length, noting the differences of textures and flavors of his dark skin.

When she made her way back to the top, Cole set his hand on her head and gently pressed. "Now suck it in." She hallowed her cheeks as she brought him into her mouth as far as she comfortably could. She didn't have much experience, but judging by his accelerated breathing and the groans flying out of his mouth, he liked what she was doing. "Fuck me, that's good." Using the hand on her head, he pushed her up and down on his cock. "I'll set the pace, and you follow. Don't stop."

For a few minutes, Danielle was lost in a world that was solely about providing pleasure to one man. She closed her eyes and sunk into the experience, dragging her tongue over his bulging veins and the notch under the cockhead and squeezing his length with the suction of her mouth.

"Beautiful sight, isn't she?"

Cole's voice brought her out of the seductive trance, and she opened her eyes. Logan stood to the side of the desk, watching her work Cole's cock. She suddenly became aware her skirt remained around her hips, giving Logan a full view of her pussy and ass. She should've been embarrassed. She should've stopped blowing Cole and yanked her skirt down to cover herself. Instead, Logan's presence made her feel hot and tingly all over, especially between her legs.

Cole didn't stop pushing her down on his cock, a silent reminder he was in control. He wanted her to continue fucking him with her mouth, knowing full well this public display was feeding the exhibitionist in her. Cole's cock swelled in her mouth, a subtle pulsing by his veins alerting her he was close to completion.

He bobbed her head harder as if he was losing control, and she fought not to gag, relaxing the muscles of her throat and breathing through her nose. "I'm going to come, and you're going to take it all, because it belongs to you." His cock jerked, and he groaned, filling her mouth with his warm release. She swallowed him down, and when he lifted his hand from her head, she released him from her mouth and peered up at him.

"You're a very lucky man, Cole," Logan said. "I've got that file for you. I'll leave it for you in the screening room, and then I'm going to review the tapes like you asked. Let me know if you require anything else." Logan disappeared behind the bookcase.

Cole grinned. "You liked getting caught, didn't you?" He dragged her up by her arms and pushed her back to his desk, which she settled on top of. "I bet you're dripping for me."

Before she could respond, he slid two fingers inside her and began steadily pumping. He added a third and twisted his hand, his thumb circling her clitoris. She gripped the edge of the desk, her body bowing and moving with the force of his hand.

"That's it. Ride my hand," he crooned. "Let me hear how good it feels. Let everyone hear it. I want them to know what I do to you."

His fingers tapped the magic spot inside her, flicking it and pressing it while continuing a thrusting motion.

Her pussy trembled as he ignited sparks deep inside. She wanted to come, but she didn't want the feeling to end. Everything centered deep inside her pussy. Her muscles quivered, coiling tighter, and heat gathered low in her belly.

The tension snapped, and her climax unwound like a spool of thread, her vaginal muscles spasming around Cole's fingers and her arousal dripping down his wrist. He wrung out every last tremor before he removed his hand and licked her juices off each finger, one by one, closing his eyes as if savoring every last drop.

She jumped off the desk and shimmied her skirt down to cover herself. With the orgasms out of the way, her thoughts turned to her main mission in being here. "Where did Logan go?"

"Screening room. Only a few of us can access it, mainly dungeon monitors and myself, but Logan's got some skills that have become necessary this past month."

"Computer skills?"

He cocked his head. "Yes, how did you know?"

"From my talk with Logan last night before you and me…you know…in the gallery." Seriously, they'd just gotten each other off, and *this* made her blush.

"Before we fucked?" He smiled, clearly amused. "Let me hear you say it."

She held his gaze. "Before we fucked."

"That sounds deliciously dirty coming from your mouth." He stood. "Would you like to see it?"

Her heart slammed in her chest, making her dizzy. "Your screening room? Yes."

He went over to his bookcase and pressed on the side panel, and the piece popped open to display a keypad. After entering the password, he swung the entire bookcase out toward his office and ushered her into the screening room, stepping right behind her.

The door automatically closed with a *whoosh*. It wasn't a very large space, no larger than twelve by ten, but almost every inch of the walls was covered by a screen. On the left side of the room, a long table lined the wall, with three plastic chairs in front and three laptops laid out with a wall of monitors behind it. She counted up and across, counting twenty screens, each divided into two to four different shots of the same room. Since it was daytime, most of the rooms were empty, but she caught sight of the class being taught by Mistress Casey and noticed Gracie in the gallery, cleaning up the mess Cole had made from his meltdown.

"Logan," Cole said, announcing their presence.

Logan looked up from where he sat on the other side of the room at a desk that looked similar to the one in Cole's office, but on a smaller scale. A desktop computer sat on top, and a three-drawer filing cabinet fit between the desk and the wall.

She trembled, knowing how close she was to his private residence. If he'd allowed her in here, he was beginning to trust her. Would he finally break his rule and bring her upstairs to his bed?

Scanning the monitors, she was able to view the upstairs fantasy rooms. She whistled low. Gracie had been right. This room was a voyeur's wet dream. "Can you see all the rooms at once?"

"We can," Cole said, taking her hand. "It still isn't enough to cover all the different camera angles, so they rotate every thirty seconds."

Straight ahead was the staircase. "And what's up there?"

He squeezed her hand. "That takes you to my private residence."

She played with her locket. "So that's how you get there. Can I see it?"

When Cole flinched, she realized that even after they'd spent most of the night together, nothing had changed. Silly how that hurt even though her real reason for wanting to go upstairs was to find the box.

Logan coughed. "Cole, I hate to interrupt, but I need to discuss some information I discovered."

Cole grew somber. "Let me walk her out, and I'll be back." He placed his hand on the bottom of her spine, steering her back into his office and the door.

The reality of the situation crashed into her. He'd never invite her upstairs. She had no choice but to slip him the pills while they were in the club. She'd do it tonight.

By tomorrow, she'd be gone.

Chapter Twenty-Two

Tick-tock.

Tonight was the night.

He paced the length of the cabin, the sweet scent of blood making his mouth water.

He didn't want to wait any longer. He couldn't. His needs had grown bigger than him. Soon he would no longer be able to control the impulses raging through his blood. The voice in his head whispered it was time to make someone scream. And right now it took every bit of strength he had not to kill the woman asleep in the bedroom.

She'd never see it coming.

He picked up the shovel and headed toward the backyard.

The others had patience. After all, they'd waited all these years. But he was ready for it to be over. He wasn't a man who enjoyed being told what to do, and the more they denied him, the stronger the urge to show them who was really the boss.

Yeah, they had him by the balls, but he was smarter than them. He had stayed one step ahead of them the whole time. Soon he'd have Danielle, and when he was done with her, he'd finally have a clean slate.

A man like him shouldn't have to bow down to anyone. He wasn't a fucking slave.

He was a god.

He decided who lived and died.

He glanced at his watch, then speared his shovel into the snow and hoisted the icy precipitation over his shoulder. It was time to clear the ground and dig another grave.

Beside all the others.

Chapter Twenty-Three

DANIELLE GLARED AT herself in the mirror. On the outside, she looked fine. Her makeup was impeccable thanks to Gracie, who had helped her get ready.

But on the inside, she was a mess, knowing that sometime tonight, she'd have to drug Cole, find this mysterious account, and give the information over to the kidnappers.

Then what? Would they release Tasha? Would Danielle leave Benediction and walk out of Cole's life forever? Did she tell Cole the truth and risk retaliation from the kidnappers? And what if they didn't release Tasha? There was nothing to keep them from killing her once they had what they wanted. Or Cole. Or Danielle for that matter.

The image staring back at her from the mirror was the face of a liar. After tonight, she didn't know how she'd ever look in the mirror again and see anything else.

She opened the locket, confirming the pills were still there. Cole would forgive her. Once he realized she hadn't any other choice, he'd have to.

What she still didn't understand was why Cole would be the trustee for an account in her name or why he hadn't told her about it.

She picked up her perfume with the intention of applying it when she suddenly remembered the scent on the note from the kidnapper. Shivering, she dropped the bottle in the trash, no longer wishing to associate herself with it.

A light knock fell on her door. She opened it to a mouthwatering Cole, who was wearing his tight leather pants and a black T-shirt with the name Benediction across the chest. He eyed her hungrily.

She wasn't wearing much since she assumed he wouldn't allow her to remain dressed for very long tonight. The sleeveless black cotton dress hugged her curves and left most of her back bare.

"How was your meeting with the bank?" she asked once she found her voice.

He snaked his arm around her waist and tugged her into him. "I'm not sure. I couldn't pay attention with your scent all over me." He pulled her out of her room and shut the door, backing her up against it. "You have a good day?" He didn't let her answer, taking her mouth in a bruising kiss she felt down to her toes. She sighed into him, treasuring his rich taste.

At the sound of a few excited trainees chattering down the hall, Danielle broke away from his mouth and turned to lock the door, although God knew it was a pointless endeavor.

Wondering what Cole had in store for her as he brought her to the dungeon, she nervously toyed with her locket. He brought her to the dungeon stage, where Adrian and Logan were laying out rope onto a small round table.

"Danielle, you know Adrian and Logan." Cole grasped her hands, rubbing them between hers. "Logan's going to introduce you to *Shibari* and at the same time instruct Adrian on it. While Adrian is my slave, he's also a switch, meaning he's willing and able to take the Dominant role sometimes. One of those times is now. You are to submit to both of them Danielle. As always, you have your safe word. Do you understand?"

She opened her mouth, and nothing came out. Adrian winked at her, probably remembering how she'd done the same upon her arrival a few days ago. She glanced around the room, catching the crowd's interest in what was going on upon the stage, and realized Cole was fulfilling several of her fantasies at once. "Yes. I think I do."

She panicked as Cole removed his arm and stepped back. "Master Cole? I'd feel more comfortable if you stayed…and watched."

"I'm not going anywhere," Cole promised, kissing her cheek. "I want this for you, and it will please me at the same time. Do you understand?"

"Yes."

Cole was her mirror.

The voyeur in him would enjoy watching her receive pleasure, and she'd enjoy herself knowing he was watching. He wouldn't get jealous. He wanted this for her as much as he wanted it for himself.

He brought her to Logan before taking a seat in the chair at the back of the stage.

"What is your safe word, Danielle?" asked Sir Logan, using the same voice he'd used when doing the verbal exercise to identify her fantasies. She suspected Logan and Cole must have discussed it and come up with this scene together.

"Red, Sir."

Adrian inched closer. "Are you familiar with rope bondage, Danielle?"

"Very little, Sir."

"Adrian, take off Danielle's dress and her wristband," Logan said. "You can keep her locket on since it won't interfere with the ropes."

She peered over her shoulder at Cole, who sat as still as a statue, his spine rigid and his hands resting on his thighs. Adrian removed her wristband and her dress, leaving her completely naked on the stage.

What were the members thinking? Were they disgusted by her body? Several club members and a few trainees gathered in front of the stage, ready for the demonstration to begin. Tonight, she was the headliner.

Whispered words of the crowd reached her ears. *Brave. Exquisite. Submissive.*

Logan spun her around so her back was to the audience, then circled behind her. "I'm going to place a blindfold over your eyes." She sucked in a breath as he tied a satin sash around her head, submerging her in total darkness. "I want you to relax and breathe slowly. Like this. In and out. In and out."

She focused on following his command, rhythmically inhaling and exhaling until all her muscles loosened and the sounds of the room melted away.

Her body betrayed her arousal. Exposed to the air, her nipples puckered, the tightness of them almost causing pain, and she grew slick between her thighs at the notion that everyone, including Cole, was watching.

Did it turn him on to see her helpless? To see other men touch her?

Without the use of her eyes, her other senses took control. The heat of both men seeped into her, enveloping her in a safe cocoon where she could surrender to their ministrations and turn herself over to a new experience.

"I'm going to start by binding your wrists together over your head and then creating a harness around your breasts. If you feel any discomfort, tingling, or numbness, I want you to let me know," the voice she recognized as Logan's said.

"Yes, Sir."

Logan proceeded to speak in low tones to Adrian, instructing him on proper knot technique as he pulled her arms up straight and tied her wrists together. A hand stroked her back, up and down, each time moving closer to her bottom. She squirmed, rising up on her toes, wanting those fingers to trail down her crack and cup her pussy.

The hand spanked her behind. "None of that."

Grinning, she recognized the voice and the slap as belonging to Adrian. "Sorry, Sir."

She wasn't.

Adrian tugged her ponytail. "You've gotten cheeky since you've gotten here."

If he thought that would deter her, he was sadly mistaken. She'd take cheeky over wallflower any day. In the last couple of days, she'd become more confident in both her body and her sexuality. No one here would judge her for her desires. She was free to be herself.

The weight of the rope slid between her breasts, its soft texture surprising her. She'd expected it to be rough against her skin, like the rope on a sailboat.

New hands worked the rope underneath her breasts, and they inadvertently brushed her nipples. Without her having sight, they felt more sensitive than normal.

Logan continued to speak to Adrian in a hushed voice, but Danielle zoned out, their words not making much sense to her and becoming simply background noise.

She swore she could feel Cole's gaze on her. That invisible tether bound her to him stronger than any rope. Her entire body buzzed, and her limbs felt sluggish.

Hands caressed her flesh. Her shoulders. Her ribcage. Her thighs. Two, four, a dozen. She didn't know. In her mind, they all belonged to Cole.

Rope pressed between her legs, spreading her open wide. Logan whispered something in her ear, and suddenly she was airborne, floating on her back as if lying on a cloud.

Fingers swept across her cheekbones and feathered down her neck. A warm wet tongue teased one nipple as a rougher tongue licked the other. Then two strong mouths simultaneously sucked those nipples into their heat.

Pressure built in her pussy, her clitoris throbbing. She tried to close her legs, but the rope kept them open. She couldn't move. All she could do was lie there and take it.

"Has she ever taken a plug?" one of the men whispered.

A gasp slipped from her chest. No, she'd never had anything other than Cole's finger in her backside. A frisson of fear passed through her at the thought of it, but since they'd discussed anal plugs last night, she trusted Cole would keep her safe.

She didn't hear the answer, but warm fluid dripped down her crack and a finger worked it inside. There was a burning. A stretching. But it didn't hurt.

The moan that fell from her lips sounded foreign to her ears.

Another finger rubbed circles on her clitoris, and it began to warm. To heat. Like cinnamon or mint. The more he touched, the hotter it got, until tears pricked her eyes. Not from pain, but from pleasure and from need.

Something thicker than a finger entered her behind and she knew instantly it was the plug. As he worked it in deeper, the odd sensation of being filled made her writhe and struggle against the ropes.

She knew the moment Cole moved to her. Her heart beat faster, and her hands tried unsuccessfully to reach for him. Then he was there, kissing her cheek and whispering in her ear. "You're so beautiful like this. I'm so proud of you."

That's all it took for her to relax her muscles and surrender. The plug slid in easier, and all the discomfort disappeared, leaving behind overwhelming arousal. More fingers massaged her clitoris and slid inside her pussy, rhythmically thrusting. A tongue laved her nipple. Hands pinched and tugged.

Her body shook, and tension coiled tight in her belly, making her toes bend and her hands clench. In the darkness, she saw a brilliant white light as the tension snapped, and she splintered into a million pieces, calling Cole's name over and over.

Her muscles went lax, and hands supported her weight. She felt the cold stage under her feet, and yet at the same time, it was as if she were still floating in the air.

Cole murmured words of praise, but each one was like a knife to her heart. He'd given her so much, strengthened her confidence, and shown her a world where she didn't have to hide. For the first time in her life, she truly believed she was beautiful on the outside.

But she was rotting on the inside, her soul darkening as she realized these would likely be their final moments together. Hot tears dampened her blindfold. Soon he would hate her, and even if he didn't, what kind of life could they build on a shaky foundation of lies and deceit?

Cole was a fantasy, a naïve girl's dream of love. Even if he forgave her and she forgave him for his part in her father's imprisonment, he'd made it clear a wife and kids were not in his future.

Benediction was Cole's life. His one true love.

Not her.

"Shh, let it out. I've got you," Cole said, holding her to his chest and rubbing her back.

The weight of the blindfold was gone, and so was the anal plug. She opened her eyes and blinked away the tears to clear her vision. Cole had her on his lap, and they were sitting on a couch at the side of the room. Someone had dressed her, and her wristband was back on her wrist.

She rested her head on his shoulder and choked back a sob. "Where did Logan and Adrian go? How did I get unbound?"

"We got you out of the ropes a few minutes ago. Logan went upstairs, and Adrian went to get us water. How do you feel?"

Remorseful and frightened. "Good. Fine."

"I thought you'd feel better than that." He tipped up her chin. "Did it bother you to have other men touch you?"

She flinched, the intensity of his gaze too over-whelming, as if he could see straight to her weary soul. "Obviously not."

"I'm not talking about your physical reaction." He placed one hand on her head and one on her heart. "I want to know what you felt in here and here."

She took a deep breath. "At first, I was apprehensive. I worried about how I looked. Then I got over it and enjoyed myself. But I'm confused. I didn't think you'd let anyone else touch me if you wanted me for yourself. You said we were exclusive."

He growled and took her mouth, slamming his lips over hers and stealing the breath from her lungs. Then he pulled back, rubbing his cheek against hers. "We are. Tonight's scene didn't change that. Sexuality is a difficult concept even in the vanilla world, but it becomes more complex in alternative lifestyles. Although Logan and Adrian were the ones touching you, it was under my direction and my control, and I got to grant you one of your fantasies. The voyeur in me found it incredibly arousing." He cupped her face in his palms. "But I'd never allow anyone to go any further with you. You take my cock and no one else's. Your mouth, that gorgeous pussy, even your ass are mine and mine alone."

Overcome with emotion, she glanced away from Cole, and her eyes locked with Rinaldi's across the dungeon.

He pointed to his watch and mouthed the words that had kept her awake at night.

Tick-tock.

Danielle's stomach dropped like a dead weight, and her throat tightened as if Logan was winding his rope around it. She didn't want to do this. She wasn't ready. Panicked, she searched the room for a sign—any sign— that would tell her what to do.

Adrian approached with two cups of water and left them on the side table next to the couch. As Cole and he spoke, she toyed with her locket, quickly and surreptitiously opening it and depositing the pills into her hand. Her heart twisted, and tears burned her eyes.

When Adrian left, Cole handed her one of the cups. "Here, drink your water."

She accepted it, took a sip, and stretched across Cole, returning the cup to the table.

She had no choice.

She knew what she had to do.

She brought her lips to Cole's and savored him, the flavor of his mouth, the softness of his lips, the groan ripped from his throat.

His eyes were closed.

Hers were open wide.

She dropped the pills into the untouched cup of water and watched as they dissolved without a trace.

Nausea, swift and strong, rolled through her. She tore herself away from the kiss. "You should drink too."

His gaze bounced between her and the cup. "No thanks, I'm good."

Did he suspect? A huge part of her was hoping he did. That he wouldn't accept the drink. That the choice would be taken from her hands. But the other part of her knew if she didn't convince him to take this drink, the kidnappers would kill Tasha and possibly Cole. Drugging him would save his life. He'd have to understand. She'd make him understand.

She tucked her head into the crook of his neck and looked up at him with what she hoped was a flirtatious smile. "I'd drink it if I were you. You don't want to get dehydrated when you fuck me."

He returned the smile as he lifted a cup. "You're right."

Ten seconds later, he'd drunk it all. He wiped his mouth with the side of his hand and grimaced. "The water has a sour aftertaste." His eyes widened, and he crushed the plastic cup in his hand.

"Are you okay? Cole what's wrong?"

He wrapped his hand around the front of his neck. "My throat is closing up. What did you do?" His eyes rolled back into his head, and his body slumped on the couch.

Chapter Twenty-Four

"Cole." She shook him by his shoulders and got no response. "Help! Somebody help!" Guilt swamped her as she quickly slipped her hand into his pocket and retrieved his key ring, wrapping her fingers around it to conceal it the best she could.

Suddenly, Gracie and Adrian were there, and Danielle jumped off his lap. Gracie kneeled on the couch besides Cole and placed two fingers on his neck, seemingly checking for a pulse. "What happened?"

Danielle shook so hard she could barely stand. "He said his throat was closing."

Gracie put her hand in front of Cole's nose and mouth then dragged him to the floor and tilted his head back. "Someone call 911. He's not breathing." She covered his mouth with hers and blew air into him.

She'd killed him. She'd thought she was helping him, but instead she'd killed him.

People gathered around her, and a couple members proclaiming their status as doctors went over to assist Gracie with chest compressions.

She had to get out of here. There was something she had to do…

With her hand over her heart, she took a step backward. Then another. And another.

Looking furious, Adrian grabbed her by the elbow. "Danielle?"

She shrugged him off and ran.

She raced out of the dungeon. She might have killed Cole. She'd left him lying on the floor as though he meant nothing to her, when in fact, he meant everything. By keeping him in the dark, she'd tried to protect him, but instead she'd only put him in danger. She should've told him the truth, and now it was too late.

The main floor of the club was in chaos as word spread that Master Cole had stopped breathing. She passed several of the dungeon monitors on the way to Cole's office, all of them headed toward the basement.

The kidnappers had given her the means to create a distraction. No one would be in the screening room, the entire staff too busy calming the masses.

She flew into Cole's office, the door of which had been left wide open, as if offering an invitation. She pounded the code into the keypad and slid inside the secret room.

Just as she'd anticipated, it was empty.

Instantly she saw Cole's body on the floor of the dungeon, Gracie's hands on his chest. Danielle couldn't stop her tears from flowing, but a voice inside her that sounded like Cole ordered her not to waste the opportunity and to find the box.

She climbed the stairs to his residence. With shaky hands, she fiddled with the keys, sticking them into the lock one by one until finally one fit.

She pushed open the door and got her first look of the space he called his own. Except for a few framed photographs of an older couple she assumed were his parents, there was nothing of Cole in the décor. Anyone could live here. There were no bookshelves or televisions or magazines laid out on the black coffee table. There was no artwork on the white walls. No mirrors.

From the gray S-shaped couch to the kitchen's stainless steel appliances, the space had a sterile environment, none of it matching the Cole DeMarco she'd come to know these past few days. The man she'd gotten to know deserved color and light, not this dark cave he'd created for himself to retire to at night.

Where would he have put the box? As she moved into the living room she spotted a manila file with her name on it resting on the couch. She sat and flipped it open on the coffee table, and hundreds of photographs spilled out. Pictures of her from her school graduation. Of her walking into the building where she'd taken her art history class. Photos of her reading by the pool in her own backyard.

Eight years of photographs someone had taken without her knowledge. Her hands trembled violently.

Cole had been watching her all these years.

Why?

"What do you think you're doing?"

She snapped up her head to an angry-looking Adrian. "I…I'm looking for something to help Cole."

"In here? I doubt it." He stalked closer and clutched her shoulders. "Tell the truth, Danielle. You were looking for your offshore bank account."

She eyed Adrian warily. How did he know about the account? "You're working for the ones who have Tasha."

"Tasha." He frowned, letting go of her shoulders. "You mean your stepmother, Natasha Walker? She's been kidnapped?"

Although it was possible he was playing her, she wanted to trust him, knowing how much Cole did. Watching Adrian's bewilderment, she pinched the bridge of her nose to head off the tears. "You didn't know. If you're not working for them, how did you know about the bank account?"

A muscle in Adrian's jaw jumped. "Why did you try to kill Cole?"

"I didn't!" She ran her fingers through her hair. "I gave him a couple sleeping pills. That's it. I don't know what happened."

"An allergic reaction."

She bit down on her lip so hard she tasted blood. Her father had died from an allergy.

She sniffed. "Is he okay?"

"Why do you care? You just left him."

"I didn't want to. You have to believe that. I never wanted to hurt him. I've been trying to protect him. I've been trying to protect everyone." She curled her fingers into his shirt. "Please, Adrian. Tell me he's okay. Tell me he's alive."

Waves of pain wracked her body. She couldn't breathe, every inhalation squeezing her heart.

"Cole's fine," he said gently. "Logan and Gracie will be bringing him up here shortly."

Relief flooded through her. "How do you know about the offshore account?"

Adrian perched on the arm of the couch. "I'm not only Cole's slave. I also work for him in private security and as his bodyguard."

"Well you didn't do a good enough job. I almost killed him!" She lifted a photo of herself. "If you knew I was here for the file, why didn't you confront me about it?" She clutched it to her chest.

He sighed. "We didn't tell you because we didn't know what your angle was. We figured you'd show eventually, which was why I left Arizona and came here a few months ago to settle in and blend into the background."

"Arizona?"

"Cole assigned me to watch over you after your father died. I took all those photos."

She swallowed. "Who else is involved?

"I'm not sure I should—"

She slapped her hands on the coffee table. "Who?"

He flinched. "Logan. He's been doing some... computer work for us. And...Gracie."

Everyone she'd trusted. Each of them had lied to her.

Cassandra was right. It was all an illusion.

She heard voices right before Cole stumbled in flanked by Logan and Gracie. She flung herself at him, nearly bowling him over with the force of it, and wrapped her arms around him. "Cole, I'm so sorry."

Gracie and Logan moved away, but Cole's arms remained by his sides. "Close the door and check for bugs, Adrian," Cole said, his voice steady and strong.

Stepping back, she saw the cold expression on Cole's face.

Adrian held a device that looked like a walkie-talkie and advanced around the room. "All clear. They're not watching or listening in here."

"What is going on here?" she asked, feeling as though she was missing something vital. Cole didn't appear to have been affected by the sleeping pills at all.

Ignoring her, Cole looked to Adrian. "What does she know?"

"Nothing. Less than we do."

"I don't understand," she said. "I thought I almost killed you. That you had a severe allergic reaction to the pills I gave... You played me?"

Cole folded his arms across his chest. "I saw you slip the pills into my water, so I switched cups. I figured I was supposed to have an allergic reaction; that seems to be Rinaldi's modus operandi, so I made sure to list it on the fake electronic medical records, and surprise—he took the bait."

She felt like a fool. "All of you were in on this?" She looked at her friend. "Gracie?"

Guilt in her eyes, Gracie lowered her gaze to the floor. "At first we weren't sure why you were here or if you knew anything about the offshore account."

"And when you realized I was innocent?" Danielle asked. "What then? You all just decided to keep me in the dark without any concern for what I might be going through and putting my life in danger?"

"Since you've been here, your life has never been in danger," Cole said firmly.

"Then how do you explain the knife at my throat the other night?" she asked, staring directly into Cole's eyes.

His anger disappeared as his brows furrowed. "What the hell are you talking about?"

"Apparently he wasn't satisfied with the progress I'd made." She could still feel the cold metal against her neck. "He said the longer I stayed, the more opportunity he'd have to rape me. I didn't want to take the chance that it was merely an intimidation tactic."

Cole ran his hand over his head and sat on the couch, then gathered her into his arms. "You should've come to me. I would've protected you. You were supposed to be safe here. We've had the video cameras on you the entire time."

She pulled back. "Except for the residences, right? Everything that's happened to me was in my bedroom."

Cole slid a glance at Adrian. "Before you arrived, I had Adrian add a camera to the upstairs hallway with a view of your front door and one inside your room. Gracie, Logan, and Adrian all watched and reviewed the footage, and none of them saw anything out of the ordinary."

She put her hand up in front of her. "For the moment, I'll ignore the fact you violated my privacy, but are you accusing me of lying?"

Cole shook his head. "No, I'm saying someone messed with the recordings."

Adrian took a step toward her. "Earlier today, I found a bug in the screening room. One of the dungeon monitors has to be working for Rinaldi." He turned to Cole. "I realize you've placed your trust in your dungeon monitors, but people can be bought for the right price. Outside of the people in this room, we can't assume anyone is innocent."

Cole nodded to the others. "Why don't you three go back to the club while Danielle and I talk?"

When they closed the door behind them, Cole cradled her face in his hands. "Now, why did you really come to Benediction?"

She took a deep breath. "My stepmother was kidnapped."

Beginning with the night of Tasha's kidnapping, she filled him in on all the events leading to tonight.

"You're not to blame for any of this. Not for Tasha, and not for your father." He paused, the silence of the room deafening. "Danielle, your father didn't commit suicide." He stroked her cheek. Studying her face, he blew out a warm breath. "He was murdered."

Chapter Twenty-Five

MY FATHER WAS murdered.

The words hung in the air as if they had physical substance.

Her mind rejected it even as her gut twisted in painful acknowledgement. For eight years, she'd carried the belief her father had chosen to end his life rather than fight to return to her. He'd left her alone in this world, and she'd hated him for it.

If she'd been wrong, if he'd been murdered...

"No, that's not true. The prison said he paid off another prisoner to buy him peanuts at the commissary, and he ate those peanuts knowing he'd have a severe allergic reaction. That sure sounds like suicide to me."

Cole's jaw tightened, but his touch remained soft as he caressed her face with the tips of his fingers. "I believe he felt he had no choice."

Cold barbs of shock ripped through her, stealing the breath from her lungs. "Why?"

"Two weeks before your father's death, his lawyer brought him a message from an extremely dangerous organization."

"His lawyer? That idiot?" She remembered the greasy older man well. Her hackles went up anytime they shared space. He'd refused to entertain any notion her father could be innocent and had told them there was no way to win at trial. He'd convinced her father to take the first plea deal that had passed his desk.

"He wasn't an idiot. He was just another pawn. Who, by the way, died in a car accident one week after your father's death."

She shuddered, doubting the veracity of Cole's words, of everything she'd known for the last decade. Rage surged hot and strong. "How do you know this?"

"Because he told me when I went to visit him a day before he died. Danielle, he was the one who gave me the files to take to the FBI. It was the only way."

"The only way for what?"

"The only way to save your family's lives."

She put her hands on his chest, intending to push him away, but instead, her fingers curled into tight fists against the solid warmth. "I don't believe this. You're trying to tell me my father wanted to go to prison?" Her voice cracked, all the myriad of emotions whipping through her at once too overwhelming to process. "That he did it to protect us?"

"That's exactly what I'm saying."

She'd grieved for how she'd left things between them, but this...this stabbed at her heart like a knife. Her throat constricted. "The last time he and I spoke, we got into an argument. I had gone behind his back and found a new attorney, one who believed my father had a shot at having his plea deal reversed if he turned over evidence on some of his clients. I thought he'd be happy about it, but he wasn't. He rebuffed any suggestion of working with the government. I was angry at him for protecting his clients—strangers—over me, and I told him I'd never forgive him." She'd thought she'd expended every possible tear over her father's death, but she'd been wrong. "Those were my last words to him."

Cole let her tears fall, kneading her back and shoulders. "He knew you loved him. Don't ever doubt that."

She couldn't change the past, but she also wouldn't choose to accept it. Her father deserved justice. She'd always known that. Now Tasha deserved it as well. And the only way to get it was by learning the truth.

She rubbed her eyes and pulled back to look into Cole's eyes. "Why would he trust you with the information? Why not go to the FBI on his own?"

"Because he was being watched," he said. "I was your father's business partner. Silent, yes, but his partner nonetheless. I had access to all the same files as your father."

"So my father gave you information that supported the inane theory he'd embezzled from his clients and defrauded them with a Ponzi scheme in order to cover it up? That's ridiculous. Why would he implicate himself in the crimes without using the information he had on this organization as a bargaining chip?"

Cole squeezed her hand. "Your father got involved with a bad group of businessmen. When the stock market crashed in 2007, he lost most of his clients. I had introduced him to several members of Benediction, including Anthony Rinaldi. At the time, I hadn't known anything about Rinaldi other than he was a wealthy businessman. They brokered a deal, which resulted not only in your father becoming the Rinaldi crime family's investor, but their money launderer as well."

She closed her eyes as if she could shield herself from the agonizing truth. In all these years, she'd never once believed her father could have been guilty of the crimes. "He wouldn't have done that."

"He did. I wish to God he didn't. There's not a day that's gone by I haven't regretted playing hardball when my loan came due and for causing your father to use the mafia's money to pay it off."

None of them were innocent. They'd all made mistakes. Could she forgive Cole for his?

"He eventually dug himself into a hole from which he couldn't escape," Cole continued. "To try and recoup the money he embezzled from the mafia, he built a Ponzi scheme, using new clients' money to make false returns on Rinaldi's investments. One day, the numbers didn't add up, and Rinaldi figured out what your father had done. At that time, your father still owed the mob millions of dollars, so Rinaldi blackmailed him into taking on a Russian crime syndicate as a client. The Russians' money was used to pay off Rinaldi, and eventually, your father earned enough to pay back the Russians. But at some point, he couldn't stomach working for them anymore. He wanted to get out without endangering his family, so he hid the Russians' money and placed it in an offshore trust under your name on the condition you couldn't touch it until you got married or turned twenty-five. At the same time, I handed over the evidence of embezzlement of all clients but Rinaldi and the Russians to the FBI. The Russians couldn't touch you if they wanted their money."

Her father may have committed the crimes, but he'd loved his family and done his best to protect them. It was up to her to do the same. "Now that you know the truth of why I'm here, how do we get Tasha back? The kidnapper—Rinaldi—said he'd kill Tasha if I told anyone or contacted the police. If he discovers—"

A knock interrupted her.

Cole rose from the couch. "That should be the doctor."

"Doctor?" she asked, confused. "I thought you said you were okay."

Logan, Gracie, and Adrian walked in with a man wearing a white doctor's coat.

"The club is completely empty, and we sent the trainees to bed with word that you were recovering nicely," Gracie said, dropping onto the couch.

Adrian kept going, heading toward the back of the apartment to what Danielle guessed would be the bedrooms.

Cole shook the doctor's hand. "Agent Miller, thank you for getting here so quickly."

Agent? Did that mean he was FBI?

The man smiled. "Logan contacted me yesterday and filled me in on the case. When he called thirty minutes ago to share some new developments, I was intrigued. Never been asked to dress up as a physician for a case."

Cole gestured for Agent Miller to take a seat on the couch. "We needed a way to get you into the house without raising Rinaldi's suspicions. No doubt he's got his people watching. He's already managed to bug parts of my home." Cole took his spot beside her. "I appreciate your agreement to look the other way as to Benediction."

"I grew up with Logan. Believe me, I'm not interested in his or anyone's consensual sex life," Agent Miller said. "Besides, everyone in the Detroit FBI office has been looking to nail Rinaldi for years."

Cole slid his arm around her. "If you contact Agent Davis in the Phoenix office tomorrow, he'll provide you some details that didn't make it into James Walker's file, including his connection to the Rinaldi crime family."

Agent Miller looked at her. "You must be Danielle. It's your mother who's been kidnapped?"

"Stepmother," she clarified. "Please, if Rinaldi learns I've gotten the FBI involved, he'll kill her."

The FBI agent frowned, shaking his head. "I know Rinaldi. He doesn't believe in leaving any loose ends."

Her stomach dropped. "You think he'll kill Tasha no matter what I do?"

"If he hasn't already, then yes, I think he'll kill Tasha." He paused. "But I also believe he'll go after you."

Cole tugged her closer. "Then she needs more protection. I'll set something up for her."

"I've got a different idea," Agent Miller said. "Rinaldi has been groomed to take control of his family's crime syndicate since before he could walk. He knows when he's being tailed, and he knows how to shake one. We believe he's responsible for the disappearance of several young women who have gone missing. Their bodies have never been found."

She shivered at the thought that the man who'd possibly murdered several women had kidnapped her stepmother. "Then how do you know he's involved?"

"Rumors from a couple rival associates of his," Agent Miller explained. "A couple of the girls had been part of a kinky dating agency he owns. He pretends to pair up sexually like-minded people, but usually he takes the clients' money and sets them up with prostitutes who can't say no to whatever kink the clients want. The problem is since they're runaways and junkies, no one reported these girls as missing. And we can't figure out where he's taking them." He leaned toward her. "But you can."

Cole shot to his feet. "No way in hell are you using Danielle as bait."

Agent Miller rose from the couch and put up his hands. "Hear me out. She'll wear a wire and a GPS. Logan filled me in on some of the specifics of what Rinaldi was looking for. Once Danielle gives him the account information, he'll think he's won. And he'll be looking to tie up those loose ends. I think he'll kidnap Danielle and bring her back to wherever he's been taking the other girls. Danielle could help us finally put this guy away for good."

Cole shook his head. "You'll have to find another way—"

"I'll do it," she said, standing and ignoring the concern in Cole's eyes. "What do you need me to do?"

Adrian handed her a square sterling silver box decorated with sapphires. "This was your mother's."

Her heart ached, and a tear escaped her eye. In his grief after Danielle's mother died, her father had given everything that had belonged to her to charity. Danielle had grown up with no more than a few photographs of the woman she'd never gotten to meet.

She didn't understand why her father hadn't given this to her years ago or why he'd hidden the bank account information in it, then given it to Cole, but at the moment, it didn't matter.

She unclasped her necklace and clutched the locket in her hand. The tip of the key shaped locket fit perfectly into the lock of the box. She heard a click and flipped open the top. Inside was a folded document. She took it out, unfolded it, and read. Just as Rinaldi and Cole had said, her father had left fifty million dollars for her.

Blood money.

She didn't want it. Then again, she doubted her father actually intended for her to keep it. This was an insurance policy. Too bad it had expired the moment she'd turned twenty-five.

She looked at Agent Miller. "Now what?"

"How are you supposed to contact Rinaldi?" he asked.

"I'm supposed to call him."

The agent pulled a phone from his pocket. "What's your cell number?" As she gave it to him, he punched the numbers into his phone. "I've programmed my cell to make it look like it's coming from your phone." He handed his cell to her. "Call him."

Cole soothingly rubbed the back of her neck as she dialed. After one ring, Rinaldi answered. "You have it?"

"I do." Trembling, she read off the account number.

"Now inside your locket is the password," Rinaldi informed her. "What is it?"

She didn't have to open the locket to check. She knew the inscription by heart. It was her parents' names and anniversary. "James and Jessica 2-21-85." She grabbed Cole's hand. "When will you release Tasha?"

"As soon as I've got the money safely in my account. See you soon, Danielle," Rinaldi said in a way that made it sound like a threat.

When the call went dead, she returned the phone to Agent Miller. Her body began shaking violently, and her legs buckled. Cole caught her before she hit the floor, swept her up into his arms as if she weighed nothing, and carried her back to the couch. Once settled, she took a few steadying breaths and addressed Agent Miller. "Now what do I do?"

"We'll try and trace the wire," he said. "Unfortunately, there are procedures we have to follow. Because it's overseas, it's a time-consuming process, but we'll do our best. We want to nail him just as much as you. I'll swing by tomorrow and get you wired. You don't want to make it too easy for him to nab you, but this place is like Fort Knox."

Logan whispered something to Adrian, then got up from the couch and nodded once to Cole before walking out the door.

"Tomorrow night, Danielle and I have an invitation to meet friends for drinks," Gracie said. "It would get her out in the open, but we could have Adrian come so it appears as though he's watching out for us. Would that work?"

That's right. She'd forgotten Kate had issued her an invitation.

Sitting beside her, Cole turned her to face him and caressed her cheek. "Danielle, we'll find another way—"

"You heard Agent Miller." She took Cole's hand and interlaced their fingers. "They've already tried and failed. If there's any chance that Tasha is alive, I have to do this."

Chapter Twenty-Six

AFTER GRACIE AND Adrian left with Agent Miller, Danielle rested her head on Cole's shoulder. She curled her hand around his thick biceps, marveling at the steely strength beneath his satiny skin. "Why do you have all those pictures of me?"

He brushed his hand down her hair, re-creating the intimacy she'd worried she'd lost earlier tonight by drugging him. "When your father died, I took it upon myself to hire someone to watch over you. If they got to him, what would keep them from coming after you? My only hope was they had no idea where the money had gone or who had access to it." He kissed the top of her head. "But that has nothing to do with why I kept the photos or why I spent hours staring at them."

She looked up at him, her lips parting in invitation. "Why, Cole?"

He swept her up into his lap and grasped the nape of her neck. "Because I've wanted you since the moment I saw you on the stairs of your home all those years ago when you were seventeen. I kept your photos because it was the only way I could have a piece of you." Sadness shone from his eyes. "I understand if you never forgive me for getting your father mixed up with Rinaldi."

They'd both carried their burdens alone. It was time for forgiveness.

"It wasn't your fault," she said. "I've wasted years blaming you and, at the same time, hating myself for wanting you." She shifted to wrap her thighs around his hips.

She was done with the guilt. Done with the tears.

Right now, she didn't want to worry about tomorrow. She wanted to escape for a few more hours and live in the fantasy world where everything would work out. She wanted to believe her stepmother was alive, Rinaldi would go to prison, and she and Cole would live happily ever after.

"Make love to me," she whispered, her impatient fingers working to unbutton his leather pants.

"I want you, Danielle." His hands slid to her butt. "I want your ass. Will you let me?"

The earlier plug had only given her a brief taste of what it would be like. He'd promised to prepare her, but their time was running short. What if they didn't have another chance? He wasn't the first man she'd made love to, and he might not be her last. But she wanted to give him something she'd given no other man. "There's nothing I'd refuse you. Take it. It's yours."

"Hold on to me," he ordered, lifting them both off the couch and carrying her through the living room and down the hall into a bedroom. He deposited her onto her feet and pulled her dress over her head, leaving her completely naked. Then he pushed her back onto his mattress, but rather than join her, he crouched down and pulled something from under the bed.

As she waited, she took in the room. It was similar to the rest of his personal space. White walls. No décor. For the most part, his residence was just a place for sleeping. The exception was his bed. Hearing Cole fiddling with something metallic, she studied it. Made of steel, it looked similar to a four-poster bed, but there were cross bars and built-in hoops along the headboard and on all four posts.

Cole stood, holding what she recognized from the dungeon as a black leather sex sling. Her nipples hardened and her pussy fluttered as he connected the metal chains supporting the sling to the four top corners of the bed frame.

"Time for a ride," he said, once the sling was attached. "Lay on your stomach. There's a cut-out at the head for you to breathe through. Line up your mouth over that hole."

The commanding tone of his voice made her shiver with arousal and her juices drip from her pussy. As she climbed into the sling, she realized she was so wet, her thighs were slippery. She rested on her stomach, careful to place her mouth over the hole in the head rest. Once she was situated, he spread her arms and legs wide, then restrained her ankles and wrists to the sling. She heard a tearing noise right before he positioned himself between her legs.

Cool liquid dribbled down the crack of her ass. Cole pushed a finger into her back hole, plunging it in and out until he had her gasping for more. Adding another one or two well-lubricated fingers, he stretched her muscles, slicking the inside of her ass with lubrication to ease the path for his cock. She moaned at the burn, and her nerves lit on fire, fueling her need for him to fill her.

His fingers disappeared, and a whirring noise began. He slid something into her pussy, and it didn't take her a second to recognize it was a vibrator. The head of the vibrator swirled near her G-spot, and another part of it vibrated and flicked her clitoris. Moaning from the overload of sensations and the direct contact on her clit, she tried to move away, but the restraints held her in place.

Cole slapped her ass. "Surrender to the pleasure, Danielle. You can't escape it or me." She hissed as his thick length nudged the entrance. "You're mine, and now I'm going to prove it to you." Inch by inch, he worked his thick cock into her ass until she was filled in both her holes.

Once he was fully seated, he used the sling to move her back and forth, relentlessly forcing her up and down his cock. She'd never felt so helpless or submissive. He fucked her as if she was a plaything for him to use solely for the purpose of getting himself off.

Yet at the same time, he'd ensured she would enjoy herself too. As the head of the vibrator rubbed the sensitive tissues inside her pussy, the nub of the toy worked its magic on her clitoris.

Pleasurable sparks danced down her spine, and lightning flashed in her eyes as the first orgasm broke over her in a wave of heat, smashing her into a million little pieces. But rather than give her a moment to rest, Cole continued to yank her onto his cock, keeping her arousal at a fever pitch and sending her directly into another earth-shattering climax. Tears from the pleasure drenched her cheeks, and her heart beat as if she was running a marathon. She rolled from one orgasm to another, the pleasure becoming almost unbearable as her pussy continuously contracted around the vibrator and the muscles in her ass clamped down on Cole's cock.

Cole's fingers dug into her hips. "One more for me, baby. This time I'm going to come with you." She tried to relax her body, but everything inside of her grew tighter and tighter until on a scream, the tension snapped and she soared into the strongest orgasm in her life. Only seconds later, groaning, Cole flew over the edge as well, his motions slowing as his cock jerked inside her ass.

She didn't know how much time passed before Cole removed the restraints from her ankles and wrists and lowered her to the bed. He unhooked the sling from the frame and dropped it on the floor. He disappeared into an adjoining room, and she heard water running. After returning with a washcloth, he gently cleaned her up, then gathered her into his arms.

The night flew by in a tangle of warm lips and sweaty limbs, dirty words and tender touches. Her mouth worked his cock until he jetted his release on her breasts, and he rubbed it into her skin, marking her. She'd fall asleep only to be woken with his tongue between her thighs or his cock entering her from behind. They couldn't get enough of each other, hungry and frantic to possess and claim, their bodies speaking words neither could say.

But in her head, as he brought her to the peak of another climax, three little words repeated over and over again. And when he snored in the crook of her arm, she finally allowed herself to whisper, "I love you."

Chapter Twenty-Seven

IT WAS ALMOST over.

By now, the money filled the coffers of some of the scariest sons of bitches in Eastern Europe, which meant his debt would be erased. Soon he'd have his reward.

He wasn't going to let them stop him. They could kill him, but his wife and children were untouchable. At least the Italian mafia lived by a code, but those Russian fuckers would murder their own mother in her sleep to prove a point.

They had no honor.

By tomorrow, Danielle would join him for a brief stay in his cabin. He'd finally have a woman who could withstand his torture and quench his thirst for blood and pain. Then she'd vanish like all the other whores.

Tonight he'd have to make do with the slut he'd tied up in the extra bedroom. It meant having to dig another grave, but what was one more when there had been so many he could barely remember what each of them had smelled like as their lives drained from their eyes?

This one was a screamer. He'd kept her doped and drunk for days, but tonight, he'd sobered her up in time for the party to start.

He opened his kit, laying the needles beside the defibrillator's paddles. When everything was set, he grabbed his knife, and with a shallow cut to her cheek, woke his prey from her drug-induced slumber.

Her hazy eyes instantly cleared as they focused on the blade in his hand. She screamed, her emaciated body fighting against the restraints keeping her locked in place on the mattress.

She was nothing but an appetizer.

By later tonight, no matter what it took, he'd have his main dish.

Chapter Twenty-Eight

HOLDING UP HER cable-knit sweater that Cole had given her to wear, Danielle stood still as Agent Miller wired her. He'd already inserted a tiny GPS tracker into her locket.

"You're certain the GPS will work?" Cole asked Agent Miller, who'd dressed up as a doctor again.

This morning, they'd spread the rumor to the trainees that Cole had nearly died from an allergic reaction to an unknown substance and was recovering in his residence. No one would blink at a physician coming to check on him. Also Gracie had announced that she was taking Danielle for a night out with the girls to cheer her up. They hoped the information would spread to the dungeon monitors and then to Rinaldi, letting him know that Danielle would be unguarded tonight.

Agent Miller finished taping the wire to her skin and pulled her sweater back down. "I doubt Rinaldi will suspect a thing, but we'll only be a couple blocks away from

Danielle at all times, just in case. Don't worry, we've done this plenty of times. Danielle will be perfectly safe."

"Were you able to figure out where he hid the money?" she asked.

The agent shook his head. "We're working on it."

Logan got up from the couch. "Rinaldi transferred the funds using CHAPS to another UK bank and converted the money into Bitcoins. Then he wagered the entire lot of them on a hand of poker on a Darknet gambling website and lost. It will take some time to trace from there. Not impossible, but I'll need some special software for it. I've got my contacts out west on it, but it will be at least twenty-four hours before they can hack into the gambling site and access the block chain, then follow the network map."

Agent Miller's jaw dropped as if he was shocked, but he quickly recovered, even going so far as to grin. "Hacking? I'll pretend I didn't hear that."

Logan had mentioned he was into computers, but from the sound of it, he could do things that the FBI couldn't.

"Are we almost ready to go?" Gracie asked. "The girls are expecting us in a half hour."

She nodded. "Just give me a minute alone with Cole."

After Logan and Gracie left with Agent Miller, she turned to Cole. All day, he had been on edge, stuck inside his residence as if it was a prison. They hadn't spoken much about tonight, but he'd made it clear that he didn't want her to do this.

"You heard Agent Miller," she said, wrapping her arms around his waist and resting her head against his chest. "I'll be fine."

He tipped up her chin. "I've spent eight years watching over you and trying to keep you safe."

"And now it's out of your control, right?"

He walked backward to the couch and sat, bringing her onto his lap. "Yes, damn it. If I felt protective of you before you even walked into Benediction, do you have any idea of how I feel now that I've claimed every part of you? You said that you belonged to me, but if that was true, you wouldn't be doing this. You'd let the FBI find another way to find your stepmother and get Rinaldi."

"Cole, I meant what I said." She pressed a hand over his heart. "I do belong to you. But I'm not your slave. I'm free to make my own decisions. And besides, even slaves have a safe word." She gave him a little smile. "You can't control everything. Sometimes, you have to have faith that it will all work out in the end."

"I told you before, I put my faith in science." He plunged his fingers into her hair at her nape and cradled the back of her head, pushing her toward him. He stared into her eyes. "If something goes wrong tonight, don't worry about ruining this operation. You do whatever it takes to make it home to me."

"I promise."

She kissed him lightly on the lips before she forced herself to walk out his door. Gracie showed her to the garage, and for the first time in days, Danielle left Benediction. They made small talk as Gracie drove, and Adrian followed right behind them in his car.

"I hope you don't hate me," Gracie said as she parked in the darkened lot behind the restaurant. "I never meant to lie to you. Master Cole always had your best interests at heart, and so did I. Can you forgive me?"

Danielle clutched her locket between her fingers. "We all kept secrets. There's nothing to forgive."

The snow swirled all around, the wind biting and bitter. They strolled into the Spanish-style tapas bar, pretending as if this was really just a girls' night out. Ceramic tiles colored in blue, gold, and white were used in accents on the walls and floors, and curved arches gave it a Western European feel.

Danielle immediately spotted Kate sitting at a round table with two other women. But like a storm cloud on the horizon, a sense of foreboding hovered over Danielle, chilling her even though they'd left the frigid temperatures outside.

Kate got up from the table and welcomed Danielle and Gracie with hug. "Rachel, Lisa," Kate said, motioning to each of them with a wave of her hand, "I'd like to introduce you to Gracie and Danielle."

Danielle sat beside the woman Kate had identified as Rachel, a stunning brunette wearing heavy eyeliner and a blouse unbuttoned enough to show her perfect cleavage. Rachel picked up her glass of wine, and a slight grin appeared on her face. "Are you both attorneys?"

"Uh, no," Danielle said, catching Adrian sitting alone in a nearby booth. She scanned the restaurant looking for someone who looked suspicious, her knee bouncing nervously.

"Then you're members of Benediction." Rachel leaned over, resting her forearm on the table. "Tell me, what really goes on behind closed doors?"

"Uh-uh, Rachel." Like a mother admonishing her child, Kate shook her finger at her. "You know all members have to sign a confidentiality agreement. Even if I did know them from Benediction—and I'm not saying I do—they aren't permitted to disclose the details."

Rachel rolled her eyes. "Spoken like an attorney. One of these days, I'm going to get in there."

"Rachel's a reporter," Lisa said as if it explained everything. She was equally as pretty as Rachel but in a less in-your-face way, with her straight medium brown hair, glasses, and simple makeup.

Rachel straightened in her chair and flashed her a million-dollar smile. "I'm sure they're aware of that already."

"Sorry." Danielle shrugged. "I'm from Arizona, and I haven't watched any television since I've arrived in Michigan."

"And I don't watch the news," Gracie said, chiming in with her usual peppy manner. "It's too depressing. Now reality TV, that's another story."

"It's so nice to meet you both," Lisa said, the area around her eyes crinkling from her amusement. "Arizona, huh? What part?"

Danielle tried to concentrate on the conversation, but she became distracted every time someone new walked through the door. "Scottsdale. Have you been?"

Sipping her wine, Lisa shifted in her seat. "No. I've heard it's beautiful."

"It is, but I've come to appreciate Michigan too. Cole's neighborhood—"

"Cole DeMarco, Cole?" Rachel asked. "The owner of Benediction?"

"Rachel, heel," Kate said.

Danielle could've kicked herself for slipping up and giving Rachel a hint about how she knew Kate. Rachel most likely assumed it anyway, but Danielle felt as though she'd broken a rule.

Rachel crumbled up a cocktail napkin and threw it at Kate. "Damn it. If you would get me a guest pass for one night, I wouldn't have to hound your friends here."

Kate sighed dramatically. "Fine."

Rachel's jaw dropped. "Excuse me? Did you agree?"

"I did," Kate said. "Next month, Benediction is having an open house for prospective members. No nudity or sex allowed, but you'll be able to tour the facility and ask questions. If you sign a confidentiality agreement, Cole will grant you an interview. But if you out anyone, I guarantee—"

"No, no. Of course I won't," Rachel said, clapping her hands. "Oh, thank you. Thank you. I could kiss you."

Lisa lifted her cell off the table and waved it around. "If you do, let me get my camera ready. I'm sure Jaxon would love to see that."

"What about you?" Rachel asked Lisa. "Are you coming with us to the open house?"

Lisa frowned, her gaze dropping to her lap. "No. That's not my thing. You know that."

"Actually, I have no idea what your thing is," Rachel said. "You never date. Are you secretly married or something?"

Lisa's eyes widened. "Why would you say that?"

Rachel rolled her eyes as if it was obvious. "Because married people are notorious for not having sex. You fit the criteria perfectly."

Lisa sighed and shook her head. "I'll think about coming with you. Okay?"

"I'll be happy to show you the ropes," Gracie said in her usual perky manner. "Speaking of ropes, there's this guy who does some awesome bondage scenes."

Rachel pursed her lips. "Let me guess? Logan, right?"

"Her and Logan rub each other the wrong way," Kate said, a ghost of amusement on her lips.

Gracie's eyebrows arched. "Probably because they haven't rubbed each other the right way. One night at Benediction could change that."

Clearly annoyed and ready to change the subject, Rachel ignored the previous comments and turned her full attention to Danielle. "Are you planning on staying in Michigan?"

Her heart jumped a beat. If Cole asked her, would she stay? "I'm not sure. It depends…"

Rachel sipped from her drink. "Let me guess. It depends on a man, right?"

Danielle bit her lip and tried to decide how much to say. All the women watched her with interest, especially Gracie. "I'm not sure if it's going to work out. There are issues I'm not sure we'll ever see eye to eye on."

"Hey, if Kate and Jaxon could make it, anyone can," Rachel said.

Kate glared at Rachel. "Thanks for the glowing endorsement."

From across the room, Adrian rubbed his chin, giving Danielle the sign that it was time to move. She glanced at Gracie and nodded. "I'm going to the ladies' room. If you'll excuse me."

"Oh, I'll go with you," Rachel said, grabbing her purse.

"No!" Gracie said. "I mean, if you really want to hear about Benediction, you don't need to interview Cole. I've been his slave for years. I'll answer your questions."

Her stomach churning with nerves, Danielle hurried to the bathroom and washed her hands, wondering if Rinaldi would take the bait. After a couple minutes, she walked out of the ladies' room and smacked into Master Michael in the hallway, holding a rag in one hand and in the other, a similar gadget to the one Adrian had used to detect bugs.

"I'm sorry," Michael said, "but he's got my sister. I don't have a choice."

In a flash, he yanked her necklace until it broke and ripped off the wire. Panicked, she tried to fight him off, kicking and punching him, knowing without the GPS in her locket, the FBI might not be able to find her once he took her from the restaurant. He slapped her face, and before she could scream, he covered her mouth and nose with a sweet-smelling cloth.

Her body crumbled, and as the darkness took her, her last thoughts were of Cole.

Chapter Twenty-Nine

"DANIELLE? WAKE UP."

Her head pounded. She tried to open her eyes, but it felt as though someone had sprinkled sand in them and glued her eyelids together. All the moisture had dried from her mouth, leaving behind a bitter, acidic flavor, and she could've sworn her tongue had swollen to twice its size.

She turned her head toward the voice, and nausea slammed into her, bile burning her throat. Everything seesawed, and she tried to hold onto something, but she couldn't move. Swallowing, she cracked her lids to a blurred view.

As she rapidly blinked, her vision cleared. A dim lamp swung from the ceiling, and the yellowish paint was peeling from the walls. They were in a wooden shack or a cabin of some sort. The coppery scent of blood was overpowering in the small space. Danielle lowered her head and realized the reason she couldn't move was because she was tied to a chair with rope.

Her heart jumped at the sight of her stepmother sitting next to her. She was similarly bound with bruises and scratches on her cheeks. A blood-stained bandage covered the part of her hand where her ring finger had been.

She was alive.

"Tasha." Tears welled in her eyes. "Oh, thank God. I thought I'd never see you again."

"Danielle, I'm so glad you could make it." Smiling as if greeting her for dinner, Anthony Rinaldi stepped out of another room. "I must apologize for the accommodations. It's not up to par with what you deserve, but it's been very convenient for my purpose."

His calm demeanor scared her more than the fact that she was tied to a chair. "What purpose? Why are we here? What did we ever do to you?"

He dragged a chair over to her, its metal legs scratching the hardwood floor along the way, the grating noise like nails on a chalkboard. He placed it backward in front of her and casually straddled it. "Your father got me into a mess with some dangerous Russians. He owed them quite a bit of money, but rather than pay it back, he turned himself in to the Feds and hid that money overseas, leaving me on the hook with the Russians. He thought we wouldn't find it, and I admit, I almost would've believed the money had all been lost in the stock market if it weren't for the information I got stating otherwise."

"What information?" The rope around her wrists chafed her skin as she wiggled her hands to test the strength of the restraints. Without the GPS, there was a good chance the FBI wouldn't be coming to save her, which meant she was on her own.

Tasha whimpered, tears rolling down her cheeks. With glazed eyes, she silently pleaded for Danielle to stop talking, obviously trying to protect her.

"Sorry, dollface," Rinaldi said, glancing at Tasha. "Not my story to tell."

"You killed my father," she said, keeping him talking to distract him from her attempts at loosening the ropes.

"I did no such thing." He sounded offended. "James Walker was a coward. Rather than face prison, he took his own life and left you to fend for yourself." His hand reached out toward her face. She flinched, prepared to feel its sting. Instead, when he tenderly stroked her cheek, she tamped down the strong urge to bite him. "A beautiful girl like you should be treasured."

The fear whipping through her had nothing on the anger and disgust she harbored for this man. "You got your money. So why didn't you release Tasha? Why am I here?"

He hurdled to his feet, kicking away the chair with a crash. "And deprive myself of your company? No, Danielle." Crouching in front of her, he slid his hands up her thighs. "Since the night in your bedroom, I've been waiting for you. You're aware I'm a sadist, but lately, I haven't found the same pleasure in inflicting pain while at Benediction. Cole's constant monitoring of my activities limits how far I can go and hasn't afforded me the ability to test my newest creations." His eyes were wild, and his pupils shrunk into pinpricks as his fingers pressed into the flesh between her legs. "Did you know you can run electricity through a knife? Double the pain, double the pleasure. By the time I'm done with you, Danielle, you'll beg me to kill you." He licked his lips. "Just like the others."

"No, please," Tasha cried. "Let Danielle go and keep me instead."

Rinaldi jumped up and leaned over Tasha, wrapping his hands around her throat and squeezing. "You misunderstand. I have no intention of letting either of you go. But I've had my fun with you, and I'm ready for a newer model. It's been a pleasure." He laughed. "Well, at least for me. When you see your dead husband in hell, don't forget to tell him I said hello."

He relinquished his grip, leaving a red-faced Tasha gasping for air. "Michael," he shouted.

Skin slick with sweat, Michael ran his hand through his hair as he stepped into the room.

She narrowed her gaze on him, realizing now that although Rinaldi had been the one who'd woken her up from her bed in Arizona, Michael was the one who had threatened her at Benediction. "You broke into my room at Benediction. How did you get in?"

He wiggled his fingers. "Made a copy of your key. Just needed somewhere to hide on your floor. Luckily, Cassandra was more than willing to lend a helping hand with that. Easy in. Easy out. Girl was more trouble than she's worth though." His gaze darted everywhere but on her, as if he was afraid to look her in the eyes.

"Stop talking," Rinaldi said to Michael. "Take Tasha outside, kill her, and throw her in the grave I dug this morning. We wouldn't want anyone to stumble upon her while Danielle and I are enjoying our time together." He winked at Danielle. "We need some privacy, right babe?"

Her throat thickened with terror. "You're crazy."

He tsked and shook his head. "Actually, I'm perfectly sane. That's why I never get caught. That and the powerful people I have in my back pocket." He pounded his chest. "I'm invincible. I can set this cabin on fire and watch you burn without answering to anyone. Some people think taking a life is playing God, but they're wrong. I don't play God." He widened his arms. "I am God."

"Crazy," she repeated, unable to stop herself.

Rinaldi rushed toward her, his face turning purple with rage, and with a crack, her head knocked back into the chair, fire exploding across her cheek from the punch. "That's just a taste of what I'm about to do to you," he shouted. He craned his neck around to Michael. "What are you waiting for? Get the old bitch outside and shoot her in the head."

Tasha cried, swinging her head back and forth. "No. No. No."

The front door crashed open, and a storm of heavy footsteps pounded into the room, bright lights blinding her. "FBI! Drop your weapons, and hands up where I can see them." Through her star-filled vision, she made out several shapes dressed in navy and white.

Her face throbbed as she frantically glanced around searching for Cole. Was he here?

As her eyes adjusted to the lights, she witnessed Agent Miller and another agent cuffing Rinaldi's and Michael's hands behind their backs. "Anthony Rinaldi and Michael Malone, you are under arrest for the kidnapping of Natasha Walker and Danielle Walker. You have the right to remain silent. Anything you say can and will be used against you in a court of law. You have the right to speak to an attorney and to have an attorney present during any questioning. If you cannot afford a lawyer, one will be provided for you at government expense."

"Agent Ryan, it's good to see you again," said Rinaldi calmly. "How's your daughter? Celia, right? I bet she's got to be around sixteen now. As I remember, a beautiful girl like her mother."

The agent swung him around and pushed him against the wall. "Is that a threat?"

"Just making conversation. I don't need to make threats," Rinaldi said, seemingly unperturbed by his arrest.

"Yeah. Apparently he's a god." Danielle inhaled, relieved the FBI had shown when they had. "Michael busted the tracker and the wire. How did you find me here?"

Agent Miller grinned. "You're buddy Logan sewed a tracker and transmitter into your sweater. It activated as soon as the other GPS was destroyed. He called us with your coordinates and patched the feed from it into our system. You did a great job, Danielle. We got enough to help put them both away for a long time, and I have a feeling we'll find the bodies of those missing girls on this property."

"Oh, Miller." Rinaldi sighed dramatically. "You know there's no amount of evidence that could ever keep me behind bars. DeMarco." At the name, Danielle followed Rinaldi's line of sight, and her heart danced from the vision of Cole striding toward her. "Didn't think you'd let her out of your sight for a minute, but to wire her and allow her to get kidnapped? You and your little subbie have some major balls. Enjoy your time together, and I'll see you both when they drop the charges and I not only walk out of jail, but get a big, fat apology from Agents Ryan and Miller."

"Fuck you, Rinaldi," Agent Ryan said, pulling him toward the door. "There's nothing that would ever get me to apologize to a thug like you."

Rinaldi bared his teeth like a wild animal. "We'll see."

"Hey, I'm innocent in all this," Michael protested as another agent led him away. "He made me do it. Took my sister, Lynette. Said he'd give her back if I helped kidnap Danielle." He looked over his shoulder at Rinaldi. "Well, I did it. Now where is she?"

Rinaldi pursed his lips as if he was thinking. "Lynette... Lynette. Oh yes, I remember her." He shook his head. "Nasty heroin addict, if I recall. Poor thing probably OD'd. I bet if you made your way to the county morgue, you'd find her. The morgue is filled with unidentified bodies. At least she died doing what she loved best." He grinned, his face turning into nothing but gleaming white teeth. "Well, second best."

Michael's face paled. "You son of a bitch." He looked at Danielle. "I swear, I never would've hurt you. I was only trying to get you to work faster at getting that bank account information. You have to understand. He has…" Michael hung his head to his chest. "Had my sister. I just wanted to get her back." His eyes burned with rage at Rinaldi. "I don't care if I have to spend the rest of my life behind bars. I'm going to testify and make sure you get what's coming to you."

"Don't worry," Rinaldi said. "You won't have to spend very long in jail. I look out for my people." Danielle shivered at the deadly promise of his words. Rinaldi's gaze narrowed on Cole. "DeMarco, we're not finished."

Cole puffed out his chest as he got into the mobster's face. "I think it's safe to say your membership has been revoked, and if you ever step foot on my property, I'll have you arrested."

Rinaldi smirked. "We'll see, DeMarco."

It was as if the moment Rinaldi stepped out of the cabin, the oxygen in the room was restored, and Danielle could breathe again. Only a minute had passed since the FBI had first arrived, and yet it felt as though it had been a lifetime. A few police officers came through the door along with a team of EMTs.

Her eyes locked with Cole's, and everything else disappeared.

A couple agents kneeled behind her and Tasha and began to cut the ropes.

Cole cupped her face between his hands, inspecting her cheek. "Are you okay? When I realized he'd hit you…"

She didn't care about her face. She just wanted them to get the damned restraints off her so she could return to Cole's arms. "It hurts, but I'll be fine. You gave me a sweater with a GPS tracker sewn inside. Very clever."

He shrugged and smiled. "I told you I have faith in science."

Science had certainly saved her life tonight. She jutted her chin toward her stepmother. "Tasha needs medical attention."

A female EMT crouched by Tasha. "Ma'am, we're going to take you to the hospital and have you checked out. Is there anyone we can call?"

"My son, Roman," Tasha whispered, "but he's in Russia." Tears flowed down Tasha's face as she too gained freedom from the ropes. She turned to Danielle. "It's all over now, darling. We'll go back to Arizona and put this whole disaster behind us."

The rope fell away from Danielle's legs, and she sighed, flexing and pointing her feet. "Did you know about the money?" she asked Tasha.

Tasha winced as the female EMT helped her to her feet. "No, I had no idea. Your father told me were broke. We've been living off his life insurance policy, but it's almost gone now. Roman has been helping with the bills. Maybe it's time to sell the house and move into a small condo."

Danielle tried to stand, the room spinning and the floor tilting under her feet. "I'm going to go with her in the ambulance."

Cole caught her, snaking his arm around her waist. "Tomorrow morning she'll be there," he said to Tasha. "Right now, I want to get her home so she can rest."

Her heart fluttered at his reference to home. Where was her home now?

The danger was over. Once they gave their statements to the FBI and Tasha was released from the hospital, there was nothing to keep her from returning to Arizona.

She rested her cheek against Cole's chest, inhaling the soothing leather scent of his coat, comforted by his warmth. They were living on borrowed time, the clock ticking down to the moment when they'd each have to choose what they couldn't live without.

She only wished she knew what that was.

Chapter Thirty

THE SUNLIGHT STREAMED through the window, stirring Danielle from her sleep. She sighed into the pillow and burrowed in closer to the man behind her, relishing the experience of waking up in his arms.

After they'd given their statements to the FBI, she'd fallen asleep on Cole in the backseat of the car as Adrian drove them home. The next thing she knew, they were in Cole's bed, naked under the covers, limbs entwined as if they were one. She wasn't sure who had turned to who first, but within moments, he'd been inside her, driving her to the brink of ecstasy over and over before finally pushing her off the edge and tumbling down the cliff along with her, his body shuddering and trembling before they both collapsed into a deep slumber.

She'd guess by the sun's position in the sky that it was probably early afternoon. Cole's arms were wrapped around her waist and his leg thrown over hers, his solid chest cradling her back and his erection nudging between the cheeks of her ass. She pushed back, eliciting a groan from him.

She wanted to ignore the reality waiting for them outside his bedroom and spend the day making love here in this room, where they could pretend nothing else existed but the two of them and that reality wasn't ready to tear them apart at their fragile seams.

"Good afternoon," he said, grinding against her backside and tweaking her nipple between his fingers.

After last night, she thought she'd be sated, but her pussy moistened and her clitoris throbbed. "It is now."

He rolled her onto her stomach, his weight pinning her to the bed, and tugged her arms behind her back. Holding her wrists with one hand, he notched his cock to her entrance and pushed inside. She was trapped, unable to move, and there was nowhere she'd rather be. Funny how providing consent to bondage changed the way her mind and body reacted to it.

With shallow pumps, Cole moved his cock in and out of her pussy, the position limiting its depth. She clenched her vaginal muscles as if she could trap him as well. As if she could suck him deeper inside her and keep him there, becoming one, never to be separate again. The slow and steady rocking of their bodies rubbed her clitoris on the sheet, throwing her into a state of fevered desperation, her core tightening as heat built into a blazing inferno, and she toppled into climax, taking him with her, his hot essence dripping down her inner thigh. He lifted his weight off her body, dragging her with him and her in the crook of his arm.

She watched his chest rise and fall with his breaths and traced his tattoo with her fingertip. "What happens now?"

"I was thinking of taking a shower." He kissed her forehead. "Taking *you* in the shower. Lunch followed by a visit to the hospital to check on Tasha. Then—"

"I mean with us." A lump lodged in her throat. "It's all over. Once they release Tasha from the hospital, I can go back to Arizona."

He tipped up her chin, his eyes laced with breathless intensity. "Is that what you want?"

She had nothing for her out there. But what choice did she have? "I can't stay here. This isn't who I am."

A muscle jumped in his cheek. "Maybe it wasn't a week ago, but you can't tell me you don't belong here."

Did she belong anywhere? She felt as though she was caught between two worlds, with one foot in each, belonging to neither. Could she leave Roman and Tasha? "And what would I do?"

"Whatever you wanted. Open your own art gallery. Make your dreams come true. Stay here with me at Benediction."

What were her dreams? Only one came to mind.

Cole.

She searched his eyes, seeing her reflection, and realized she dreamed the impossible. Nothing had changed. His fear of going blind, of losing control, of depending on someone he loved, continued to drive a wedge between them. She accepted his lifestyle. Accepted his need to give back to the community that had saved him when he'd hit rock bottom. But what she couldn't accept was being the only one to make sacrifices.

"I want to say yes, but I want to get married and have kids someday. If I stayed and things worked out between us, would that be something in our future?"

Storm clouds gathered in his eyes, darkening his expression as he braced her face in his palms. "No. I just can't commit to you like that. I love you too much to turn you into my nursemaid, Danielle. I love you more than I thought I could ever love anyone. I don't want you to go, but I can't give you what you want."

He loved her.

And she loved him. Loved him enough to walk away from him, knowing that conceding to his limitations would mean a lifetime of unhappiness for them both. Unable to return his words of love, she blinked back the threatening tears and dug inside herself for strength. "I don't want to go, but I want it all. It wouldn't be enough for me to be one of your slaves. I want marriage. I want your children. It would be different if you couldn't have them, but this is your choice, and I can't stay knowing I don't have all of you."

He flinched. His throat worked over a swallow as he trailed his fingers down her face as if memorizing it. "You have every part of me there is to give. I'm sorry I can't give you more. You deserve more."

She inhaled, sealing the pain deep inside where he couldn't see it. "Yes, I do. And so do you. Will you at least give me a chance tonight to change your mind?"

He nodded. "I'd give you a dozen chances." He reached over to the nightstand and grabbed the silver box. "This was your mother's. Your father wanted me to give it to you."

Her heart ached, and a tear escaped her eye.

"Thank you for keeping it safe." She kissed him lightly on the mouth and tore herself away before she changed her mind and promised to stay forever.

After she dressed, she left Cole's and returned to her room to pack the few things she had brought as well as her mother's box. Before she got ready for the club, she called Tasha, who had been discharged from the hospital and was spending the night at a hotel.

She and Cole had one final night together. One night left to convince the other they were making the wrong choice. Tonight she had a few lessons to teach her voyeuristic lover. She may walk out of his life tomorrow, but she'd hopefully leave him with the idea that there was more to voyeurism than the visual.

Gracie helped Danielle set up everything she needed, then sent word to Cole to meet Danielle in the kitchen.

Wearing a silver beaded corset and matching panties with enough bling to see from outer space, she greeted him as he stepped into the kitchen. "Welcome to the grand opening of Café DeMarco. I'm Danielle, and I'll be your slave for the evening. Please have a seat." His gaze ate her up as he climbed into one of the tall chairs situated at the island. "I've prepared a special feast for you."

"I hope you're part of that feast."

She leaned on him, pressing her breasts into his arm, and whispered in his ear. "If you play your cards right, you can eat me all night long." At his shudder, she pulled away. His breathing quickened, and he made a low rumble deep in his throat.

She nabbed the black scarf she'd left dangling off the other chair and twisted it around both her wrists, stretching the fabric taut. "Tonight, Master, I'd like you to use your other senses. Do you consent?"

Nervously biting her lip, she held her breath. The skin around his eyes and lips crinkled as he weighed the decision of turning over that little bit of power and control to her.

"Yes," he said, his voice raspy. "I consent."

She draped the scarf over his eyes and tied a knot in the back. Her nipples hardened into tight peaks at the sight of him blindfolded, his rosy lips slightly parted and the flutter of his pulse evident in his neck.

Glancing at his lap, she was encouraged by the impressive bulge tenting his pants. The loss of his vision hadn't tampered his arousal. If anything, it had enhanced it.

That was a good sign. Wasn't it?

She snagged the bottle off the marble island, popped the cork, and poured a single glass of wine. "You must be thirsty. I took a tour of your wine cellar. Would you care for a sip?"

His mouth quirked up at the corners. "Yes, I believe I would."

She dipped her index finger into the Bordeaux and painted his lips with it. "Do you recognize the vintage?"

His tongue snaked out and licked a complete circle around his mouth, leaving his rosy lips glistening. "I'll need a little more to ascertain that."

She tipped the wine glass between her lips, allowing it to pool in her mouth before slanting her lips over his to share it. He growled, tangling his fingers in her hair and pushing her head closer, tightening the seal of their mouths. Their tongues glided and danced as he sampled the wine, his dizzying kiss more potent than any alcohol she'd consumed. Panting, they broke apart.

"What did you taste?" she whispered, resting her forehead on his.

He licked his lips. "Black cherry. Vanilla. Plum." He paused and smiled. "You."

Unable to stop herself, she trailed soft kisses down the side of his face before lifting the glass under their noses and swirling the wine around, releasing its essence. "What do you smell?"

"Truffle. A hint of tobacco." He buried his nose in her neck. "You."

She raised the glass to his lips. "Drink." His hand covered hers and together they tilted the glass to his lips. "What does it feel like in your mouth?"

"Soft." His fingers caressed her knee, then brushed the inside of her thigh. "Rich." She trembled as his fingers continued to explore, pushing away the fabric of her panties and sinking into her core with ease and precision. "Silky like the inside of your pussy."

"Can you identify the vintage yet?" she asked on a moan, wondering how he'd turned this game around on her.

"It's a Bordeaux. *Chateau L'Eglise Clinet*?" His thumb worked her clit, pressing and rubbing just enough to heighten her arousal but not enough to shove her over the edge.

She choked down a plea for more. "You're right. You have an excellent palate."

"I agree. And right now, my palate wants you." He tore his fingers from her pussy and sucked them into his mouth, groaning. "There's nothing in this kitchen that could possibly taste any better."

"If you don't behave, I may have to punish you," she said, trying to sound serious.

Apparently she wasn't convincing, because Cole laughed as if she'd told him a joke. "Baby, you'd never make it as a Domme."

"So you'd never let me top you one night? Allow me to tie you up?" As soon as the words left her mouth, she wanted to take them back.

They both knew there would never be another night.

"If it was something that excited you, sure, I'd let you tie me up," he said calmly. "I might even let you think you're topping me, but in truth, I'd still be dominating you. Right now, you've got me blindfolded. Do you feel as though you're the one in control?"

"No." She laid a hand on his cheek. "I can't explain it, but when I'm with you, I don't want to be in control. I know I'm safe to let go and trust you to take care of me. I answer to no one else but you. But right now, this is about showing you there's more to sex than sight. Please let me continue, Master."

"Of course. Besides, I'm curious what else you have for me to taste."

"Nothing but the best for you." She cupped a crostini with caviar in her hand and held it under his nose. "What do you smell?"

He inhaled. "The ocean. It's caviar."

"Very good." She rubbed it up against his lips. "Now take a bite and describe the taste to me."

He sampled the appetizer and chewed. "A bit salty like the sea."

She poured the fizzy liquid from the other bottle into a glass and brought it to his mouth. "Now take a sip of this."

His hand wrapped around the glass and sampled the bubbly liquid. "Champagne. The good stuff. I'd recognize *Dom Perignon* anywhere."

She unwrapped a square of chocolate and waved it under his nose. "Can you smell this?" She slipped it onto her tongue and sealed her mouth with his, letting the creamy chocolate melt from the heat of their kiss.

He hooked his arm around her waist and tugged her into his side. "I know what you're trying to impart to me. That when I go blind, I'll still find pleasure through my other senses. And you're right." He slid his hand up the inside of her trembling thigh and delved his fingers between her swollen folds, thrusting them inside her. "There's nothing I enjoy more than the slick, hot feel of your tight pussy. Or the wet sucking sound of it as I move my fingers or my cock inside it." She whimpered when he brought his drenched fingers to his nose and inhaled. "The sweet scent of your arousal." On a moan, his tongue laved a path down one finger and up the other. "The spicy, addictive taste of you. Nothing more I enjoy…" He ripped off his blindfold, his brown eyes somber. "Except the sight of you."

Chapter Thirty-One

"ARE YOU READY for my surprise?" Cole asked as he took her hand. At her nod, Cole led her out of the kitchen and up the staircase to the fantasy rooms.

Danielle choked down her disappointment. What had she expected? That Cole would instantly change his mind and fall to his knees with a marriage proposal? He'd made his choice not to marry years ago. It would take more than a few minutes for him to process that he could still experience sexual fulfillment without his sight.

When they got to the top of the stairs, Cole opened a door and guided her into a hallway with a window on the left side that gave them a view of a trio of women making love on a bed. Chairs for viewing were set up along the wall on their right. At the end of the hall, they came to another door, and going through it, she looked into this window, observing a man dressed up as a vampire fucking the ass of a man dressed as a werewolf. Continuing into the next hallway, they stopped in front of a room that had the shades drawn.

Cole pushed open the door, and she stepped inside. The room was like something out of a historical romance. Candles flickered, and the smell of incense filled in the air. Square pillows made from foreign fabrics in royal purple and gold covered the floor. Netting hung down from the ceiling like a ceremonial veil. The room looked endless, and that's when she realized the walls were lined with mirrors.

Cole swept his fingers down the length of her neck and across her collarbone. "I want to make love to you here. I want you to see every facet of me so you know there's not a part of me that doesn't love every part of you. I didn't used to believe in love at first sight, but it was as if something inside me woke up when I caught you looking at me from the stairs of your house. I hadn't known what to call it back then, but now I think it was love—or at least the realization I would love you one day."

A warmth filled her chest. He'd felt the same connection as she had all those years ago. He loved her, and she loved him. Why couldn't that be enough for her?

She ventured farther into the room and caressed the gauzy netting. "I would have thought a mirror room would look more like one of those rooms in a funhouse, but this…I've never seen anything more beautiful."

He moved in behind her, surrounding her with his heat, his steely erection prodding her backside. "I have. Every time I look at you."

She glanced over at the covered window. "I'm frightened."

"Of what?" He captured her chin between his thumb and finger and tipped up her head, stealing her ability to look away. "Of me?"

A shiver ran down the length of her spine, hardening her nipples. "Of how much I want this." She'd bared herself in front of the members when Adrian and Logan had tied her up, but that time, she'd been blindfolded.

Cole and Danielle breathed in sync, as if they were one, their chests rising and falling together.

"What is your safe word?" he whispered in her ear, his dark and delicious voice sending tingles straight to her clitoris.

She turned in his arms. "Red, Master."

He hissed through his teeth, and his pupils dilated, his body jerking as if the word *Master* had taken physical form. "When the music begins, you will strip. Slowly. Seductively. Dance and move your body as though a thousand hands are touching you." He jutted his chin toward the window. "Tease those men and women out there with what they cannot have. What they cannot touch. Show them how drenched your pussy gets knowing they can see you. And when the moment is right, your Master will fuck you so hard and so good, they'll hear your screaming in the dungeon."

Her vaginal muscles clenched, and arousal spread to her outer folds, her pussy preparing to be filled. She felt weightless, as if she was floating a foot off the floor, and her body buzzed with need from the awareness of those who waited behind the covered window. She couldn't see them yet, but she sensed their anticipation like a beacon in the sky on a starless night.

"Will you do something for me? Wear the blindfold as I dance. Imagine me dancing for you. My hands on my breasts. My pussy drenched with my arousal. Can you do that for me? Please?"

"Yes. As long as you include some vocals for me. We'll hear you in the hall through an audio feed." Cole seized her lips, staking his ownership of her. Without warning, he tore himself away and strode out of the room, leaving her panting and desperate for release.

The door closed, and the window blinds began to rise, giving her glimpses of the crowd that had gathered in the hallway. They were shadows, outlines of people without defining characteristics—only eyes—while she was in the spotlight, no longer hiding her true self.

Soft music began to play, a familiar song about sex and desire. The rush of her pulse roared so loudly in her ears that she could barely distinguish the beat of the music from her own heart.

She moaned and sighed as she ran her hands down her sides and swiveled her hips in a seductive imitation of sex. Heat built in her pussy as she caught the flames of desire in her audience's eyes. She dragged her corset down until it lay on the floor, baring her breasts to the eager voyeurs. Cole's words played in her head, a whisper of instructions she had no choice but to obey. She pinched her nipples and massaged her generous breasts, and it was as if there were a dozen other hands on them in addition to her own.

Five minutes. Ten minutes. There was no measure of time.

Her body was on fire.

She dipped her hands into her panties and rubbed her finger over her clitoris. "Oh, Master. My pussy is soaking wet, and my clit is swollen. It feels so good to touch it, but my fingers aren't enough."

The crowd wanted more. They wanted to see. So she tugged the drenched fabric down her legs and gave it to them.

Power swept through her, emboldening her, and it was being fed by the slack-jawed response of her audience at her naked body. Her legs trembled, and she wobbled on her Prada heels.

She lowered herself to the floor and crawled to the center of the room, catching sight of herself in the mirrors all around her. Her breasts hung heavy, and the muscles in her ass flexed as she moved on her hands and knees.

What did they see when they looked at her?

She settled on the pillows and spread her thighs wide, her greedy fingers instantly going between her legs. Her eyes sought Cole. "I've pushed three of my fingers inside my pussy, and I'm stroking the pearl of my clit with my thumb while my other hand is pinching my nipple hard, just the way I like it. I'm fucking myself, Master, but it's not enough. I need your cock."

New sounds entered the room, quiet moans and smacking noises, telling her she wasn't the only one masturbating. Cole had turned on the audio so she could hear the observers out in the hall. Now the exhibitionist was also the voyeur, both roles feeding off each other and driving her arousal even higher.

But only one person really mattered. Was her dirty talk arousing him? Could he visualize what she was doing to herself? Was he touching himself right now?

Her muscles tightened and her body shook, the fire in her core burning out of control. "I'm coming, Master. I'm coming." Heat gathered in her pussy, burning hotter and hotter until she exploded and the heat rushed through her, leaving no part untouched.

A door slammed, footsteps stomped across the floor, and then Cole was there, the blindfold in his hands. He stood over her, ripping off his clothes.

Naked before her and those who remained in the hallway, he motioned to the mirrors. "I get it. I didn't need to see you to visualize what you looked like as you fucked yourself to an orgasm. Lesson learned. But now I want you to watch me claim you."

"No." She got to her knees, leveling her mouth with his cock. "First I want you to watch me claim *you*."

He jolted as her tongue swirled around the head of his cock, exploring the sensitive underside. She licked her way down to his heavy testicles, then back up to the tip, where a drop of pre-come awaited her. Squeezing and jacking him with a firm grip, she lapped up the tangy essence before sucking the head of his cock into her mouth.

When he groaned and pushed his cock deeper into her mouth, she took it as a sign she was doing something right. He cupped the back of her head, his fingers winding into her hair, but he didn't force himself any further or control her speed.

The taste of him, a mix of salt and musk, drove her wild. Made her pussy ache for him. A buoyancy filled her at the idea of pleasing him. Making him insane with pleasure and making him come.

His hand tightened on her head, and suddenly he wrenched away.

"Did I do something wrong?" she asked.

"If you had kept up much longer, I would've come in your mouth."

She smiled. "That was the general idea of me giving you a blow job."

His hands went to her shoulders, his fingers possessively digging into her flesh. "I want my cock inside your pussy. I want to feel your heat. Your wet, velvety flesh as I drive myself in you over and over again. I want to feel you ripple around me as you climax."

He moved behind her and kneeled on the pillows, facing her toward the audience. She looked at the mirrors.

Six Coles wrapped their dark tattooed arms around the pale skin of her middle.

Six Coles notched their cocks to Danielle's slippery entrance and sank their rigid lengths into her.

Six Coles arched their necks and palmed her breast. "Fuck. Never felt so good."

Each Cole commanded her body as if it belonged to him, dominance and control in every thrust.

He pulled at her nipples until she tore her gaze from the mirrors and cried out his name. "Every time I think it can't get better, it does. You undo me, Danielle."

Her thighs burned, and sweat trickled between her breasts. Hunger showed on each of the voyeur's faces, moans and sobs spilling from their lips. Hunger for her. Hunger for release. Cole swept his hand to her clitoris, and she watched as his nimble fingers worked her. An electric current shot down her spine, zinging to her fingers and her toes. It was too much, the mirrors and the candles and the eyes dizzying, overpowering her ability to believe she was anything less than beautiful.

"I'm going to come," she said breathlessly, unsure whether she was supposed to ask for permission.

He bit her neck in response, and the pleasurable pain of it sent her careening into a full-body climax, her muscles turning liquid and hot as her core pulsed and throbbed. Seconds later, Cole joined her, his own body still except for the twitch of his cock as it released inside of her.

She didn't know how, but as if right on cue, the blinds lowered over the window and the audio feed quieted, so that the only sound in the room was their panting. They collapsed onto the pillows, and he kissed her tenderly, leisurely, as if they had all the time in the world.

But time was not on their side.

He pulled back, that knowledge mirrored in his eyes. Tomorrow morning, she'd be on a plane back to Arizona.

Cole planted a trail of kisses down her spine, and she felt herself responding, her body softening and moistening as if it hadn't just climaxed. She peered over her shoulder, viewing the erotic sight of it in the mirrors, and she sighed.

She loved the strong, confident man Cole was, but she was greedy. It wasn't enough that he loved every part of her. Until he could accept all the parts of himself, he'd never truly belong to her.

And she wouldn't settle for anything less.

He didn't have to say it.

Tonight had changed nothing.

Here in this room, they'd made love one final time.

This night was their good-bye.

Chapter Thirty-Two

Two Months Later

DANIELLE STARED OUT her bedroom window at the surrounding mountains and desert landscape, wondering how she'd ever thought she could have a different life.

Two months had gone by without a single word from Cole. He'd not only let her leave Michigan, he'd provided her and Tasha with his private jet to take them back to Arizona. Up until the plane had lifted off into the air, she'd held some hope he would change his mind and beg her to stay in Michigan with him.

The minute the plane touched down in Phoenix, she'd started to cry. After receiving word about his mother's kidnapping, Roman had flown back from Russia. He'd been Danielle's rock, listening to her vent and holding her when she cried. It would have made it so much easier if she'd been angry at Cole or hated him, but she didn't. She couldn't.

Unsurprisingly, she had lost her job at the art museum. Barely sleeping, she found herself having trouble getting out of bed in the morning. Her appetite diminished, and she started losing weight without trying. When she did eat, she'd sometimes get sick right after. For weeks she'd thought her symptoms would improve once she adjusted to life without Cole.

If only it had been that simple.

After closing the shades, she dropped back into bed and drew the covers over her, her gaze falling on the original Degas paintings on the wall. They'd arrived a week after she'd moved back to Arizona, delivered by special courier. No note.

She'd started to drift off when a knock fell on her door. It creaked open. "Can I come in?"

Roman.

She wiped her eyes and sat up, resting her back against the headboard. "Of course."

He settled beside her, stretching his legs out and sliding his arm around her back. "I'm worried about you. Since you came back from Michigan, you haven't been yourself."

She played with a thread of her blanket, her chest tight with tension. "What do you mean? I'm doing what I always did. I read. Lay by the pool. Rinse and repeat."

"I'm talking about the fact that you barely eat anything. You have no energy. And you never smile." His expression grew serious. "I think maybe you should see a doctor. You went through a traumatic event. It's normal to suffer some effects after something so scary. Not to mention, you're nursing a broken heart. It's natural for the physical body to show symptoms of depression."

She sighed. Of course Roman had noticed. "You want me to see a psychiatrist?"

"It wouldn't hurt. He could prescribe some medication—"

"I don't need an antidepressant, Roman." She looked up at him. "I'm pregnant."

His jaw dropped. "What?"

That had been her reaction to the doctor's diagnosis too. She'd chalked up her symptoms to her broken heart until one day she came across her unused pack of birth control pills and remembered she had missed a few while in Michigan. Two store-bought pregnancy tests and a doctor's appointment later, she finally accepted the truth. "Ten weeks. My gynecologist said the fatigue and nausea should pass in a couple more weeks."

"Is it DeMarco's? Or someone—"

"It's Cole's. There's no other possibility." She hadn't gone into details with Roman about her time at Benediction because talking about it, thinking about it, was too painful for her. At least now she knew there was more at work than simply a broken heart. The hormones had wreaked major havoc on her emotions as well.

"Have you told him?" Roman stood, his jaw set in anger. "If he thinks he can just turn his back—"

"No. He doesn't know." She kicked off the blankets. "And he wouldn't turn his back on me or the baby, but it's also not what he wanted. I won't go into the reasons, but the subject did come up, and he doesn't want a wife or children."

Roman paused and ran his fingers through his thick blond hair, seemingly at a loss for words. After a moment, he grew somber. "You're going to keep it from him?"

She'd briefly considered it, but it didn't take more than a moment to decide she would never keep the truth from Cole or lie to him again. He deserved the chance to know his child. "Of course not. I wouldn't do that. I'm just trying to figure out the best way to handle it. I don't want to be his obligation. He's a good man, and he loves me." She hung her head and blinked back the tears. "He'll do what's right, and in his view, that means marriage. But I'll always know he preferred a life without me or the baby over a life with us."

"You can't know that," Roman said softly.

"Yeah? Where is he?" She looked up at her stepbrother. "I've been home for weeks now."

He got up from the bed and stuck his hand in the pocket of his jeans. "Gracie says he's miserable."

"You've been talking to Gracie?"

"More like Gracie's been talking to me," he said, reminding her of Gracie's chatterbox nature. "She was worried about you because you sounded so depressed on the phone. So she's been calling me. Daily. Apparently Cole isn't doing well either. She said he hasn't been the same since you left."

The thought of Cole suffering didn't give her any satisfaction. "Then maybe he should do something about it rather than allow his fears to rule his life." She sprung to her feet. "You're not going to say anything to Gracie about my pregnancy, are you? Promise me you won't tell her."

Roman pulled her into a hug. "I promise, but only because it's not my place to tell. Anyway, congratulations." He nudged her under the chin. "With or without DeMarco, I think you're going to make a terrific mother."

"Thanks, Roman." She gave him a kiss on his cheek. "So you and Gracie?"

Smiling, he stepped back with his hands up in front of him. "She's just a friend. But actually, the reason I came to your room was because she called with some news this morning you should know." The smile slid from his face. "Michael Malone is dead."

She covered her stomach, thinking about the child growing within her. Rinaldi had sworn that Michael would pay for testifying against him. "Was he murdered?"

He slowly shook his head. "Not officially. Officially he died of an allergic reaction to penicillin for the treatment of a sinus infection. His parents swear the allergy information should've been in the system and that Michael never would've taken it, but there was nothing in his records about the allergy."

Biting her nails, she nervously paced the room. "Rinaldi did it. He's got someone on the inside. Killed from an allergic reaction, just like my father. He said he'd walk. Jesus. If he had someone inside the prison change Michael's records, he's invincible. No wonder the man thinks he's God." She stopped and took a breath. "Does Cole know?"

He went to her and rubbed her arms. "He does."

"And he's still not here." The excruciating truth knocked her for a loop. Even when she'd thought she'd convinced herself he wasn't coming for her, a part of her had held onto a tiny shred of hope he'd change his mind. That he loved her enough to fight his fear. Baby or not, they were truly over. "Out of sight, out of mind, right? What if Rinaldi comes after me next?"

He tucked her hair behind her ear. "Gracie doesn't think that will happen. But just in case, I've arranged for a bodyguard to stay here. He should be here in a couple of hours."

She pushed his chest. "You did that without asking me first?"

"Is this some emotional pregnancy thing?" He scratched his head. "Because one second you're worried Rinaldi will come after you, and the next you're mad at me for protecting you. You're not going to send me out for pickles and ice cream, are you?"

Annoyed, she growled. Why did men always have to blame the hormones? Wasn't it possible to go from sad to scared to angry in only a couple of minutes because the situation warranted it? "It's not pregnancy. I don't want some stranger here. I mean, where did you find him? Did you open up the yellow pages and look up bodyguards?"

"Give me a little credit. It's someone I know. I wouldn't trust some random stranger with you."

Why hadn't he said that to begin with? "Oh. Okay then. And no, I'm not going to send you for pickles and ice cream. That's disgusting." Besides, she wouldn't limit herself to sweet and sour when there were so many other available flavors. Her mouth watered. "But I would kill for some Wynters Confectionary jelly beans."

He gave her a grin reminding her why they'd been such good friends all these years. "I'll make you a deal. I'll go out and get you the jelly beans if you promise to keep an open mind when you finally do talk to DeMarco. Because the man you've told me about—the man you fell in love with—would do anything to keep you safe, even if it cost him everything. If you're honest with yourself, you'd know that."

Her eyes burned as she held back the tears. She wished she could believe that. "I promise. Now go get me my candy, and if you're lucky, I'll share them with you."

He ruffled her hair. "You're my best friend, Danielle. I'm glad my marriage proposal didn't mess that up."

"Nothing ever would." She squeezed his shoulder. "But Roman, why did you propose?"

"My mom put it in my head that because you and I were already such good friends, we'd also work romantically."

"Tasha said that?" Her stepmother probably worried if she didn't marry Roman, she'd spend the rest of her life living with her. She patted her belly. "I'm sure once she learns about the baby, she'll forget all about the idea."

"I think she forgot the idea about ten seconds after she spoke it out loud to me." He laughed as he walked out Danielle's bedroom door, but she knew a lifetime of his mother's indifference still hurt him. It hadn't taken Tasha long after her kidnapping to forget all about her ordeal and go back to raising money for her charities.

She wiped her eyes, a ball of sorrow, anxiety, and resentment lodged in her throat.

How would she tell Cole he was going to be a father in less than eight months? She couldn't imagine picking up the phone or sending a letter. It had to be done in person. She supposed she could wait until her belly was round with his child and waddle into Benediction. Then she wouldn't need to say a word. But it wouldn't be right to wait that long. He deserved to know now. Their lives would forever be connected through their baby. But as much as she wanted Cole in her life, she didn't want him by default. She wanted him to choose her and their child. Otherwise, he'd never completely belong to them.

She wandered aimlessly around her room, dragging her fingers across her dresser, stopping at her mother's silver box. "Mom, I wish you were here to tell me what to do." She picked it up and sat on the edge of the bed, holding it in her hands as if it would give her the answers through osmosis.

Sighing, she raised the lid. She pressed her palm to her belly again. Someday, she'd give this box to her daughter. She knew in her gut she was carrying a girl. There was nothing she wouldn't do to keep her safe, even if it meant having a stranger guarding her twenty-four/seven.

The box slid off her lap onto the carpet. When she picked it up, she noticed the fabric lining on the inside bottom had shifted, and it looked like there was something below it. She dug her fingers underneath and felt a rectangular-shaped object. She pulled it out and laid it flat in her hand.

A flash drive.

It was longer than the ones presently sold.

Her mother had died before flash drives were invented. Had this belonged to her father? Had he hidden this in the box for Danielle to find?

A sense of unease banded around her chest, constricting her lungs. She held the flash drive as if it was a deadly snake ready to strike if she made a sudden move. She didn't want to know what was on this harmless piece of plastic, because she knew whatever it was had gotten her father killed and set the wheels into motion that had resulted in Tasha's kidnapping.

She and her baby were in danger.

She had to find out what was on this drive. She needed a computer.

For a moment, she hesitated and considered waiting for Roman to return, unnerved by the idea of doing this alone. But she couldn't wait. She had to know the truth. With the drive in her hand, she raced to the den down the hall, where she and Tasha shared a computer.

The house was quiet except for the sound of her bare feet brushing along the carpet. She entered the den and, sitting down at the desk, woke the computer from its hibernation.

She stuck the flash drive into the USB port and clicked on the drive to open the files.

She held her breath, her heart speeding like a freight train, and waited. One file titled "Important" and dated from eight years ago popped up on the screen, and she opened it.

It was gibberish, a bunch of odd-looking symbols, letters, and numbers filling the computer screen. She studied it, wracking her brain for some way to decipher it. Was it a corrupted file? Or was she missing something?

"Danielle? What do you have there?"

She jumped, startled by Tasha's voice coming from behind her. She whipped her head around to see her stepmother standing in the doorway, her perfectly groomed eyebrows furrowed as she squinted at the screen.

Should she lie? She didn't want to involve her, but as she'd learned from before, not having all the information put them both at risk. "My father left it for me. It's a list of some kind."

Tasha hummed in her throat and moved into the room. "What language is that?"

"I'm not sure." She frowned. Some of the letters looked like the modern-day Roman alphabet. Was it a code? All the numbers were backward. "Wait. I have an idea. Leonardo Da Vinci used mirror writing in his notebooks. He wrote from right to left."

Tasha stood right behind her now. "But some of those figures don't look anything like English letters."

"They're not." She typed in a search into her web browser, brought up a couple samples of foreign alphabets, and compared them to the file. There were similarities to a few Eastern European languages, but only one stood out to her. "I think...maybe they're Russian."

"Russian. Why would your father leave you a document of Russian written backward? No one could read it."

"No, not at first glance." Nervous excitement shot through her. She quickly found a program on the Internet which would reverse the text for them. Then she copied and pasted a section of the list into the site. The symbols morphed before her eyes. She highlighted the text once again and plugged it into an online Russian-to-English translation program.

The list was converted into what appeared to be names, dates, and locations along with notes about drugs, murder, and human trafficking. "It's a list of crimes. My father was working for the Russian mafia. That's who Rinaldi convinced to invest with my father. I don't think Rinaldi was working alone." She peered up at Tasha, who had paled from a golden tan to a snowy white. "I think your kidnapping was about more than the money. They were probably looking for this. We need to call the FBI."

Tasha nodded. "I'll do it."

As Tasha left the room to make the call, Danielle swerved back around to read more. Wanting to protect the information in case something happened to her, she sent the file in an email to Cole.

She caught a flash of black from the corner of her eye, and at the same moment, excruciating pain exploded at her temple. She tumbled off the chair and onto the floor, her hands folded over her abdomen to protect her child.

Tasha stood over her with a gun.

Pointed it at her head.

Then blackness.

Chapter Thirty-Three

THE HARSH SCENT of acetone invaded Danielle's nose, rousing her from unconsciousness. Her head bobbled as if she couldn't control her muscles, and a searing pain shot through her skull. A warm, sticky wetness dripped down her cheek. She tried to remember what had happened, but she felt as if she was hitting a brick wall and the memories were on the other side of it. Was she in a nail salon? Had she been in an accident?

Nausea choked her.

Her baby. Was her baby okay?

Frantic, she opened her eyes to slits and fought against the pitching of the room. Her stepmother was splashing nail polish remover on the window drapes.

"Tasha?" she asked, her voice cracking.

"Sleep well, my darling?"

She swallowed and wiggled her body, awareness of the dire situation sinking in. "What's going on? Why am I tied to a chair? *Again*?"

Tasha turned to her and slammed the plastic bottle of acetone down on the desk. "I thought you enjoyed being bound. When you whored yourself for DeMarco, I'm sure you allowed him to use his filthy ropes and chains on you."

This didn't make any sense. Tasha couldn't be involved. She'd been married to Danielle's father. Danielle had lived in the same house as her for ten years. They were family.

"I didn't whore myself," Danielle snapped. "I was there to save you."

"Were you?" With a hand on her hip, Tasha arched a brow. "You didn't enjoy yourself and have sex with your crush, Cole DeMarco?"

"Why are you talking like that? Is Rinaldi behind this?"

Tasha folded her hands over her heart. "I think it's adorable you're so worried about him when the person who should scare you is standing right in front of you."

"But your finger…"

She wiggled her remaining digits. "Rinaldi was actually squeamish, if you can believe it. For days while we stayed in that cabin, he tortured Michael's sister yet he balked at cutting off my finger. I told him it would get you working quicker to find the account information. Losing a finger was a small sacrifice to make for my cause. At first, I worried how the society women would view it. They can be so catty. But then I realized it would be a great opportunity to start yet another charity I can use to fund my real cause." Before Danielle's eyes, the woman she'd known disappeared, leaving a monster in her place. "These women are such idiots. All they do is spend their husbands' money and donate to fake charities just so they can feel good about themselves. America is truly the land of opportunity for people like me."

She shook her head, the pain of it making her stomach rebel. "I'm confused. You are one of those women."

"Really?" Tasha snagged a red pillar candle from the top of the desk. "How many of them could stage their own kidnapping and get away with it? How many of them could manipulate a man like Rinaldi into doing her bidding?"

Fear for her life and her baby's life swept through her. "You didn't stage it. You couldn't. It was Rinaldi. He took you." As she witnessed the look of pride on Tasha's face, understanding struck her like a lightning bolt. "You were partners?"

She fluffed her layered blonde hair. "Partners implies we had an equal amount of power in the relationship. He worked for me." Her jaw tightened. "Well, 'worked' makes it sound as though he had a choice. He owed me and my friends a great deal of money. Cole DeMarco convinced Rinaldi to invest, and Rinaldi convinced us. Even a sadistic psychopath like Rinaldi can be blackmailed with the people he loves. In return for his cooperation, we let his wife and children live."

"But he ordered Michael to shoot you."

Tasha sighed and shook her head as if pitying Danielle for her stupidity. "All part of the plan. Michael would have roughed me up a little before letting me go. I would've told the police I escaped, but couldn't save you. And, of course, I couldn't identify the man who kidnapped me because he kept me blindfolded."

Although she'd heard some of this from Cole and Rinaldi, there were missing pieces to the story. "Why did you marry my father?"

Tasha's eyes narrowed. "To keep him in line. Contrary to what you've always believed, your father was no saint. His hands were as dirty as the rest of ours. He could handle the money laundering, but when he learned about where that money came from, he got nervous, not only for his future but for yours."

Using a match, she lit the candle and held it in her hands. "By then, I had married him and become his confidante. He told me was going to turn over the evidence he had on the Mikhailov *Bratva*, which, unbeknownst to him, was my family. I convinced him instead to put the money in an offshore account with me as the trustee and beneficiary. No one could touch it. We'd move away and take you kids with us. I don't know why, but instead he gave the evidence of his Ponzi scheme over to Cole to give to the FBI. To protect you from the families, the official statement was Cole had discovered the embezzlement and mismanagement of the funds and that your father burned all his records of the Rinaldi and Mikhailov accounts. Then he left the trust to you."

Tasha's story made Danielle ill. How had she lived with this woman all these years and not known her true nature?

"And if he had run off with you and the money?"

Tasha rolled her eyes. "After I had control of the money, you and he would have met an untimely demise."

She thought when she'd left Benediction, she'd returned to reality, but in truth, her entire life had been an illusion. Her only hope was if Cole sent for help when he received her email. *If* he received her email. Unless…

"Is Roman working for you?"

Tasha's expression grew stony. "No, he knows nothing, and I plan to keep it that way. Before he left, I made sure to send him on a few errands to keep him busy for the next couple of hours." She sighed and shook her head. "If you would've only married him, it would have made things so much easier. Once you rejected him, I had to initiate plan B."

"And if I had married him?"

The flames of the candle flickered in Tasha's eyes. "You would've died in an accident, leaving my son a widower. A wealthy one who shared everything with his mother, including his bank account." She set down the candle and waved her finger at Danielle. "But no, my Roman wasn't good enough for you. You had the silly infatuation with Cole DeMarco that I helped fan into an obsession. You blamed him for your father's death when his real killer held you as you cried."

Odd that Tasha saw herself in the role of consoler when she'd barely managed as much as a hug over the years. If anyone had held her, it had been Roman. "My father would never have left me with you if he thought I was in danger."

Tasha's lips curled into a cruel smile. "Oh, but he did. No, he didn't realize I was the one pulling the strings. I got a message to him through an associate of mine. It was either him or you. He thought by killing himself he'd keep you safe. And to a point, that was true. I had to wait until you either married or turned twenty-five before the trustee of the money could turn over the assets to you. I couldn't even find out where he'd set up the account. All I knew was he had told DeMarco to keep the information in your mother's jewelry box for you and that the password was engraved on your locket. Rinaldi and Michael both tried to get into DeMarco's private residence, but of course, they failed. That's when I thought about sending you."

Danielle tracked the candle's smoke as it snaked a path across the room to the window. Her pulse flew into overdrive, her brain finally making the connection between the acetone and the flame. Tasha wasn't going to let her out of this house alive. A gun sat on the edge of the desk, blood on the handle.

That was the sticky substance on the side of her face. If she could wriggle one of her hands out of the rope, she might be able to reach the gun. She had to keep Tasha talking. "But even if I hadn't shown up at Benediction, wouldn't Cole have released the money to me since I'd turned twenty-five?"

"I couldn't take the chance he'd hold onto it. All I knew from your father were the conditions of release. That trust kept you safe because if you died, the money was to go to charity."

She twisted her wrists back and forth, trying to break free. "So you had yourself kidnapped and blackmailed me into finding the account. Why were you so sure I'd get into the room where he kept it? How did you even know about it?"

Tasha picked up the gun and cradled it in her palm like a fragile bird. "Rinaldi had kept tabs on him for years, and I'm guessing it worked both ways. DeMarco knew Rinaldi had something to do with your father's death, but he couldn't prove anything. Over the years, DeMarco would drop little hints, as if daring Rinaldi to make his move." She ran the barrel of the gun down the side of Danielle's face. "We knew he'd do anything and everything to protect you. He was as obsessed with you as you were with him. You walking into Benediction was like handing him his fantasy on a silver platter." She sighed wistfully. "I was going to allow you to live, but unfortunately, you stumbled on a very important list. A list that in the wrong hands would shut down my organization." With the gun in one hand, she raised the candle in the other and neared the drapes. "So I'm sorry to tell you this dear, but your world is about to go up in flames."

Danielle yanked at the ropes, tears streaming down her cheeks. She couldn't die. "Don't do this. I promise I won't tell anyone, and you can destroy the flash drive. Just please don't kill me."

"Mother?" Roman strode into the room carrying a plastic shopping bag. Shock registered on his face as he took in the scene. "What's going on here? Why do you have Danielle bound to a chair?"

"Roman," Tasha whispered, her eyes wide. "You weren't supposed to come home yet. The errands I sent you on should've kept you out of the house until this afternoon."

His eyes narrowed on his mother. "I'd promised Danielle I'd bring her jelly beans. I was going to drop them off to her before I started on that ridiculous list of errands you made for me. But I don't need to explain my actions." He dropped the shopping bag to the carpet and shook his hands in front of him. "You're the one who is standing there with a gun."

"Roman, your mother was working with Rinaldi," Danielle said, using the distraction of his arrival to work harder on the bindings. "She's been behind everything from the beginning."

Tasha's eyes flashed with anger before she schooled her face into that of concerned mother. "Dear, she's lost her poor mind. You've seen how depressed she's been lately. She attacked me and pulled this gun out, and I was able to overpower her and tie her to the chair. I was just about to call the police."

Danielle had to convince Roman she was telling the truth. He was the only one who could save her and the baby. "That's not true. She told me she wanted us to marry because then you'd inherit the money when I died in an accident. She's part of the Russian mafia."

Roman's expression hardened. "You told me we left that life behind when we left Russia."

Tasha's innocent mask melted away, revealing the dangerously angry woman underneath. "Oh, please. Where do you think all your business in Moscow came from?" She paused. "My brothers." At Roman's shake of his head, she sneered. "Yes, Roman. Part of you knows it's the truth. Part of you has always known. It's time for you to choose between the family who loves you and this whore."

Roman gave Danielle a sad smile before turning his attention to his mother. "Danielle is not a whore. She's my family. Not you."

He rushed toward Tasha. A boom reverberated against the walls, and Roman's eyes widened as crimson stained his shirt. Then there was another boom, this one muffled as if Danielle was underwater, and Roman crumbled to the floor, his blood flowing and flowing and flowing.

Danielle screamed, the sound of it foreign to her ringing ears, as if it was coming from someone else. "Roman! Oh my God. You killed him. You killed your own son."

Tasha didn't shed a single tear. "He made his decision," she said coldly. "He's no longer my son."

Roman lay lifeless on the floor, his blood pooling on the carpet. How could a mother destroy her own child?

Danielle's body shook violently. A sharp spasm wracked her lower abdomen, stealing her breath, and she tried to curl into herself, wrenching against the restraints.

Was she losing her baby?

Tasha was speaking, but Danielle couldn't understand her, and it took a moment to realize her stepmother was speaking in her native Russian tongue. Danielle was helpless as she watched the woman she'd once called family lift the candle to the curtain and the fabric go up in flames. Billows of smoke instantly filled the room as the fire roared to an inferno of blazing heat. She coughed, her lungs burning as hot as the drapes, and another cramp squeezed her belly.

Her life couldn't end this way.

She'd never gotten the chance to tell Cole about the baby. When he learned about her death and that of their unborn child, would he mourn them? Would he blame himself for not protecting them? She didn't blame him. Not one bit. She should've stayed in Michigan, fought harder for their love, rather than give up on him and retreat into a shell like a turtle. She'd allowed life to pass her by when she should've held onto it as tightly as she could with both hands. She was a coward. Too afraid of rejection that she hadn't even taken a chance. She'd thought her old life would keep her safe, but instead it would kill her.

A child's face flashed before her eyes. A little girl with skin the color of café au lait and a gap-toothed grin that lit up her face. Her daughter laughed as her daddy sent them careening down the hill in their sled, her braids peeking out from under her pink snow hat.

Her child.

Cole's child.

Another contraction wrapped around her middle. Danielle cried out, the pain of it almost unbearable, and tears streamed down her face.

Tasha pointed the gun at her.

Danielle's laugh, nothing like her unborn child's musical one, mixed with her coughs. At least she wouldn't burn to death.

She squeezed her eyes shut, preparing for the shot. In her mind, she pictured Cole. His image was so vivid, she could almost smell him beneath the smoke. Hear his voice through the rumble of the flames. He was talking to her. Telling her to hold on. That he'd get her out.

Tasha screamed.

Danielle opened her eyes.

And Cole was there, fighting with Tasha for the gun. His fist plowed into Tasha's face, and the gun fired, its bang drowned out by the thunder of the blaze engulfing the curtains. Tasha flailed backward, the bullet's force knocking her into the fire, and she dropped to the floor, the flames licking at her skin.

May she rot in hell.

Danielle opened her mouth to call to Cole, to tell him she loved him, to tell him about their child, but she could only cough, the smoke suffocating her. Spasms rocked her abdomen, one after the other. A heavy weight crushed her chest, and her throat constricted. Despite the bright flames, the room dimmed, swirling like a merry-go-round.

Suddenly, she was shrouded in warmth and floating as if weightless. The acrid air disappeared, and she sucked in a breath.

Her eyes opened to a soot-covered Cole looking down at her, the sun at his back. "Cole," she said hoarsely. "Am I dead?"

He cradled her face in his hands. "No, baby. I'm really here. Everything's going to be fine. The ambulance is on its way."

She scanned her surroundings, processing she was outside, in front of her house. How long had she been here? "Tasha tried to kill me. I found a list my father left for me in the music box. I sent it to you by email. It's got everything we need to bring her Russian crime family down." Feeling as though she was missing something important, she slowly sat up. "I just sent it to you a little while ago. How did you get here so quickly?"

He supported her with his arm around her back. "I was already on my way here from the airport. I told myself I was protecting you by giving you up, but you were right. I was only protecting my stupid pride. I've lived in a hell of my own making these last ten weeks. Even with my sight, I'm blind without you. So after Gracie spoke with Roman this morning about Michael and Rinaldi—"

She hurtled to her feet, stumbling with dizziness. "Roman is inside the den! He might still be alive!"

Cole's head snapped up toward the house. Sirens sounded in the distance. He plunged his fingers into her hair and cradled her head in his hands, then kissed her hard on her lips. Before she could respond, he tore away from her. "I love you."

He darted across the driveway and up the steps of the porch into the entryway. He turned and waved to her, then disappeared inside.

"Cole, I love you. Come back to me," she shouted as the sirens' wails grew louder. "To us. I'm pregnant."

Searing pain rippled through her abdomen. Feeling a sticky wetness between her legs, she doubled over and fell to her knees.

She was losing their baby.

Glass shattered, and flames shot out of the den's window, the fire spreading to the roof.

The ground tipped under her, and she toppled over, cracking her head on the pavement.

She'd lost everyone.

There was nothing left for her now.

She cried for Cole as the darkness stole her sight.

Chapter Thirty-Four

COLE LAY IN a hospital bed, all sorts of wires and tubes connected to him. Danielle sat in a hard chair beside him, the beeping of the monitor lulling her into a trance, her eyelids growing heavy as she continued to watch Cole's chest rise and fall. She knew it was irrational, but she worried if she left him, something bad would happen. She couldn't lose him.

The staff and her friends had all tried to get her to get some rest, but she'd refused, her butt glued to that chair by his side since her examination with the doctor. Eventually, they'd accepted there was nothing they could do to get her to leave, short of arresting her.

It had been forty-eight hours since the fire. He'd suffered from smoke inhalation and some second-degree burns, but he'd passed the critical stage, and the doctors felt confident that he was healing well. So why hadn't he woken up yet?

"Danielle," Gracie said, handing her a cup of coffee, "you need to get some rest. Why don't you—"

"No." Without looking away from Cole, she took the drink from her friend. "I have to be here when he wakes up. He'll need me." She took a cautious sip. "How's Roman?"

"He's worried about you."

"Me? He's the one recovering from bullet wounds, third-degree burns, and smoke inhalation. He's the one whose mother tried to kill him."

She still couldn't believe Tasha had been responsible for everything. What kind of woman would shoot her own child?

Danielle wanted to be there to comfort Roman, but as hard as she tried to convince herself to go down the hall and see him, she couldn't. Not until Cole opened his eyes and she made certain he knew about the baby.

Even if Cole didn't want her and his child, she needed him to know how she felt. He deserved to know how much she loved him and that out of their love, they'd created a life.

Gracie dragged a chair next to Danielle and plopped herself down. "At least he's allowing the hospital staff to take care of him. Since you saw the doctor a couple of days ago and received the IV for rehydration, you haven't done a single thing to take care of yourself. You need to eat something and get some rest."

"I can't leave him, Gracie," she said hoarsely, tears blurring her vision. She rubbed her eyes. "What if I leave and something happens to him? What if I have one chance to tell him how much I love him and I miss it?"

"How much do you love me?" she heard Cole whisper.

She blinked away the tears to see Cole had opened his eyes. "Cole!" She jumped up from the chair and leaned over him. "I love you. I love you so much I could spend every second of every day telling you I love you, and it still wouldn't come close to the amount of love I feel for you." She caressed his cheek with her trembling fingers. "You're awake."

"What happened?" he asked, his brows furrowed.

"You ran back into the burning house and carried Roman out. You're a hero."

Gracie stood. "He's recovering a few rooms down from here. I'm going to go tell him you're awake and that Danielle will be visiting him soon."

Needing to be closer to Cole, Danielle lowered the side rail and sat on the edge of the bed. "From my phone, I e-mailed Agent Miller the file I found. He's going to work with Interpol on it. And he told me that thanks to Logan, they were able to locate and seize the money Rinaldi had wired. They're still working on identifying the owner of the accounts, but I'm guessing they'll match the names in my father's file. I told Agent Miller that once they no longer require the fifty million as evidence, they should donate it to a research and treatment association for the visually impaired."

He placed his hand on her thigh. "I remember something. You were shouting to me as I went inside for Roman. I could've sworn you said something about a baby. Danielle, are you pregnant?"

Her chest tightened, and she burst into tears. "I'm sorry. I'm so sorry." She grabbed a tissue and wiped her eyes.

"I've been extremely hormonal." She took a deep breath. "Yes, Cole. I'm pregnant. You're going to be a father."

The beeping of his monitor accelerated.

She covered her belly. "I had some cramping and bleeding from the stress of the ordeal with Tasha, but the doctors here did an ultrasound, and the baby is fine. I'm ten weeks along, and she's growing perfectly. I know you don't want children—"

"Danielle?" He yanked his oxygen tube from his nose and ripped the wires from his chest. Then he sat up and hoisted his legs over the side before dropping to his knees in front of her. "Eight years ago, I set my eyes on the most beautiful woman I'd ever seen. She was too young for me then, and circumstances kept us apart, but she was never far from my thoughts. I watched from a distance as she bloomed, dreaming about a life I could have with her if only things were different. Then one day, her application landed on my desk, and I realized I'd finally have the chance to touch her and have her in my life, even if it was only temporary. But I didn't want to show her how much I cared, so I tried to intimidate her that first day and push her past her comfort zone." He smiled. "She met every challenge I threw at her. Every minute I spent with her, I fell deeper in love, but I let my fear keep me from giving her all of me."

She fell to her own knees and took his hands as he continued. "These last weeks without you have been hell, and I never want to go another day without you again. So even though I don't deserve you, I'm asking…Danielle, will you marry me?"

A nurse ran into the room. "Sir, are you okay? Our monitors indicated you flat-lined."

"I'm alive right now, but if the love of my life refuses my marriage proposal, she'll break my heart."

Her pregnancy hormones were working overtime, and the waterworks started again. "Are you sure you want to marry me? It's not just because I'm pregnant?"

"The baby is just a bonus. I love you, and I love the child growing inside of you. Say yes, Danielle."

She smiled. "Yes. I'll marry you."

Epilogue

INHALING THE SCENT of freshly cut grass, Danielle rested her e-reader on her rounded belly and closed her eyes, enjoying the moment. The birds sang, and the breeze rustled the leaves on the trees. It was so peaceful out here right now. Too bad it wouldn't last.

After all those years of living a solitary life, she wasn't used to having people around her all the time. And not just people, but friends. Cole had assigned Gracie to serve as Danielle's private bodyguard, a task the woman took way too seriously considering the threat to her life was gone. But Cole insisted, overprotective of not only her, but their baby girl, who'd make her entrance into the world in only a few short months.

Until the new house was built, the only privacy Danielle could get outside of her bedroom was here inside the gazebo. Because it was on the grounds, she could leave Gracie behind and enjoy the peace and quiet. Both a blessing and a curse, there was never a dull moment at Benediction.

Gracie had taken her shopping for maternity clothes and even managed to find her maternity fetish wear, something she would never have thought existed until Gracie surprised her with a visit to the store. And when Danielle took her business class at the nearby university, Gracie remained in the hallway and hit on the professors, male and female.

She rubbed her thumb over the diamond on her ring finger as if checking to make sure it was still there. It didn't make a difference because the ring didn't make the marriage, but the certificate they'd signed and filed at the courthouse the day Cole had gotten out of the hospital had.

A smile tugged at her lips. She'd never grow tired of being called Mrs. DeMarco or, as she was known at the club, Master Cole's.

"What's that smile for?"

She looked up at her husband, who was still as handsome as the day she'd first seen him nine years ago. Wearing jeans and a Detroit Tigers T-shirt, he sat down beside her on the bench and exchanged the e-reader for his hand. For a man who'd insisted he never wanted children, he spent hours each day waiting to feel the kick of his daughter's foot or the punch of her little hand.

She covered his hand with her own. "I was thinking how much my life has changed this year."

"All for the better, I hope?"

A blush crept over her chest. "I think I proved that to you in the mirror room last night."

The morning sickness had finally disappeared around week fifteen, after which, to Cole's delight, she'd moved into a long-lasting phase of having an insatiable sexual appetite.

He chuckled. "You certainly did." His hand slid out from under hers and glided up toward her breasts. "Enjoying the solitude?"

"I was until you arrived. Now I'm enjoying some quiet alone time with my husband."

His eyes sparkled with mischief as his hand continued its way up her chest, playfully flicking open the buttons along the way. "Yes, well, I came out to tell you the workmen have arrived, and the noise will start up in approximately fifteen minutes."

She sighed and arched into his palm. "That's fine. I'll enjoy the few minutes we have."

His fingers swept over her sensitive nipple. "You will if I have anything to say about it."

"How are you going to ensure that? You gonna act like Gracie and guard my body?"

He spread the opening of her dress and pulled down the cup of her bra, revealing her breast to his view. "No, I have an entirely different plan for your body."

She bit down on her lip. "Now? You just told me the workmen are here."

"They are."

The folds of her sex grew slick with need. "They'll see us…"

He tugged her onto a picnic blanket set out on the floor of the gazebo and laid her on her back. "Making love? Probably. Is that a problem?"

Her breathing quickened. "I'm pregnant. No one wants to see my naked ass right now."

"I do." He stretched her arms over her head and restrained her wrists by tying the nylon rope attached to the bottom of the gazebo bench around them. "I've been fantasizing about sinking my teeth into it all day."

Arousal trickled down her thighs. "You did that this morning before you went to breakfast with Roman."

"Exactly. And I couldn't wait to do it again." After binding her arms, he grabbed a spreader bar he'd conveniently left by the gazebo entrance. "Your body is fucking incredible. I think I'll have to keep you pregnant for the next ten years or so."

She sucked in a breath as he spread her wide open and cuffed her ankles to the bar. "Let's get through the first one before we start thinking about more."

"I've been dying for it to be warm enough to use this gazebo with you." He hovered over her body and, being the sly pervert that he was, pulled scissors from his back pocket. In seconds, he'd cut away all her clothes, leaving her completely bare.

"Hey, I liked that dress."

He nuzzled her swollen breasts. "I'll buy you a new one."

"And more underwear."

He slid his tongue across her nipple. "No. You're not supposed to be wearing panties while you're home. Consider this your punishment for breaking the rules."

Pressure built inside her pussy, but she was helplessly bound and at the will of her Master. "I was outside in a sundress that happens to ride up when I lie down on the bench to read. I thought it was prudent to cover up in case the workmen showed."

All thought of propriety fled the moment he sucked her nipple into his mouth. Heat flowed through her. They'd been so sensitive since the third month of her pregnancy, she could actually orgasm without any contact to her pussy. Her clitoris throbbed, the breeze on it like a dozen tiny fingers.

And then she heard them. Men's voices coming from down the hill and getting louder by the second.

The building crew had arrived to work on the new house.

She sunk her teeth into her bottom lip to keep from making too much noise.

But as her Master, Cole would never allow her to remain quiet. He knew what got her excited, and he refused to allow her to stifle it. He looked into her eyes, his pupils dilated and his nostrils flared. "You hear them? They've got a prime view of that sopping-wet pussy of yours right now. I bet they're hard as a rock seeing you spread out like that, bound and vulnerable. They've heard rumors about this place, and now that they see you, they're hoping I'm going to share you with them. That they'll get to feel your hot pussy, your tight ass, your sinful mouth around their dicks. And the thought of that makes you horny as hell, doesn't it?"

It did. When Cole took control, she could embrace her inner exhibitionist.

"Yes," she said breathlessly.

"Yeah, I bet it does." He pinched her nipple. "But do they get to touch you?"

"No, Master."

He unzipped his pants and, holding the center of the spreader bar, lifted her bottom off the ground. "Why, my beautiful slave?"

"Because I'm yours."

With one thrust, he seated himself inside her pussy. "That's right. And no one touches my wife but me. Every part of you belongs to me, just as every part of me belongs to you. But I understand your desire to be watched, and how I love to watch you, my sweet. I want to hear you. I want the workmen to hear you. Fuck, I want the guy delivering the mail down the street to hear you."

He wasn't gentle, driving into her over and over, swerving his hips in frantic motion. The noise of their lovemaking sent her careening toward climax. His skin slapping against hers. Her pussy's wet suction of his cock. His groans. Her cries. Those workmen could hear everything. They could see everything. See her.

Her body trembled as everything in her tightened, and nothing else existed except for the throbbing electric spot high inside her pussy only Cole could touch and claim. On a scream, she unraveled, pleasurable spasms clenching around Cole's cock as she came and came and came. She was still coming when he shuddered, bathing her inner tissues with his hot release. He collapsed on top of her; then, after catching his breath, he rolled off and removed the restraints from her arms and legs.

She sighed as he massaged her wrists. "I can't believe we did that. Even with the confidentiality agreement, the workmen are going to tell everyone they know what goes on here."

He shrugged. "Those aren't the builders. I requested a few of the male slave trainees take a walk by the gazebo."

Of course. Cole would never risk harming her in any way. "I should've guessed."

"There's something I wanted to discuss." He sat her up and kneeled beside her. "Before I met you, I lived in the dark. But since you've come into my life, even the darkness is filled with your light. I don't know how much time I have until I lose my vision completely. Before I do, I want to see you walking down the aisle of the church wearing white like the angel you are. Danielle, would you do me the honor of marrying me?"

She cocked her head. "That was a beautiful speech, but your memory must be fading along with your sight because we're already married."

"I want to do it right. You deserve more than a five-minute ceremony at the courthouse. This morning, I officially asked Roman for your hand. I never thought I'd get married, and now that I am, I want it all. The church wedding with our family and friends, the reception at the house, the honeymoon." He took her hand. "Say yes, Danielle. Even when I'm blind, I'll still see you. I don't need working eyes or photographs for that. You are my light."

She cupped his cheek. "And you are my mirror. I'll always say yes. Of course I'll marry you again."

Don't miss Shelly's first sexy and suspenseful
novel featuring Benediction!

The four-part serialized erotic thriller
that started it all…

WHITE COLLARED

Parts One–Four

available now from Avon Red Impulse!

Read on for an excerpt…

An Excerpt from

WHITE COLLARED PART ONE: MERCY

Chapter One

THE SINGLE-TAIL WHIP sliced through the air, leaving behind the thirteenth bloody line on a canvas of black and blue skin.

Did she understand the significance?

"Please," she begged, her blonde hair muffling the sweet music of her cries. Her body shook as she whimpered and moaned in agony.

No, she had no idea.

She would.

Soon.

With the hunting knife in hand, he stalked to her and pressed it against her carotid. He inhaled the pungent scent of fear emanating from her sweat-soaked pores. "Do you like my new knife? I bought it for you."

She shuddered. Oh yes, she definitely enjoyed his new-est acquisition. Too bad he wouldn't be able to keep it.

Prone and hog-tied with thick blue rope that criss-crossed over her face and knotted around her arched neck, she waited for his next move, blood trickling from the soles of her feet as a result of the final lash. She panted, her lungs barely inflating.

After a brutal beating with both a cane and whip, most in her position would have tired and dropped their neck, strangling themselves on the rope. Her strength and determination surprised him.

Perhaps she required another challenge.

He rested his knife on the bed beside her and picked up his black duffel bag. Rummaging through it, he found the final torture and smiled. The thick, four-inch-tall, white leather posture collar would look beautiful on her. He buckled it around her neck, squeezing her windpipe with the rope.

"Why?" she gasped, the porcelain skin of her face red-dening from the lack of oxygen to her blood.

"What motivates anyone to kill?" He lifted the knife. "There's greed." He carved several shallow cuts on her torso. "Envy, anger, passion, self-defense, necessity."

She stared at him in horror.

That simply wouldn't do.

"Identification." With a lover's touch, he gently shut her eyelids. "But we can't forget the two most important reasons," he whispered, slashing the bare mound between her legs.

"Revenge."

She remained silent, her dusky bluish, mottled body frozen. His eyes teared at the realization that he'd never feel her lips on him again.

"And mercy."

Then he plunged his new hunting knife straight into her nonbeating heart.

Chapter Two

Fourteen Days to Elections...

AFTER THREE HOURS of computer research on piercing the corporate veil, Kate's vision blurred, the words on the screen bleeding into one another until they resembled a giant Rorschach inkblot. She lowered her mug of lukewarm coffee to her cubicle's mahogany tabletop and rubbed her tired eyes.

Without warning, the door to the interns' windowless office flew open, banging against the wall. Light streamed into the dim room, casting the elongated shadow of her boss, Nicholas Trenton, on the beige carpet.

"Ms. Martin, take your jacket and come with me." He didn't wait for a response, simply issued his command and strode down the hall.

Jumping to her feet, she teetered on her secondhand heels and grabbed her suit jacket from the back of her chair. As Mr. Trenton's intern for the year, she'd follow him off the edge of a cliff. She had no choice in the matter if she wanted a junior associate position at Detroit's most prestigious law firm, Joseph and Long, after graduation. Because of the fierce competition for an internship and because several qualified lackeys waited patiently in the wings for an opening, one minor screwup would result in termination.

Most of the other interns ignored the interruption, but her best friend Hannah took a second to raise an arched eyebrow. Kate shrugged, having no idea what her boss required. He hadn't spoken to her since her initial interview a few months earlier.

She collected her briefcase, her heart pounding. As far as she knew, she hadn't made a mistake since starting two months ago. Other than class time, she'd spent virtually every waking moment at this firm, a schedule her boyfriend, Tom, resented. To placate him, she'd used her dinner break last Saturday to drive to his place and give him a quick blow job before returning to work. She didn't even have time for her own orgasm.

She raced as fast as she could down the hallway and found her boss pacing and talking on his cell phone in the marbled lobby. He frowned and pointedly looked at his watch, demonstrating his displeasure at her delay. Still on the phone, he stalked out of the firm and headed toward the elevator. She chased him, cursing her short legs as she remained a step or two behind until catching up with him in the elevator.

When the doors slid shut, he ended his call and slipped his cell into the pocket of his Armani jacket. She risked a quick glance at him to ascertain his mood, careful not to visually suggest anything more than casual regard.

He was an extremely handsome man whose picture frequently appeared in local magazines and papers beside prominent judges and legislative officials. But photos couldn't do him justice, film lacking the capability of capturing his commanding presence. Often she'd had to fight her instinct to look directly into his blue eyes. At the office, his every move, his every word overshadowed anyone and everything around her.

Standing close to him in the claustrophobic space, she inhaled the musky scent of his aftershave, felt his radiating heat. Her trembling body instinctively angled toward him.

Mr. Trenton spoke, fracturing the quiet of the small space with his deep and powerful voice. "This morning, our firm's biggest client, Jaxon Deveroux, arrived home from his business trip and found his wife dead from multiple stab wounds."

About the Author

SHELLY BELL writes sensual romance and erotic thrillers with high emotional stakes for her alpha heroes and kick-ass heroines. She began writing upon the insistence of her husband, who dragged her to the store and bought her a laptop. When she's not practicing corporate law, taking care of her family, or writing, you'll find her reading the latest smutty romance.

Shelly is a member of Romance Writers of America and International Thriller Writers.

Visit her website at ShellyBellBooks.com.

Discover great authors, exclusive offers, and more at hc.com.

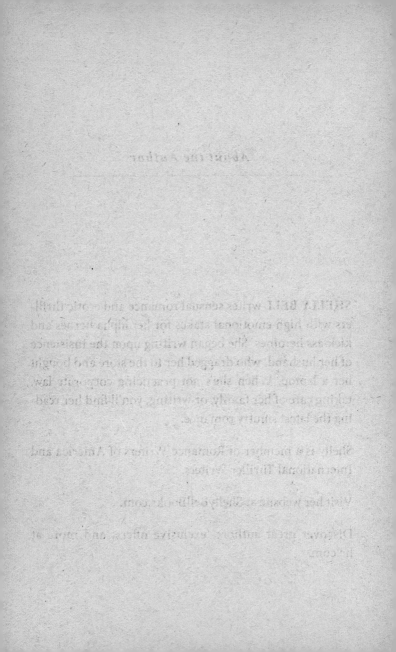

About the Author

SHELLY BELL writes sensual romance and—mercifully—ers with high emotional stakes for her alpha heroes and kick-ass heroines. She began writing upon the insistence of her husband, who dragged her to the store and bought her a laptop. When she's not practicing corporate law, or reading some other sexy or exciting stuff, you'll find her reading the latest smutty romance.

Shell is a member of Romance Writers of America and International Thriller Writers.

Visit her website at ShellyBellbooks.com.

Give in to your impulses . . .
Read on for a sneak peek at six brand-new
e-book original tales of romance
from HarperCollins.
Available now wherever *e*-books are sold.

WHEN GOOD EARLS GO BAD
A Victorian Valentine's Day Novella
By Megan Frampton

THE WEDDING BAND
A Save the Date Novel
By Cara Connelly

RIOT
By Jamie Shaw

ONLY IN MY DREAMS
Ribbon Ridge Book One
By Darcy Burke

SINFUL REWARDS 1
A BILLIONAIRES AND BIKERS NOVELLA
By Cynthia Sax

TEMPT THE NIGHT
A TRUST NO ONE NOVEL
By Dixie Lee Brown

An Excerpt from

WHEN GOOD EARLS GO BAD
A Victorian Valentine's Day Novella
by Megan Frampton

Megan Frampton's *Dukes Behaving Badly* series
continues, but this time it's an earl who's meeting
his match in a delightfully fun and sexy novella!

"**W**hile it's not precisely true that nobody is here, because I am, in fact, here, the truth is that there is no one here who can accommodate the request."

The man standing in the main area of the Quality Employment Agency didn't leave. She'd have to keep on, then.

"If I weren't here, then it would be even more in question, since you wouldn't know the answer to the question one way or the other, would you? So I am here, but I am not the proper person for what you need."

The man fidgeted with the hat he held in his hand. But still did not take her hint. She would have to persevere.

"I suggest you leave the information, and we will endeavor to fill the position when there is someone here who is not me." Annabelle gave a short nod of her head as she finished speaking, knowing she had been absolutely clear in what she'd said. If repetitive. So it was a surprise that the man to whom she was speaking was staring back at her, his mouth slightly opened, his eyes blinking behind his owlish spectacles. His hat now held very tightly in his hand.

Perhaps she should speak more slowly.

"We do not have a housekeeper for hire," she said, pausing

between each word. "I am the owner, not one of the employees for hire."

Now the man's mouth had closed, but it still seemed as though he did not understand.

"I do not understand," he said, confirming her very suspicion. "This is an employment agency, and I have an employer who wishes to find an employee. And if I do not find a suitable person within . . ." and at this he withdrew a pocket watch from his waistcoat and frowned at it, as though it was its fault it was already past tea time, and *goodness, wasn't she hungry and had Caroline left any milk in the jug? Because if not, well,* "twenty-four hours, my employer, the Earl of Selkirk, will be most displeased, and we will ensure your agency will no longer receive our patronage."

That last part drew her attention away from the issue of the milk and whether or not there was any.

"The Earl of . . . ?" she said, feeling that flutter in her stomach that signaled there was nobility present or being mentioned—or she wished there were, at least. Rather like the milk, actually.

"Selkirk," the man replied in a firm tone. He had no comment on the milk. And why would he? He didn't even know it was a possibility that they didn't have any, and if she did have to serve him tea, what would she say? Besides which, she had no clue to the man's name; he had just come in and been all brusque and demanded a housekeeper when there was none.

"Selkirk," Annabelle repeated, her mind rifling through all the nobles she'd ever heard mentioned.

"A Scottish earl," the man said.

Annabelle beamed and clapped her hands. "Oh, Scottish! Small wonder I did not recognize the title, I've only ever been in London and once to the seaside when I was five years old, but I wouldn't have known if that was Scotland, but I am fairly certain it was not because it would have been cold and it was quite warm in the water. Unless the weather was unseasonable, I can safely say I have never been to Scotland, nor do I know of any Scottish earls."

An Excerpt from

THE WEDDING BAND
A Save the Date Novel
by Cara Connelly

In the latest *Save the Date* novel from Cara
Connelly, journalist Christina Case crashes a
celebrity wedding, and sparks fly when she comes
face-to-face with A-list movie star Dakota Rain . . .

Dakota Rain took a good hard look in the bathroom mirror and inventoried the assets.

Piercing blue eyes? Check.

Sexy stubble? Check.

Sun-streaked blond hair? Check.

Movie-star smile?

Uh-oh.

In the doorway, his assistant rolled her eyes and hit speed dial. "Emily Fazzone here," she said. "Mr. Rain needs to see Dr. Spade this morning. Another cap." She listened a moment, then snorted a laugh. "You're telling me. Might as well cap them all and be done with it."

In the mirror Dakota gave her his hit man squint. "No extra caps."

"Weenie," she said, pocketing her phone. "You don't have time today, anyway. Spade's squeezing you in, as usual. Then you're due at the studio at eleven for the voice-over. It'll be tight, so step on it."

Deliberately, Dakota turned to his reflection again. Tilted his head. Pulled at his cheeks like he was contemplating a shave.

Emily did another eye roll. Muttering something that

might have been either "Get to work" or "What a jerk," she disappeared into his closet, emerging a minute later with jeans, T-shirt, and boxer briefs. She stacked them on the granite vanity, then pulled out her phone again and scrolled through the calendar.

"You've got a twelve o'clock with Peter at his office about the Levi's endorsement, then a one-thirty fitting for your tux. Mercer's coming here at two-thirty to talk about security for the wedding . . ."

Dakota tuned her out. His schedule didn't worry him. Emily would get him where he needed to be. If he ran a little late and a few people had to cool their heels, well, they were used to dealing with movie stars. Hell, they'd be disappointed if he behaved like regular folk.

Taking his sweet time, he shucked yesterday's briefs and meandered naked to the shower without thinking twice. He knew Emily wouldn't bat an eye. After ten years nursing him through injuries and illness, puking and pain, she'd seen all there was to see. Broad shoulders? Tight buns? She was immune.

And besides, she was gay.

Jacking the water temp to scalding, he stuck his head under the spray, wincing when it found the goose egg on the back of his skull. He measured it with his fingers, two inches around.

The same right hook that had chipped his tooth had bounced his head off a concrete wall.

Emily rapped on the glass. He rubbed a clear spot in the steam and gave her the hard eye for pestering him in the shower.

She was immune to that too. "I asked you if we're looking at a lawsuit."

"Damn straight." He was all indignation. "We're suing The Combat Zone. Tubby busted my tooth and gave me a concussion to boot."

She sighed. "I meant, are *we* getting sued? Tubby's a good bouncer. If he popped you, you gave him a reason."

Dakota put a world of aggrievement into his Western drawl. "Why do you always take everybody else's side? You weren't there. You don't know what happened."

"Sure I do. It's October, isn't it? The month you start howling at the moon and throwing punches at bystanders. It's an annual event. The lawyers are on standby. I just want to know if I should call them."

He did the snarl that sent villains and virgins running for their mamas.

An Excerpt from

RIOT

by Jamie Shaw

Jamie Shaw's rock stars are back, and this time
wild, unpredictable Dee and sexy, mohawked
guitarist Joel have explosive chemistry—but will
jealousy and painful memories keep them apart?

"**K**iss me," I order the luckiest guy in Mayhem tonight. When he sat next to me at the bar earlier with his "Leave It to Beaver" haircut, I made sure to avoid eye contact and cross my legs in the opposite direction. I didn't think I'd end up making out with him, but now I have no choice.

A dumb expression washes over his face. He might be cute if he didn't look so. freaking. dumb. "Huh?"

"Oh for God's sake."

I curl my fingers behind his neck and yank him to my mouth, tilting my head to the side and hoping he's a quick learner. My lips part, my tongue comes out to play, and after a moment, he finally catches on. His greedy fingers bury themselves in my chocolate brown curls—which I spent *hours* on this morning.

Peeking out of the corner of my eye, I spot Joel Gibbon stroll past me, a bleach-blonde groupie tucked under his arm. He's too busy whispering in her ear to notice me, and my fingers itch to punch him in the back of his stupid mohawked head to get his attention.

I'm preparing to push Leave It to Beaver off me when Joel's gaze finally lifts to meet mine. I bite Beaver's bottom lip between my teeth and give it a little tug, and the corner of

Joel's mouth lifts up into an infuriating smirk that is *so* not the reaction I wanted. He continues walking, and when he's finally out of sight, I break my lips from Beaver's and nudge him back toward his own stool, immediately spinning in the opposite direction to scowl at my giggling best friend.

"I can't BELIEVE him!" I shout at a far-too-amused-looking Rowan. How does she not recognize the gravity of this situation?!

I'm about to shake some sense into her when Beaver taps me on the shoulder. "Um—"

"You're welcome," I say with a flick of my wrist, not wanting to waste another minute on a guy who can't appreciate how long it took me to get my hair to curl like this—or at least make messing it up worth my while.

Rowan gives him an apologetic half smile, and I let out a deep sigh.

I don't feel bad about Beaver. I feel bad about the dickhead bass guitarist for the Last Ones to Know.

"That boy is making me insane," I growl.

Rowan turns a bright smile on me, her blue eyes sparkling with humor. "You were already insane."

"He's making me homicidal," I clarify, and she laughs.

"Why don't you just tell him you like him?" She twirls two tiny straws in her cocktail, her eyes periodically flitting up to the stage. She's waiting for Adam, and I'd probably be jealous of her if those two weren't so disgustingly perfect for each other.

Last semester, I nearly got kicked out of my dorm when I let Rowan move in with me and my roommate. But Rowan's asshole live-in boyfriend had cheated on her, and she had nowhere to go, and she's been my *best* friend since kindergarten. I ignored the written warnings from my RA, and Rowan ultimately ended up moving in with Adam before I got kicked out. Fast forward to one too many "overnight visitors" later, I still ended up getting reported, and Rowan and I got a two-bedroom in an apartment complex near campus. Her name is on the lease right next to mine, but really, the apartment is just a decoy she uses to avoid telling her parents that she's actually living with three ungodly hot rock stars. She sleeps in Adam's bed, his bandmate Shawn is in the second bedroom, and Joel sleeps on their couch most nights because he's a hot, stupid, infuriating freaking nomad.

"Because I *don't* like him," I answer. When I realize my drink is gone, I steal Rowan's, down the last of it, and flag the bartender.

"Then why is he making you insane?"

"Because *he* doesn't like *me*."

Rowan lifts a sandy blonde eyebrow at me, but I don't expect her to understand. Hell, *I* don't understand. I've never wanted a boy to like me so badly in my entire life.

An Excerpt from

ONLY IN MY DREAMS
Ribbon Ridge Book One
by Darcy Burke

From a *USA Today* bestselling author
comes the first installment in a sexy and
emotional family saga about seven siblings
who reunite in a small Oregon town to
fulfill their brother's dying wish . . .

Sara Archer took a deep breath and dialed her assistant and close friend, Craig Walker. He was going to laugh his butt off when she told him why she was calling, which almost made her hang up, but she forced herself to go through with it.

"Sara! Your call can only mean one thing: you're totally doing it."

She envisioned his blue eyes alight with laughter, his dimples creasing, and rolled her eyes. "I guess so."

He whooped into the phone, causing Sara to pull it back from her ear. "Awesome! You won't regret it. It's been waaaaay too long since you got out there. What, four years?"

"You're exaggerating." More like three. She hadn't been out with a guy since Jude. Easy, breezy, coffee barista Jude. He'd been a welcome breath of fresh air after her cheating college boyfriend. Come to think of it, she'd taken three years to get back in the game then too.

"Am I? I've known you for almost three years, and you've never had even a casual date in all that time."

Because after she and Jude had ended their fling, she'd decided to focus on her business, and she'd hired Craig a couple of months later. "Enough with the history lesson. Let's talk about tonight before I lose my nerve."

"Got it. I'm really proud of you for doing this. You need a social life beyond our rom-com movie nights."

Sara suspected he was pushing her to go out because he'd started dating someone. They seemed serious even though it had been only a couple of weeks, and when you fell in love, you wanted the whole world to fall in love too. Not that Sara planned on doing that again—if she could even count her college boyfriend as falling in love. She really didn't know anymore.

"I was thinking I might go line dancing." She glanced through her clothing, pondering what to wear.

"Line dancing?" Craig's tone made it sound as if he were asking whether she was going to the garbage dump. He wouldn't have been caught dead in a country-western bar. "If you want to get your groove on, Taylor and I will come get you and take you downtown. Much better scene."

No, the nearby suburban country-western bar would suit her needs just fine. She wouldn't be comfortable at a chic Portland club—totally out of her league. "I'll stick with Sidewinders, thanks."

"We wouldn't take you to a gay bar," Craig said with a touch of exasperation that made her smile.

"I know. I just don't want company. You'd try to set me up with every guy in the place."

"I'm not that bad! Taylor keeps me in line."

Yeah, she'd noticed. She'd been out with them once and was surprised at the difference in Craig. He was still his energetic self, but it was like everything he had was focused on his new boyfriend. She supposed that was natural when a relationship was shiny and new. "Well, I'm good going by myself. I'm just going to dance a little, maybe sip a lemon drop, see what happens."

Craig made a noise of disgust. "Don't ass out, Sara. You need to get laid."

An Excerpt from

SINFUL REWARDS 1
A Billionaires and Bikers Novella
by Cynthia Sax

Belinda "Bee" Carter is a good girl; at least, that's
what she tells herself. And a good girl deserves
a nice guy—just like the gorgeous and moody
billionaire Nicolas Rainer. Or so she thinks,
until she takes a look through her telescope
and sees a naked, tattooed man on the balcony
across the courtyard. He has been watching
her, and that makes him all the more enticing.
But when a mysterious and anonymous text
message dares her to do something bad, she
must decide if she is really the good girl she has
always claimed to be, or if she's willing to risk
everything for her secret fantasy of being watched.

An Avon Red Impulse Novella

I'd told Cyndi I'd never use it, that it was an instrument purchased by perverts to spy on their neighbors. She'd laughed and called me a prude, not knowing that I was one of those perverts, that I secretly yearned to watch and be watched, to care and be cared for.

If I'm cautious, and I'm always cautious, she'll never realize I used her telescope this morning. I swing the tube toward the bench and adjust the knob, bringing the mysterious object into focus.

It's a phone. Nicolas's phone. I bounce on the balls of my feet. This is a sign, another declaration from fate that we belong together. I'll return Nicolas's much-needed device to him. As a thank you, he'll invite me to dinner. We'll talk. He'll realize how perfect I am for him, fall in love with me, marry me.

Cyndi will find a fiancé also—everyone loves her—and we'll have a double wedding, as sisters of the heart often do. It'll be the first wedding my family has had in generations.

Everyone will watch us as we walk down the aisle. I'll wear a strapless white Vera Wang mermaid gown with organza and lace details, crystal and pearl embroidery accents, the bodice fitted, and the skirt hemmed for my shorter height. My hair will be swept up. My shoes—

Voices murmur outside the condo's door, the sound piercing my delightful daydream. I swing the telescope upward, not wanting to be caught using it. The snippets of conversation drift away.

I don't relax. If the telescope isn't positioned in the same way as it was last night, Cyndi will realize I've been using it. She'll tease me about being a fellow pervert, sharing the story, embellished for dramatic effect, with her stern, serious dad— or, worse, with Angel, that snobby friend of hers.

I'll die. It'll be worse than being the butt of jokes in high school because that ridicule was about my clothes and this will center on the part of my soul I've always kept hidden. It'll also be the truth, and I won't be able to deny it. I am a pervert.

I have to return the telescope to its original position. This is the only acceptable solution. I tap the metal tube.

Last night, my man-crazy roommate was giggling over the new guy in three-eleven north. The previous occupant was a gray-haired, bowtie-wearing tax auditor, his luxurious accommodations supplied by Nicolas. The most exciting thing he ever did was drink his tea on the balcony.

According to Cyndi, the new occupant is a delicious piece of man candy—tattooed, buff, and head-to-toe lickable. He was completing armcurls outside, and she enthusiastically counted his reps, oohing and aahing over his bulging biceps, calling to me to take a look.

I resisted that temptation, focusing on making macaroni and cheese for the two of us, the recipe snagged from the diner my mom works in. After we scarfed down dinner, Cyndi licking her plate clean, she left for the club and hasn't returned.

Three-eleven north is the mirror condo to ours. I straighten the telescope. That position looks about right, but then, the imitation UGGS I bought in my second year of college looked about right also. The first time I wore the boots in the rain, the sheepskin fell apart, leaving me barefoot in Economics 201.

Unwilling to risk Cyndi's friendship on "about right," I gaze through the eyepiece. The view consists of rippling golden planes, almost like . . .

Tanned skin pulled over defined abs.

I blink. It can't be. I take another look. A perfect pearl of perspiration clings to a puckered scar. The drop elongates more and more, stretching, snapping. It trickles downward, navigating the swells and valleys of a man's honed torso.

No. I straighten. This is wrong. I shouldn't watch our sexy neighbor as he stands on his balcony. If anyone catches me . . .

Parts 1 – 8 available now!

An Excerpt from

TEMPT THE NIGHT
A Save the Date Novel
by *Dixie Lee Brown*

Dixie Lee Brown concludes her thrilling
Trust No One series with the fast-paced
tale of a damaged hero and the sexy
fugitive he can't help falling for.

She pursed her lips and studied him. "That's deep, Brady." A crooked grin gradually appeared, erasing the worry wrinkles from her forehead. Then, without any encouragement from him, Mac took a step closer and leaned into his chest, sliding her arms around his waist.

He hesitated only a second before wrapping her in his arms and pulling her close. A groan escaped him.

She shifted her head to glance up. "Do you mind?"

A soft chuckle vibrated through him. "Sugar, I'll hold you anytime, anywhere."

Mac snuggled closer, and he tipped her head with his fingers, slowly covering her mouth with his, giving her plenty of time to change her mind. When she didn't, he drank of her sweetness like a man dying of thirst. Again and again he kissed her, his tongue pushing into her mouth, swirling and dancing with hers. He couldn't get enough of her full, soft lips, her sweet taste, and the bold way she pressed against him.

Brady couldn't say which of the day's events was responsible for her change in temperature where he was concerned, but it wasn't important. They were taking steps in the right direction, and he wasn't going to do anything to screw that up. He wanted her warm and willing in his hands, but he also wanted her there for the right reasons. The decision was hers to make.

When he lifted his head, there were tears on her eyelashes, but her smile made his heart grab an extra beat. He let his fingers trail across the satin skin of her cheek as he kissed her neck tenderly and breathed in her sweet scent.

"God, you smell good." He kissed each of her closed eyes, then leaned his forehead on hers and took a deep breath. "I'd love for this to go on all night. Unfortunately, Joe wants us to meet with Maria." He steadied her as she straightened and took a step back.

Mac's gaze was uncertain. "We could meet later . . . if you want to . . ."

"Aw, sugar. If *I* want to? That's like asking if I want to keep breathing." He threaded his fingers through her hair and brushed his lips over hers. "I've wanted you since the first time you lied to me." Brady chuckled as her eyes lit up.

She punched his chest with a fisted hand. "Hey! That was the only time I lied, and I had a darn good reason. Some big galoot knocks me down, pounces on me, and then expects me to be truthful. Nuh uh. I don't think so." Her eyes sparkled with challenge.

"*Galoot*, huh? No more John Wayne movies for you, sugar."

She sucked in a big breath, and he could tell by the mischief in her eyes that she was getting ready to let him have it. He touched his fingers to her lips to silence her. "Let me say this, okay? There's a good chance we'll go in and meet with Maria, and sometime before, after, or during, you'll think about us—about me—and decide we're not a good idea. I want you to know two things. First . . . it's the best idea I've had in a long time. Second . . . if you decide it's a mistake or that you're not ready to get any closer, that's okay. No pressure."

He stepped back and gave her some room. It struck him that he'd just lied to her. What he said would have been true for any other woman he'd ever known, but he damn sure wasn't going to give up on Mac that easily.

A grin made the sparkle in her eyes dance as she slipped her hand into his. "Obviously you're confusing me with some other woman, because I don't usually change my mind once it's made up, and I'm a big girl, so you can stop worrying that your charm, good looks, and sex appeal will bowl me over. As for thinking about you—yeah." She stepped closer and lowered her voice to a silky whisper. "You might cross my mind once or twice . . . so let's get this meeting over with."

"You got it, sugar." Brady couldn't remember when he'd been so contented—or when he'd ever used that word to describe himself before. Whether or not tonight ended with him in bed with this amazingly beautiful and brave woman didn't really matter. The last few minutes had made it clear that his interest in her went way beyond just the prospect of sex. He wanted everything she had to give. *Shit!* She'd turned him upside down and inside out until he doubted his own ability to walk away . . . or even if he wanted to.